Fortune of Emerald and Salt

Monroe Wildrose

Copyright © 2021 by Teapots and Stolen Souls Publishing

All rights reserved.

No part of this book may be reproduced in any form by an electronic or mechanical means, including information storage and retrieval systems, without permission in writing from the publisher, except by a reviewer who may quote brief passages in a review.

This is a work of fiction. Names, characters, places, and incidents either are the product of the author's imagination or are used fictitiously. Any resemblance to actual persons, living or dead, events, or locales is entirely coincidental.

Cover Illustration by primegpx *on Fiverr* Copyright © Teapots and Stolen Souls Publishing

Canva images/edited/ Canva license held by Author

First edition was first published in 2021

Print ISBN 9780578253398

Teapots and Stolen Souls Publishing contact information:

teapotsandstolensoulspublishing@outlook.com

Contents

This book is dedicated to Willow and Chile.
Without you, I wouldn't know the
life-altering magic of marvelous siblings

The night is darkening round me,
The wild winds coldly blow;
But a tyrant spell has bound me
And I cannot, cannot go.
The giant trees are bending
Their bare boughs weighed with snow.
And the storm is fast descending,
And yet I cannot go.
Clouds beyond clouds above me,
Wastes beyond wastes below;
But nothing drear can move me;
I will not, cannot go.

-Emily Bronte

Trigger Warnings

S ome content in this book may be triggering and/or disturbing for some. As an Author, I aim to give my readers the best experience possible while being kind and courteous. Therefore, here is a list of possible triggers to be found in the pages beyond:

- Knives/Swordplay

- Blood (light)

- Physical Violence

- Drinking

- Suicide (attempted)

- Kidnapping

- Talk of sexual encounters (light)

One

Georgette

"Excuse me, sir, but I need to get up so I can murder my brother. So, if you wouldn't mind, please move out of my bed," I insisted, but the sleeping man didn't move.

The hammering at my door continued, and I stared at it as if my twin on the other side would be able to sense my irritation. If he could, he didn't seem to mind it in the slightest. I nudged the snoring heap of a man next to me, rather impressed that the pounding had not woken him. His head lifted, and I gave him a small encouraging smile. He didn't seem to be the brightest lad, though I hadn't brought him to my bed for his wit. I gazed at his naked form and admired it one last time. Meanwhile, the banging continued.

I exhaled and pulled up a thin sheet that had bunched at the bottom of my feet and climbed over him. Halfway falling out of bed, I tripped and barely caught myself on the way to the door. I knew it had to be my brother because no other soul on our ship would dare knock at my quarters at this hour.

I opened the door clutching the sheet to my body.

"What, Elias, what could be so pressing that you are knocking on my door before the sun has risen?" I asked.

"Morning, Captain," he said with a smile on his face.

He pushed past me with no regard for my lack of clothing. He stood in the middle of my room, staring at the guest in the bed.

"Oh." The smile on his face unwavering in a way that drove me to the edge of madness. "I didn't realize you had company."

"Sir, please grab your belongings and vacate the ship. If you refuse, I will have to ask one of my crew to remove you by force." I avoided using his name because I could not recall it.

I was suddenly exasperated by my brother's intruding, and the man's determination to sleep was becoming less impressive and more irritating by the second. I began to tap my foot against the wood floor of my ship. The headache I had was beginning to throb to the tempo of my pulse.

"I'd do as she says, mate," Elias mocked me. "The last lad went over the side of the ship in nothing but his unmentionables."

The man sprang up then and started gathering his clothing and accessories carelessly strewn about the room. He had the good sense to look both mystified and ashamed as he put on enough layers to be semi-presentable. I had a pursed-lip smile for him as he left, but that was all. Elias clapped him on the shoulder and wished him a good day.

I bolted behind my dressing curtain before he had cleared the door. I located fresh undergarments and shoved my legs into trousers, belting in a white long-sleeve shirt. I swept a sea-green jacket from off the ground while looking around for stockings. I picked up my boots and peered inside them as if they held answers to life's problems. All the while, I did my best to ignore my self-satisfied brother in the middle of the room.

"There," Elias said, pointing to where a pile of stockings and underthings were littered by the side of my bed. I mumbled a curse, threw a rude gesture his way, and snatched the socks off the floor. I shoved my stocking-clad feet and the bottom of my trousers into the boots.

"Shall I follow you, Captain, to wherever our urgent business is?" Mocking, I bowed, gesturing to my quarter doors.

"I didn't say we had any business." He stepped out onto the main deck of The Siren, our ship.

"I assumed that your attempt to shame me in front of last night's company was instigated by some errand you couldn't do on your own." I followed him and slammed the door behind me.

I acknowledged some of the crewmen who milled about. The sun promised to rise, though most of the crew had been up for over an hour. I usually would have been up with them, but I had drunk too much the night before. A litany of greetings trailed behind us as we passed.

"I don't think you have a drop of shame in you, George." We walked down the ship's docking stairs onto the pier below. "Also, Master Church would be rather miffed if I showed up alone: He does adore you so."

"Absalom didn't mention a meeting with his father," I said, trying to walk while taming my hair into my signature tight crown pleats on either side of my head.

"I doubt he knew." Elias's tone had gone from casual to bothered. "I think he fancies his son too close to us to trust him fully. Our mutual arrangement with King Kosdel is still young and untested."

"You think that's what the meeting is about?"

He walked faster than I, with more determination. He stood only four inches taller than me, but he took the steps of a giant. He would slow if I asked, but it wounded my pride to request it of him. If I ended up in a horrible place when I died, I knew it would be my pride that would get me there.

"I'm unsure. The correspondence was very vague, with not much more than a time and place to meet. Master Church's lackey delivered it this morning."

"I don't think he would like hearing you refer to him as a lackey," I mused, thinking of the red-faced man that answered Master Gerald Church's every call.

We made our way through the port town of Odie. All port towns bustled with life, but because of Odie's proximity to other nations' ports, it was substantially busier. It was close to the capital, which meant we were closely watched by the king's guard when we arrived. Our ship didn't have a home, but it spent a fair amount of time in this port. More frequently since we had sold our souls in the agreement we made with King Cyril Kosdel, who was the monarch over all of Northern Ralice.

We knew the streets of this place as well as we knew our ship. We had explored each cobblestone and hidden alley shortcut as children. Elias and I had fancied ourselves roughish adventurers with Absalom at our side. We had gotten ourselves into a fair amount of trouble, and our parents had always been there to get us out. I thought of a time when we had stolen a dress from a clothing line. The order officers had chased us around the city until we hid in the back of a butchery. The memory of Absalom's worried face as a child elicited a smile from me. He had always been there to make sure we didn't do anything too wild.

Odie also always smelled of saltwater and brick. It comforted me like a fire-warmed blanket in the winter. The previous night Absalom and I had walked the streets, reminiscing at some of our old spots, until he had left me to my favorite tavern and further debauchery.

"It's only been six months since the start of our contract with King Kosdel, and he's already running us ragged. If this is another request, the crew will be furious. We haven't been at port for even a full two days," I complained.

"They'll make do. We all know what the goal is. If we remind the crew of what lies at the end of this, they won't complain about the short dockings," Elias said as we happened up to a familiar tavern that had attached rooms for nightly rent.

In the evening, lots of raucous, drunken sailors looked to spend their money on fresh food, alcohol, and the pleasure of a woman's company. During the day, none of that changed.

"Perhaps they will make do, but my patience is frayed." I walked into the tavern's front and began to scan the gorged room for the Master of King Kosdel's armies and his son.

"I don't think you would be petty enough to jeopardize the biggest yield of our pirating career." Elias almost had to yell at me to hear over the noise.

"I'm not sure you're aware of what I would do for a warm bath and food without mold on it, Elias." I noticed Master Gerald Church and Absalom resting on the same side of a corner table shoved in the back of the room.

We made our way over to them, sidestepping drunks and skirting tables. I stopped momentarily to make deliberate eye contact with the woman at the bar, who nodded at me. I hoped that meant she was going to bring us some food. We sat down on the opposite side of the table from the two men. I winked at the younger, eliciting an exasperated shake of his head for my benefit. Gerald opened his mouth to speak first, but Elias held his hand up.

"We had better wait until George gets something to eat. She may faint without a proper breakfast," he said, and Absalom smirked again, knowing us both too well to play the fool.

To anyone else, it sounded as if Elias thought me a delicate female incapable of discussing anything on an empty stomach. Absalom and I knew the tactic shifted the conversation to be on our terms. Though, to be honest, I did prefer to talk business on a full stomach.

"Quite," Absalom agreed and stared directly at me as I tried to smother the smile that surfaced.

I saw a small fire come to life in his eyes. He knew I loathed being painted with the strokes of common female assumptions, and his mouth quirked up, daring me to contradict them. However, I wouldn't rise to his challenge. I hated to play the feminine counterpart, but the effectiveness of it won out over my pride.

"If you wouldn't mind, Master Church." I smiled sweetly at the man.

My tenderheartedness for him surfaced without much effort. I thought him a good soul who happened to be too dedicated to his king and country. He also fancied me, though perhaps not my closeness with his son.

"Not at all, Captain Georgette. I must admit I find myself worried about your daily ritual often. Such a burden this life must be on a young lady."

Absalom started coughing, seeming to struggle with his drink.

"Don't choke," I said to him dryly as he covered more laughter with coughing.

Elias and Gerald started talking about the exorbitant price of ship loaning. I said nothing, but listened with half an ear and kept my gaze on Absalom. Having been friends since childhood, we could communicate wordlessly. We did it almost as well as Elias and I did.

I asked him, in our familiar language, why he had come. He pushed both his shoulders up and shook his head, looking at his father. He didn't know any more than we did and gave me an unimpressed look while running his fingers through sandy hair, which meant he truly didn't know anything, but his fingers tapped nervously about whatever was afoot.

Absalom's features had a way of making him look friendly. He looked youthful, and his freshwater eyes held kindness. It didn't work out in his favor as he also tended to be tirelessly courteous as well. He usually preferred contemplative silence to banter, but his good manners got him into unwanted situations often. Though, his normally light features had darkened with concern, his eyes shifted over to his father's frequently, with questions that the man would never answer.

The woman from earlier had made her way over to our table, and she offered a fresh-baked loaf of bread, a block of grey-toned cheese, and a small tray of fruit. She also brought two mugs of hot liquid for Elias and me.

"You're a vision," I said to her, pressing a silver coin to her palm.

The woman scurried away without a word, but I had grown used to it. The fear people had of us was part of what it meant to be one of the Captains Baine. People generally avoided interaction with pirates as a rule.

"Carry on." I ripped a rather large piece of bread off the loaf and used a small knife I kept at my belt to slice some cheese.

"What errand has Cyril for us now?" Elias asked Gerald directly.

Gerald looked uncomfortable at the informal use of his king's name. Though we worked for the King of Northern Ralice, he wasn't our king. Pirates didn't have homes, so they didn't have kings or queens to pay respects to. To us, all men were equally capable of being a means to an end.

"It's a pirate's ship he's after," Gerald said, dropping his tone as if he suspected someone in the tavern might be interested.

"A pirate ship?" Elias asked, annoyed. "Our agreement didn't include pirate ships; that would be quite the gamble of our crewmen's lives as well as our own."

He wasn't wrong. While a pirate's code was to steal anything you could get your hands on, including other pirates' bounty, it would be an excellent way to start a war with another crew. It could be dangerous, bordering on idiotic, depending on the ship's captain.

"They stole something he wants back very badly; it's sitting aboard that ship."

"Master Church," I spoke up, "It doesn't matter what they stole. We cannot go to war with another pirate ship. Especially because if another crew found out about our bargain with your king, we would be marked."

"He's offering twenty-five pounds of gold before your voyage and twenty pounds when his property is returned." He went on as if he hadn't even heard me. "When you secure the cargo inside the ship, you are to bring it back here. From there, our guard will transport it safely to the capitol and the King."

"Gold isn't of any use to the dead," I interrupted more forcefully. "What exactly was stolen?"

Absalom and Elias focused on Gerald and awaited his answer. The army master shifted under the scrutiny. He glanced around again at the other tavern patrons rubbing his hands together. I knew he was nervous not only to discuss business in a public place but also to be seen with us, even at his king's request. Though fond of me, he found our profession distasteful. Most people found our work offensive.

"I can't say."

"You can't say, or you don't know?" Elias countered, taking one of the pieces of cheese I had sliced.

"Nobody does," he admitted.

"If we accept this voyage, how are we even to know where this ship is? Are we to travel all of Marecult looking for it?" I asked.

"They intercepted it between Molina shores and the Forgotten Mountains along Urorah's borders weeks ago. Our military has spotted it heading toward the divide at Hesterna."

"They would have to be going downriver," I guessed.

"With it being spring, that's what we assumed."

"If you know where it is, I wonder why the king doesn't send one of his military ships after it." Elias composed a cheese and bread stack and handed it to me.

His tone had warmed a little, and only I knew why.

I sipped the liquid in the mug and found it to be a spicy tea. It thawed my insides as I clutched my hands around it. If we pursue a ship going downriver on Hesterna, we would be forced to sail down past Hestiege and Southern Ralice. It would be too challenging to sail upriver. We would have to come up and around Northern Ralice's east shores and back down to Odie. It would be a long voyage, but one that we had been waiting for.

"We were hoping there would be less resistance from one pirate ship to another. Perhaps saving the cargo from danger or being lost," Gerald answered, sitting back.

He was no fool. He saw the shift in Elias, and though he didn't know why, he grinned self-satisfied.

"As if pirates just overtake each other's vessels and open our holds for one another," I laughed.

Gerald merely shrugged as if the King and he had thought precisely that. I fought the urge to snort at him and instead finished my tea. It was easy to take a merchant ship because they weren't prepared for attack. They may bear arms in one way or another, but they were less willing to part with their lives to protect cargo. Pirates were always on guard for attack and ready to die defending what they had stolen. Though there would be a much greater risk, we would take our chances. Elias and I didn't even need to discuss it.

"Very well," Elias agreed. "We shall recover whatever it is that is so precious and bring it back to Odie."

"Sending correspondence at each port," Gerald reminded him as Elias waved him off dismissively.

Stopping at ports at regular intervals slowed a voyage drastically, but it was one of the stipulations of our agreement.

"The first when we have the King's property and then regularly after that. If we are going to catch that ship going downriver, we have no time to waste. They will have a lead on us."

"That seems reasonable," Gerald agreed. "There is one more condition King Kosdel has insisted upon."

I had been about to stand up so that we could start preparing. We had done eight raids for King Kosdel. Though we were using him for our benefit, he was still about as slippery as any other king. Looking out for his self-interest, no matter the cost to anyone else. You couldn't blame them; it ran in their blood.

"Out with it," Elias sighed.

"Absalom is to accompany you during your voyage."

My eyes flicked to Absalom's for half a moment. He blanched before replacing his initial reaction with casual interest. Since his mother's passing at the tender age of twelve, Absalom learned to hate the ocean. In his eyes, the sea had taken her from him. It had been almost ten years, and he still wouldn't walk along the beach on a sunny day. He had told me once that he hated standing on the deck of a ship and seeing nothing but a glass ocean before him. Though I knew he hated it, he wouldn't refuse his father's request.

"We do not need a watchdog," Elias ground out.

"The King insisted on a man from his company. I convinced him that Absalom is right for this. I figured you would be more amiable to him than any other. It will be more comfortable, don't you agree?"

"A comfort for yourself or us, I wonder." I bit into another piece of fruit, and Absalom glanced at me, shaking his head.

"Absalom, have you any trouble with this?" Elias asked.

The table went silent. I knew full well that Absalom would protest if he could. He needed to prove to his father that he wasn't as much like his mother as Gerald believed him to be. That mission alone would drive him to do a great many things, including going on a voyage that would take several weeks. Neither Elias nor I would do him the dishonor of saying anything about it out loud.

"None at all. I am eager to learn how your ship runs so well. I doubt I would ever get an invitation from either of you. I shall be glad to take the opportunity."

His smile might have convinced someone who knew him less. His father seemed pleased with his answer and gave his son a proud grin. It was as affectionate as Gerald ever acted toward his son.

"Good lad. I shall have the gold sent to your ship before the end of the day, along with any documentation we have on the sighting of the ship," Gerald said as if everything had worked out perfectly.

"We leave tomorrow before first light." I stood up before Gerald could throw any more surprises. "We have a lot to do if we are to be ready before then. Absalom, if you come tonight, we can show you your quarters, and you can get settled."

We said our goodbyes, and Gerald wished us well. We parted ways outside the tavern. Elias and I walked in silence for a bit. The spring air had finally warmed the streets a little, but frost still lingered. I wished I had another mug of warm tea from the tavern.

Elias waited for me as I went to a few shops on the way back to pick up the new clothes I had ordered the last time we had been there. Aside from my jacket, my attire was little more than rags and holes. I got several new pairs of trousers, an almond leather vest for everyday wear, several plain linen shirts, undergarments, and hosiery.

At the counter of the undergarment shop, the woman tried selling me a dainty silver ring on a chain. I turned it down as I had only ever worn my nine gold hoops: four in each ear and one in my nose above the bow of my lips. Besides those, I never donned any other jewelry. They were the same piercings my mother had worn and what marked me as a pirate woman in a sea of people. It wasn't fashionable for ladies to wear so many hoops, especially not in their noses.

When I came out of the cobbler carrying a freshly oiled pair of boots, Elias stared absently at a woman setting up her loomed rugs for selling.

"Done," I called, and he fell in step with me as we headed for the docks. "What will we do about Absalom?"

"I suppose, once we get to the moment where the decision has to be made, we shall make it," he said, relieving me of a few of my boxes. "I am not yet sure if having him aboard will work to our advantage."

"Shouldn't we have a plan either way? The King is giving us forty-five pounds of Ralician gold to complete this witless mission. It's more than he's ever given us before; shouldn't we at least have a plan for whatever we might find?"

"George, plans for you incite worry, and we need not worry until we need to worry."

"The wisdom that comes from you is truly astounding." I glowered my displeasure.

"I astound even myself." He went on ignoring my expression.

When we got to the ship, the crew stood at attention, waiting for the day's orders.

"Men, we sail out before sunrise tomorrow," I yelled to them all. "Get her ready and restock our supplies. We have a ship to catch!"

Two

Georgette

I watched Absalom from behind the ship's wheel as he walked onto the quarter-deck and leaned back against the railing. He seemed to be taking our departure quite well, considering. When we cast off, he had come up from his quarters as presentable as ever. Elias and I had insisted he didn't dress in his military formals. If another ship were to see him, it would cause us unnecessary trouble. So, he wore plain black trousers and a cream shirt tucked into them. I chuckled at his formal vest sewn from green brocade fabric, and his cravat made him look ornamental amongst the backdrop.

"You're laughing at me," he said, looking down at his shirt and vest. "I'll have you know; I tried to come up in just my shirt and trousers. I felt completely naked and couldn't bring myself to do it."

"Well, I'm sure you would look just as handsome naked as you do fully clothed," I assured, smiling. It was the sort of flirting that he didn't bother to react to anymore. His cheeks would have colored, and his eyes darkened at one time, but years of my brazenness had seasoned him.

"I would feel flattered, George, if I didn't know you said that to every pretty lad that walked onto your ship."

"Who said I find you pretty?" I smirked.

"Why, just a minute ago, you were admiring me in my vest."

"Yes, wishing I had a vest like that. Then came the disheartening realization that I would never look quite as lovely as you."

"True," he agreed and turned away from me to look out over the ocean.

I looked after him, confused, and disappointment gripped my stomach. Usually, our verbal back and forth went on for much longer. We would only stop when one of us got too close to a line both of us knew was there. He had pulled away early, and I found myself wounded.

Though I knew he was not glad to be aboard, I was delighted to have him. Aside from Elias, I considered him my closest friend. I had always wished I could show him just a part of this life. I had longed to reveal a bit of the ocean worth loving, as I imagined it might soothe at least a sliver of his hatred for it.

"Bram!" I shouted at a middle-aged man anchoring a sail in place.

He froze and signaled to another shipmate to take over for him. He walked up and stopped just before the deck landing. Bram's barrel-shaped torso made him look stout. His nose and the bit of his cheeks that peeked out from under his beard were rosy red. He was a good sailor and loyal to my brother and me. His loyalty worth his weight in gold.

"Yes, Captain," he answered, taking his hat off to me.

Though the men didn't do that for Elias, it was something I had not been able to get them to stop doing on my account.

"Didn't we pick up a new crewman back at port?" I asked.

"Yes, Captain, his name is Jameson. He's our new surgeon to replace Gardner."

"I have yet to meet him. Send him up."

"Right away." He hastily disappeared below deck.

Jones, our quarter-master, oversaw all new hires aboard the ship. Elias and I trusted him implicitly, and as he had been pirating for well beyond our sailing years, his expertise was invaluable.

"Morning, Captain," Elias greeted me, coming up the stairs a moment later.

"Morning, Captain," I responded in turn.

We greeted each other this way every day. Our parents had done it before us, and we felt compelled to follow tradition.

"How do you feel about Absalom's vest?" I turned to the man leaning over the ship rail.

I couldn't help but wonder if he was gazing back at the shore in longing or preparing to wretch over the side. Elias turned to assess Absalom as well and grinned. He was close enough to hear our conversation but chose to ignore us.

"I rather like it; do we have a formal meal planned that I wasn't informed of?"

"Forgive me if I don't take my fashion direction from two people who spend their lives on a ship surrounded by half-dressed men," Absalom said, abandoning his previous silence.

"Wounded, truly." Elias passed us and motioned to the navigation room.

"Jones, take the wheel, please," I called to our Quartermaster.

Jones looked as well dressed as Absalom and was the best Quartermaster I had encountered. He had been our parent's Quartermaster as well. He was the only member of their crew we had kept on. He tipped his hat to me in answer, smiling in a way I often thought ladies would have swooned over in his prime. While he was probably twenty-five years my senior, he was a handsome and polished man, for a pirate.

A large table sat in the middle of the navigation room, illuminated by the sun streaming through the windows behind it. The room was modest in size but still my favorite. It held a small library of books on a single shelf-lined wall and under a bench that looked out the back windows. I often took my breakfast there to read. I felt most secure there when I wasn't on solid ground.

Elias sorted a few maps before choosing one with the most detailed rendering of the Hesterna. The Hesterna was a large river, and during spring, it dashed downstream. The only possible way we would catch the other ship on the river was if it happened to be much larger than ours or carrying more cargo. The Siren was a sizable ship. It had been initially intended for military use and converted into a thieving vessel when our father had won it in a game of cards.

"We are making our way to the divide now. It's a risk to assume that they are going downriver, but it would be almost impossible right now to force a ship up Hesterna. Though I've heard of men doing it," Elias said, his eyes following our course.

"They'll take the quickest exit," I put in, leaning over the map. "If this cargo is as precious as the claims, it would be foolish of them to waste time."

"And no one would ever expect foolish behavior from pirates." Sarcasm drenched Absalom's statement.

"No more foolish than any other man," I said.

"Or woman," Elias added.

"I have found that women are substantially less foolish than men," I said with a smile. "Though this is a fool's errand, we agreed to it. We have almost no information about this ship other than the flag it flies and the rough coordinates of its last sighting. We also know nothing of the cargo we seek and if it will be a hassle to load it aboard our ship."

"At least not many merchant ships will be sailing downriver right now," Elias said.

"A small comfort."

Absalom poured over the map with a critical eye and followed the river with his finger. He skipped all over the map, touching things at points here and there with seemingly no order.

"What if they come up by the shores of Coranthia? How do we know they will head south and not north when they exit Hesterna?" His eyes never left the map.

"The Coranthians are intolerant of pirates docking at their ports. Their laws are stringent. There are a few ports where you can dock for a short time, and you must know the port master to even consider it," I said.

"All nations have anti-piracy laws."

"They do, but the people of Coranthia truly believe that their lands are better off without pirates." My eyes grazed the shores on the map.

"They take pirate eradication very seriously," Elias added. "Land in the wrong port, and you will find yourself hanging from a gin displayed as a warning to others."

"So, the chances are unlikely. The safest ports at Coranthia aren't immediately after you exit the river. The most neutral are in Puddle Island, but they wouldn't sail for that long without resupply. If they don't port along the Hesterna, then they will have to shortly after," I said, "and if their ship is weighted with enough supplies to make that kind of journey, we will have no trouble catching them before they make it to the mouth of the river."

"I didn't realize that the subjects of Coranthia were so united in King Vaxa's feelings about piracy," Absalom said, and I ignored the impressed tone of his voice.

"It's gotten worse in the last five years. George and I would find it difficult to count the number of men we know branded pirate and executed there."

Elias looked to a spot on the map where a particularly nasty port rested. I exchanged a grimace with him and shoved down the emotions of losing friends I had known who had ported in the wrong place.

"I suppose worse is a matter of which side you stand on. To the Coranthian government, it would have gotten better. I know many of the men in my company would consider that a great victory," Absalom said, and his words weren't unkind but a reminder of another's viewpoint, a viewpoint we wouldn't fault him for.

There would always be a bit of a divide between the three of us. While we were the best of friends, Absalom could not support our lifestyle. He was a military commander, and we were often on warring sides of political issues. One man bound to uphold the law, and two taught to break it, bound by stout friendship.

"Death to one is life to another," Elias agreed and looked up, "the wind and current are with us now, but that means it is with our prey as well. We will keep the crew up tonight and rotate shifts as to not lose any speed."

"Aye," I agreed.

"Absalom, prepare for your first hunt on The Siren, mate." Elias put his arm around the military commander and shook him good-naturedly.

"I am rather interested to see you both in action." Absalom's mouth said one thing, but his eyes spoke of fear.

He looked up, and I tried not to show the pity I felt for him. Pity was a useless thing, and it helped neither the one feeling it nor the one who you were feeling it for. I also felt a sense of pride in him for coming aboard. Though he was two years older than us and a full-grown man, my heart swelled with the feeling. I focused on that and hoped that was what he saw on my face.

"I would be more comfortable sleeping with the crew than in the quarters I was given," he said, breaking eye contact with me as he headed toward the door.

I supposed his training and the relationships he had with his men back home made him think like that. Higher in rank but not so high to consider himself above the common foot soldier.

"Very well," Elias said to him. "Though if you change your mind..."

"I don't wish for them to resent me, a stranger on their ship of no rank to them, sleeping in a fine room."

Absalom nodded with a smile and opened the door to the deck stepping back out. I went to follow when Elias touched my shoulder lightly. I waited for a single breath as the door closed behind Absalom. I turned to Elias, who had soft concern written on his features.

"I mean no offense by this, George, you know," he started.

"That preface generally means what you are about to say will offend me greatly," I said, smiling. "What is it?"

"I find myself slightly concerned that having Absalom on board will have negative repercussions." He had the good sense to cringe after he said it.

I gave him an irritated look while he searched for his following line of thought.

"Negative regarding the entire crew or negative concerning me?" I asked.

"I don't mean negative," he said, waving a hand as if that would erase that he had even said the word. "I just mean..."

"Yes?" My temper flared for a moment.

"I'm not passing judgment." He looked up at the ceiling. "I merely mean I know things between you and him are..."

"There is nothing between us," I argued stiffly, and he looked at me with an eyebrow raised.

"George, you may choose to lie to yourself, but it is insulting when you lie to me. I mean no harm by asking. If you don't think it will be an issue, then I won't bring it up again."

I let my anger steep for a moment longer before letting it go. I knew Elias didn't mean any harm, and he was looking out for our future. I wasn't sure if there was any merit to his worry, but I couldn't lash out at him for asking. We had many unspoken pacts with each other, but honesty was vital to being united in front of our crew. I would have presented him with the same worries if he were in my shoes.

"I understand your concern Elias," I said, and he looked relieved. "I cannot promise his presence will not color my judgment, but I will do my best to be on guard against it."

"I have no objection to him; I hold him in the highest respect."

"Elias," I begged. "Please, I am becoming uncomfortable."

"I know. I am rather enjoying it."

I scowled at him and walked out the door, leaving his laughter behind me. In my escape from him, I ran into someone waiting just outside the navigation room.

I stepped back, and the man in front of me mumbled an apology and gathered himself. Man was too generous a word as his features lent themselves to a young boy. He would have been at least two years younger than I was with a soft face. Though he was long and thin, he had the air about him of still growing comfortable in his own body. When he finally noticed who he had run into, his brown eyes went wide, and he stepped away from me.

"My lady, my apologies."

My eyes shot to the crew on the deck below. All of them pretending not to listen to the exchange as they snickered at the boy. It was a rite of passage of sorts. The crew would conveniently leave out the fact that one of their captains was a woman, which led to awkward and often unpleasant run-ins for new crew members. I looked at Bram, who was standing behind the boy, trying to hide a smile.

Elias had come partway out of the room and witnessed him making a fool of himself in front of me and the others. He shook his head, but there was a hint of a smile on his face. Elias thought it nearly as funny as the other crew, no matter how often it happened. He stepped out, and the door closed behind him.

"That's Captain Lady to you, young lad," Elias said, standing next to me, and I fought the urge to elbow him in the ribs.

"That's just Captain or Captain George if you like," I said to him though I was warming up to the situation and smothering a small smile.

The boy's eyes got wider, and he stood stiff at attention.

"Captain...." Disbelief was evident.

"Yes."

I had long ago stopped being so irritated by men not thinking me capable of being a Captain. It made the victory sweeter when I proved them wrong. There were not very many females in piracy. A few distinguished themselves enough to leave legacies, and many that sailed pretended to be men.

"You're... beautiful." He shifted uncomfortably as the revelation left his mouth.

I did smile at him then, and his cheeks reddened when some of the crew laughed. There was no doubt about the fact that they were listening now. Elias even let out a soft chuckle. When I looked past the boy to where Absalom was standing, he was not smiling but seemed somewhat concerned.

"Thank you, though that's the last time you should say that, for your own sake." I had leaned in to say it quietly, trying to save him any further shame.

"This must be our new surgeon, Jameson," Elias said, "you look to be a bit young."

"Indeed," I agreed.

"I'm sixteen, sir."

"Captain." Elias looked amused as he gently corrected him. "Captain."

"Not so young. Don't discount Jameson for his youth." I tried to sound assuring and leaned in close to whisper, "A year older than when my brother and I took over this very ship."

I wasn't sure why I volunteered this information to him. Perhaps I felt I understood part of what he was experiencing. Obviously, his first time out on the ocean, he looked scared out of his wits. While we ran a fastidious ship and the crew had been privy to both mine and Elias's wrath, it had to be tempered with kindness and understanding to cultivate trust amongst a crew.

"Welcome," Elias said, leading him down the stairs by his shoulders. "I'll give you a tour. Though I'm sure Bram or Jones have shown you pretty much everything there is to see. Let's show you to the kitchen for some rum to calm your nerves. It gives me a good excuse to drink."

The crew dispersed now that all the fun was over. Absalom still stood at the railing but was now looking out at the ocean again. I turned to Jones, who was still at the wheel.

"How's the sailing?" I asked, and he stepped away so I could step behind it.

"Starting more slowly than I would prefer," he said. "Though once we reach the divide, we will be sailing at a pace that would make other ships blush down to their skivvies."

"I'll take over until then," I said. "We are sailing through the night. I need you to prepare the men. We can work four-hour shifts with a bone crew so that they aren't useless tomorrow."

"Yes, Captain," he said, turning and heading down the stairs, yelling orders at the others.

Absalom stepped over to me when he had gone, as I breathed the sea air and enjoyed how the risen sun was playing off the water. It was still a bit cold, and the tips of my ears stung slightly, but they would warm up in time. I shifted my tricorn hat on my head and rested all my weight on the wheel.

"I thought perhaps calling you beautiful would be a punishable offense," he said, which explained the look of concern on his face earlier. I wondered if he had worried that I would have sent the boy to be whipped or some other harsh punishment. Did he think me that cruel?

"I would be a hypocrite if I punished him for saying it, as I do not hate to hear it. I cannot punish a man for thinking my features beautiful," I said to him, "I only wish that it wouldn't be all they would think of me. I cannot take credit for my physical appearance. I would rather receive a compliment for something I can take pride in."

"Does the crew often fawn over your beauty?" He was back to teasing me now.

"Any man on this ship would be humiliated by the crew for fawning. They would be accused of trying to gain favor by appealing to my femininity, which has not gone well for men in the past."

"So, you are saying it will not work well for me?" Smiling in his way, that set me to daydreaming.

"You have never fawned over my beauty, Commander."

"Quite the assumption." His smile wavered.

He turned to walk down the stairs to the main deck but hesitated as he hovered at the top step for a moment. His hair was always so well kept as if it, too, realized it had a responsibility and wouldn't dare stray. I wanted to walk over to him and run my fingers through it. I wished to add some disorder to his otherwise pristine appearance.

He seemed to be at war with himself but shook it off quickly. He didn't so much as look back as he left. It was the second time that morning he had left me wondering what he was thinking. I scowled after him and wondered if this justified Elias's concerns.

Three

Georgette

I ducked beneath the hatch and walked down the stairs to the second level of the ship. I weaved in and out of the men's hammocks that hung on the gun deck. Some were empty as they were splitting shifts, but some held sleeping pirates. Luckily for me, the weather was cold, so they were mainly bundled up. Some seasons and along the desert line, the men would sleep almost nude, and the trek across their sleeping quarters was less than pleasant.

I peeked over hammocks at faces until I came upon the one I was looking for. The boy was not sleeping, but when I dropped down and came around to his face, he was startled and looked like he might yell. I placed my hand over his mouth and put a finger to my lips. He nodded in understanding as I removed my hand slowly. I signaled for him to follow me, and he scrambled out of his bed, stuffing his sock-clad feet into boots.

I maneuvered back through the sleeping crewmen and up to the deck. There were very few people awake. An entire crew of twenty-five, but a skeleton crew at night was not more than seven. Elias was at the wheel, looking out over the ocean in a silence that I knew better than to interrupt. When we split shifts, both Elias and I stayed up through the night. If circumstances allowed, we would sleep a couple of hours the following day, but we were used to inconstant sleep.

Two men talked loudly in the crow's nest up on the main-mast. I wondered if they were watching for the ship we were hunting or just making salty jibs about their sexual conquests. I started my ascension with anger in my veins, and it didn't take them long to stop their conversation. To his credit, Jameson started up behind me at a good pace.

"Stevie! Goose! Come down from there since all you seem to be good for is jabbering."

"Yes, Captain," they said in unison, coming down the opposite side. When they passed me, I grabbed Goose's shirt and pulled him close enough that I could smell salted fish on his breath.

"You were both loud enough to wake the dead. Tomorrow you are both on stoning duty. The entire quarter-deck better be shining by the end of tomorrow."

"Yes, Captain."

"But get some sleep first." I released him and continued my way up.

Stevie said something snide to Jameson on his way down that I couldn't hear. I crawled into the top basket of the ship and was joined shortly after by our newest young surgeon.

We sat in silence for a while as he took in the view. It was a sight that never got old. The stars over the water from atop a mast were miraculous in a way where no words could quite describe. The night was dark, the moon just a thin crescent in the sky—the glowing white stars like pieces of sand scattered across the bottomless ocean floor.

"It's rather lovely," he said first, "but also quite terrifying, Captain." He added the last bit as an afterthought, and I gazed up into the heavens.

"Very well described, Doctor."

"I'm not a proper Doctor." He turned away, "Captain."

"One Captain was plenty." I stepped back and leaned against the mast as he continued to look out over the horizon.

"I'm sorry, I have no knowledge of what to say on a ship."

"No one expects you to. Though the crew will make fun of you, many of them faltered the same way when they first joined a crew." I let him sit in the quiet for a minute before asking my question. "I trust Jones to vet the crew, but I must say, Jamie ... do you mind being called Jamie?"

"My mother called me Jamie," he said, and the affectionate longing in his voice made me think it a fond memory.

"How does a sixteen-year-old become qualified enough to be vetted by one of my toughest crew members for our new surgeon?"

"My father," his voice broke, and I waited for him to go on, "was a surgeon, a good one. I was in the room with him learning everything I could from the time I was five."

"Rather gruesome." My face twisted at the image of a five-year-old boy watching as a leg was amputated.

"My father insisted. He wasn't a bad man. My father was just ... insistent." He defended him with a rawness in his voice.

I recognized the sadness of loss on a person without them having to say anything. When he was ready, he would tell me, or maybe he wouldn't. It was his grief to do with what he wanted, and I wouldn't push him to express it.

"You have no moral conflicts about working for pirates?"

"Pirates were some of our most frequent clients." He turned to look at me. "Some of the most generous and kind people I met were pirates. Though some of the worst people we worked on were also pirates."

"You were willing to take your chances that we were the generous sort?" I asked because I could sense that he was holding something back.

"My father knew Jones."

"Ah, my Quartermaster shows his bleeding heart." My smile spread across my face, and he looked worried.

"I will work hard, and I truly have a lot of medical knowledge." He rushed the words out as if I would toss him off the crow's nest into the ocean below.

"You'll have the opportunity to prove yourself," I assured him.

"May I ask you a question?" He shuffled uncomfortably again.

"You are always free to ask a question."

"I have heard stories of The Siren my whole life. My mother told them to me when I was young. The dashing Captain Nathaniel sweeping Lady Hazel off her feet as they sailed off into the sunset. Swordfights, water sirens, hidden treasure; you aren't old enough to be Hazel."

"Not exactly a question," I said.

"Who are you?"

I chuckled. I thought of how to answer. Though Jamie wasn't asking me who I was. He was asking where my parents had gone. He wondered how I had become the captain of a pirate ship with a reputation beyond my eighteen years of life. The answer to that was part of who I was, but not all of it.

"Captain Georgette Baine of The Siren," I settled on, "The crew has many stories and explanations. My favorite being that Elias and I have found the fountain of youth and changed our names to avoid suspicion."

"Sounds like the kind of tale my mother would have told me."

"We have some excellent storytellers aboard," I said, moving to climb down the mast.

"Captain…," he faltered, looking sad to leave the perch so close to the stars.

"You take this shift, Jamie, and I'll have someone come relieve you in an hour or so. It can get cold up here, so come down if you start getting numb. We've been instructed to look out for a black and white flag with a yellow star."

"Yes, Captain." He nodded.

I swung my leg over the rail, secured my feet in the ratline, and climbed down. My boots hit the deck hard as I took the final jump down. I looked up at Elias, and he nodded, giving me the approval to come up. I made my way to him, and he left the wheel sitting across from it as I took his place. I watched as Elias pulled out a piece of driftwood that he was working on whittling down into something beautiful. He once told me that the wood spoke to him as he worked, telling him what it wanted to be.

"What will it be?" I asked, leaning into the wheel and peering over at it.

"Can't be sure yet," he said, holding it out in front of him and eyeing it carefully. "Perhaps a tree, but that's not quite right."

He went back to carving, and we sat in silence for a while. I looked up occasionally to check on Jamie but could hardly see him. I schooled myself to stop looking after him. I had already formed an attachment to him that felt protective. It was not a kindness I could afford. I had wanted to speak with him privately, covering up my real motivations by putting him to work as a lookout.

Elias either hadn't noticed or didn't say anything. It was most likely the latter as not much escaped his eye. I knew his simple careless act to be a facade. He was just as watchful as I was, just as careful with his life and emotions. He was just much better at acting nonchalant.

"What do you think they would say?" I asked, smiling up at the stars. "If we find it and it is as incredible as they told us it would be?"

My blood hummed with our quest. For as long as I remembered, our parents had chased the same treasure, the treasure of Baron Valloe. Valloe had been the captain of a pirate ship called The Forgotten, and his reputation was vaunted across all Marecult. Most people that lived on land told daring stories of him and his ruthless crew over a pint of beer. To pirates, Baron Valloe was known for his hidden treasure. Many pirates had spent their entire lives searching for it. Most thought it was more of a fairy-tale told than a treasure to find.

"I suppose they would either be incredibly happy for us or rather infuriated that they never found it. Likely a mixture of both."

"If it exists," I said, thinking of all the misleads we had followed and all the pointless locations we had sailed.

Pirates were notorious for spreading rumors of their hidden treasure as a distraction rather than actual truth. We were both aware that the prize we sought could be a rouse that Valloe had circulated himself. We were aware of it, but neither of us would ever stop searching.

"You get so ruffled every time we have a lead." He looked up at me and smiled.

"You can't tell me you aren't eager. This bit of information that we paid for dearly leads us to an uncharted island in Southern Ralice waters. At the very least, it will be a grand adventure."

"Our entire life is a grand adventure."

"Oh, go back to your whittling, don't ruin my fun." I waved him off, and we sat in comfortable silence.

Hours passed with no words between us while I imagined what it would be like to find the legendary bounty. I delved into my world of fiction, where I would take part of my share and buy a quaint house in Odie. It would be where I would stay when we were at the port. If I said this out loud to Elias, he would surely make fun of me. Pirates didn't have houses or wish to be bound by immovable stone and wood. I was sometimes ashamed when my thoughts wandered to fantasies of living in a house with a husband and children running around.

It happened more often than I would admit to anyone. I pictured myself in a kitchen with a boy pulling on my skirts and apron. I mixed up something fragrant in a bowl, spooning it into tins to be baked. A man came up behind me, kissing my neck, picked our son up, and tossed him in the air as the boy laughed, delighted. Then my daydream would change slowly. The bowl disappeared from my hand, replaced by a sword. My skirts transformed into trousers, and the boy and the man vanished. Then I woke up and was behind the wheel of a pirate ship where I would always be.

I shook my head to come out of the disappointment I felt. Elias was still whittling away as the first rays of the sun were about to peak over the horizon. I heard the crew milling around below deck, getting ready for the day and eating their first meal.

"Good morning." The man who always played the role of the husband in my daydreams came up the stairs.

"Absalom." Elias looked up at him. "How did you sleep?"

"I've had worse nights."

I had never seen him right after waking up from my imaginings of another life. I looked away from him unintentionally because I was afraid of him seeing something too intimate on my face.

"I'll get us some food," Elias said, and I heard him get up.

"I don't mind eating with the crew," Absalom said.

"I'll allow that on other days." Elias headed down the stairs, leaving me alone with Absalom.

It was still mostly dark, and the deck was lit by the lanterns hanging about. One hung just above Absalom, who was standing where Elias had just been sitting. I left the wheel momentarily unattended and walked down the stairs over to the main mast, trying to look less bothered than I was.

"Jamie, come down and eat something; the sun is about to come up."

I turned just as Bram came up from below deck. He had a piece of dried and salted meat hanging from his mouth and was wrangling a good deal of rope. He grumbled curses at it for being difficult and did not even notice that I was there. When I turned about to find Jones, he raised an eyebrow in anticipation.

"Jones! Stevie and Goose are on stoning duty until they finish the entire main deck," I said, remembering my irritation and threat.

"Aye, Captain."

"Please enlighten me who thought those two dolts assigned to the crow's nest together was a good idea?" I stopped walking now to give him a hard stare as he shifted under it.

"Captain Elias," he responded, and I sighed.

I couldn't get Elias in trouble, and Jones knew I wouldn't say anything negative about him in front of the crew.

"Very well, wake them up and get them started then." I walked back up to the quarter-deck.

Absalom stood where I had left him, and his bright eyes followed me. I sat on the ship's rail to watch the sunrise. He still said nothing, and his silence made me impatient.

I looked over, and he was still staring at me, his smile tugging on the corners of his mouth. He was waiting for me to acknowledge him; he'd known I would. I had known him long enough to realize that he was challenging me. To see how long I could sit with the silence I hated so much.

"You're insufferable." I shook my head.

"I've done nothing."

"Come here and watch this." I motioned for him to come to stand by me as we faced the horizon.

"I can't help feeling you and Elias agreed to this much too easily," he said, settling in, and my heartbeat picked up slightly as I feigned innocence. "To cross another pirate crew seems more than a negligible risk and then to be comfortable with me coming aboard. I could potentially report everything back to my father."

"Are you going to report everything back to your father?" I asked, not looking at him but instead out to the first rays of orange light grazing the water.

"I have warred over that very question."

"And which Absalom won out? The military commander or the friend of pirates?"

He ignored the question and went silent, looking out with me over the river. We were close but not touching. I could feel warmth radiating off him and longed to lean in just slightly so I would be resting against him. Neither of us moved.

"It's beautiful," he said. "Do you mean to seduce me with the beauty of the water? Would you have me forget that I loathe the very smell of its air and the sound of waves against the anchored ships?"

"Perhaps not to forget," I answered, "But to see that it isn't all as dismal as you view it."

"This sunrise certainly isn't dismal." He was back to looking at me; I felt his gaze on my skin.

"Perhaps you can accompany us more, and we shall convert you into a rascal yet."

"I can't, George," he said, his tone now serious.

Not entirely steel but something as forceful. A man that was trying desperately to explain something.

"I'm only kidding, Absalom," I assured him, turning and lifting an eyebrow at his response. "I have no trouble tracking you down on land to enjoy your company."

"George…" He was pleading with me to understand something he hadn't spoken out loud.

He opened his mouth to finish the thought, but Elias's steps came up the stairs and caused him to stop and look back out over the river. Then it was as if he hadn't said anything at all.

"Vittles for you," he called behind us and doled out cooked meat and slices of fruit.

The first three days of a voyage were always the most abundant before our meals became mainly food that didn't spoil quickly. They were my favorite days of a journey.

"We were just discussing," I said, swallowing a bit of food, "that Absalom feels we took this charge in haste, and he suspects devious motivations."

"Oh?" Elias asked, looking at me in question.

"I more than suspect you of deviousness. I know you are up to something underhanded," Absalom said humorlessly, "I just have yet to determine what you both want."

"And George is always telling me what a simpleton you are, and he's figured it out quicker than you gave him credit for."

"I've never said such a thing." My brother's good humor was infectious.

"Are you going to tell me what it is, or shall you leave me to guess?" Absalom grumbled, and it seemed that Elias's playfulness had not penetrated him. "I turn a blind eye to your roguery most of the time because it does not concern me. If you try something while I am to be supervising this voyage, it will be my neck wrung out."

"Oh, don't be so sour," Elias said, stepping behind the wheel and taking a large bite of a biscuit.

"Captains!" The single shout from one of the crewmen and our strained conversation halted.

"There she is!" It was Bram who called to us, pointing to a ship in the distance.

He had a monocular to his eye. Elias rushed down, and Bram handed it to him.

"That it is!" he shouted, and my heart raced. We shouldn't have overtaken them as quickly as we did.

"Men, prepare yourselves. All hands on deck! We don't let up until we capture that vessel!" I said, coming down the stairs and walking to stand next to Elias.

He handed me the spyglass, and I peered through it.

Not far off, I saw a large military vessel. One of the masts flew the pirate flag and a flag of three black and white stripes with a large yellow star in the center. The flag Gerald had told us was unique to this ship. A feeling of trepidation grew in my chest as I lowered the monocular and held it to one side.

Something about it felt wrong.

Four

Georgette

I had pulled Absalom and Elias into my quarters after we had gotten closer to the other ship. I was sure it hadn't escaped either of their attention that I had been obsessive about looking to the ship whenever I could. I had hardly left the front deck. Worry gnawed at my insides as The Siren crept closer.

Both of their flags were flying high. I could make out some crew moving about the top deck, but it seemed as if the ship wasn't moving, or it was merely creeping along. Certainly, moving slower than the current, and its sails were closed though the wind would be with them if opened. It did not sit well with me at all.

"Why are they stopped?" I asked once the door to my quarters was closed.

Absalom looked around with interest. He had never been in my room before, and he took everything in with intensity. Elias looked at me, now letting his controlled mask fall, and I saw the spark of worry in his eyes.

"I can't figure it, but if you keep this up, the crew will start to be concerned as well," he spoke.

"They should be. Why would the ship be stopped in the middle of the river, Elias?" I queried again, "Midday, and the ship is traveling at a speed as if its anchor is dropped."

"Do pirates ever recover or rest in the day?" Absalom asked, "Perhaps they travel at night, and their crew sleeps during the day."

"They would be much further ahead if that was the case." Elias shifted on his feet, rubbing his hand over a day's worth of growth on his face.

"You're both concerned," Absalom said, eyeing us now, "What would cause a captain to do such a thing?"

"If he wanted to be caught," I ground out and began to pace. "We have no idea what we are heading into, and something about the flag is bothering me."

"It looks familiar to me too," Absalom said. "And I can't say I've run across many pirate ships in my years."

"We must proceed with caution," Elias agreed. "We have no choice but to continue. We knew that King Kosdel could use our agreement and bend it to make us do any manner of thing. We agreed to his terms, knowing he might do something dishonest."

I couldn't argue. We knew the nature of royalty and the risks involved with our choice. It was one of our biggest hesitations and something our parents had reminded us of often. The lesson that we were only to trust each other, ingrained into us from a young age. Now it was as natural as breathing. However, our bargain had been necessary to grant us extended access to Southern Ralice's waters without attack.

"I'm not pleased with this," I said as if it changed anything. "If Cyril has put my crew or us in any immediate danger, I will..."

"And I'll help you," Elias promised me, reaching out and grabbing both my shoulders.

I looked into his eyes, and he acknowledged my worry.

"Though let's not get worked up quite yet until we are sure as to what we are facing. The reasons behind this could be endless. We will tell the crew to be on their guard. We don't have a ship full of dolts, and the men can handle themselves."

I nodded and took a deep breath. His calm washed over me, dissipating the worry slightly. He squeezed my shoulders in comfort before letting his hands drop. I went to the corner of my room and buttoned up my new coat. I put on my leather belt with my sword and toothed dagger.

"Perhaps we should tell Absalom of our true plan before we reach the ship," Elias suggested.

I weighed the merits of both options in my mind turning to them. Absalom knowing was a huge risk and was the reason we had not told him. It went against his uprightness, and asking him to keep it to himself wasn't fair of us. He was the kind of man that chose to do the right thing for its own sake. He did what he was supposed to do because he believed in ultimate justice. We would be asking him to choose between his service and his friendship. Something I knew neither of us would take lightly.

"I will not betray you," Absalom said, "I have loyalty to the King and my father, but I would not betray you."

He sounded tortured to me. As if the decision pained him to some degree, and I supposed that it did.

"We know," I said to him, smiling. "Though we don't wish to put you in such a difficult place. We were not anticipating your presence."

"I know that." Absalom dismissed my understanding with a frown. "My father pushed for this, and he has greatly miscalculated my devotion to you." He was looking at me, and his eyes went wide at the word he had used. "To you both. Our friendship seems, mostly to my dismay, stronger than the bond I have with my father."

"What do you say, George?" Elias asked.

"If you think it prudent, Elias, I trust him."

"Very well." Elias went to a small table in the corner of my room with two velvet chairs.

The chairs were anchored to the floor as everything else was. Even the bed sat nailed securely in the corner. The urge to redecorate infrequently came when it was so much trouble to do. I went to sit on my bed, though I felt rather silly sitting informally in my captain's jacket, adorned with weaponry. Absalom took the other chair, and I watched him wring his hands under the table. It was a nervous habit he had taken from his father.

"We have our motivations for allying with King Kosdel, as you have probably guessed," Elias said to him, and Absalom rolled his eyes.

"It's an unmarked island we are looking to access far off the shores of Southern Ralice. Since Cyril has a treaty with King Dalion of Southern Ralice, he has notified the King not to interfere with our ship." I picked up as Elias nodded. "Dalion has his waters pretty heavily patrolled, especially around the mouth of The Cras. We would perhaps get away with sailing through and stopping at a port. To sail in their waters for an extended period would be impossible without assurance that they wouldn't hunt us."

"What is on this island that is worth so much trouble?" Absalom leaned back in the chair.

"Treasure," Elias said, and the excitement I had tried to coax from him the previous night was now evident in his eyes.

"Please tell me that's a joke." Absalom looked between us. "What treasure? All this trouble for..."

"Valloe's treasure." I got up from my bed, feeling too vulnerable sitting where I also slept.

"Oh, Baya, consume me!" He invoked the name of the Ralician sea goddess. "Not that old children's tale. Please tell me I am not putting my life on the line so that you two can chase after some childish fantasy."

He looked between us, but neither Elias nor I said anything. He stood up, and there was a rage building on his features that I was hesitant to address. His mouth was open to say something, but Absalom didn't seem to be able to form the words around his anger. I understood why he was upset. To him, we were risking everything by chasing this lead. A lead that could turn out to be fruitless.

"How do you suppose you'll excuse your absence from porting to my father? Days' worth of silence from you? They'll suspect something, and if you try to fool the King and he finds out, he'll have a price on both your heads." I could see him trying to control himself, taking breaths deeper than necessary. "And mine! If he finds out, I'll be stripped of my rank and cast off into nothing. It will kill my father. What shall I tell him? That I lied to follow you on an absurd mission to find a treasure. It has been hidden for more than a century and was probably invented to keep fools like you entertained."

"Absalom, just let us explain," I said, stepping closer to him.

"Oh, I will have an explanation," he said to me, sitting back down.

"We paid dearly for the information that led us to the discovery of this island," Elias explained. "We also have a plan for the days we will not be at port. There will be no reason your father or the King will suspect anything is amiss."

"What kind of plan?" he asked, accusing our competence with his tone.

"We shall port at Skirttown in Southern Ralice, and then we shall leave a crew member there to travel by land to the next port. At that port, he shall send a letter to your father that the ship has been damaged. A problem minor enough to be fixed but major enough to account for a three or four-day delay."

I waited for his response. Him knowing of our plans made him complicit in our lie to the King and his father. However, the other option was to tie him up or leave him at Skirttown. I had a feeling he would take that as more of a betrayal than letting him choose to trust us or not. Though at that moment, I thought we should have tied him up after all.

"It's a plan," he said, taking another one of his deep breaths. He was visibly less irritated than he had been. "Not a great plan, but a plan."

"I'm sorry, mate," Elias said to him, and he did honestly sound sorry.

"I should expect as much," he said. "Oh, to be the companion of pirates."

It bruised me a little to hear him call me a pirate with such distaste. Pirate was usually a word that I was proud to be labeled. People threw it at us as an insult, and I would bow and accept it as praise. So, I wondered why it bothered me so much when he said it with contempt.

"Cyril isn't the brightest king we have encountered." Elias rolled his eyes. "Your father may suspect something but will feel more secure with you watching our every move."

"What a disappointment I turned out to be." Absalom was coming around now and added a smile to his words.

"That depends on who is telling the story." I walked closer to the table. "To us, you haven't disappointed at all."

"I hope," Absalom stood and headed for the door, "there is nothing on this island when we get there and that you drop this grand illusion of finding pirate treasure."

"Even if there is not." Elias stood up as well, going to follow him out.

"We won't give up our delusions," I finished.

We all stepped back out on the deck and surveyed our progress. We had almost overtaken the ship, and my anxiety reared its head. The other ship's flags thrashed in the wind, and it was so close I could see them fully. The traditional flag flown by pirate ships in Marecult were white flags with a broken anchor and three stars in the left-hand corner. The banner I stared at had the anchor but no stars.

"Elias," I said in warning.

"I see it." He strode to the foredeck, and we both followed behind him.

"If not pirates...." I stood next to him, staring at the flags, trying to get a good look at anyone who may be above deck.

They would have been aware of us by now, and with The Siren's speed and proximity, there would be no confusing our intent.

"We shall see." Elias looked at me with a question.

He always let me choose my role first when commanding. I looked to the crew, who were waiting for orders. I tried to think of what would serve us best. I weighed Elias's and my strengths.

"I'll take the quarter-deck." I turned to him. "You'll notice anything out of place before I would."

"And you're better at the wheel than I." He smirked at me because I hadn't spoken that bit aloud.

"Absalom can come with me. I'll call anchor, and you call bow shot." Absalom and I descended the stairs as I addressed the crew. "Get ready to board, lads! Keep your wits about you; something smells sour. Gunmen get below deck wait for Captain Elias' word for the bow shot. Bram, take Jamie with you to be on anchor."

I listened as Elias ordered some of the crew to release the longboat and hoist it to be at the ready. I dashed across the deck to where Jones handed me the wheel and left to go below deck with the gunmen. I hardly noticed Absalom standing behind me braced against the navigation room door. I was focused, tilting the wheel ever so slightly to prepare for the pull to come alongside the ship.

"Prepare to come along broadside, drop anchor!"

The crew carried my order below deck, and I heard the fast clicking of the anchor wheels. I waited a few breaths before turning the wheel hard in my hands, spinning it until the ship changed course to come alongside the other. I let it go to self-correct until we were sailing straight once more. The Siren shuddered as both its anchors hit the bottom of the riverbed. We slowed, and I held the wheel, watching Elias closely, expecting his order for the bow shot at any moment. The order never came.

Absalom stepped forward as I watched Elias come down from the foredeck. He never took his eye off the other ship. Absalom left me, walking toward the main deck, trying to get a better view. It was clear, even as their ship slowed down, why Elias hadn't needed to fire a shot. The entire crew of the other ship was lying face down with their hands flat against the deck and their weapons piled to one side. A small white flag waved partway up their main mast.

"Drop your second anchor!" Elias shouted over to someone that I couldn't see.

"Jones!" I called out, and a few moments later, he appeared to take the wheel.

I walked down the stairs to join Elias and Absalom, where they were standing mid-deck, looking directly onto the deck of the other ship, which now stopped as its second anchor dropped. They had an anchor down, after all. I stood frozen, calculating the situation. A man rose from where he lay, keeping his hands above his head. He walked to the edge of the rail of his ship.

"We surrender!" he shouted to us, "You may board our vessel without any resistance."

I looked over at Elias. He made an unsure noise in his throat and looked back at me. It wasn't unusual for a crew to surrender before a ship overtook them. It was unusual for a pirate ship to surrender. We had expected a fight and to be met with resistance of being boarded. It was clear that these men were not pirates, though they dressed as comical versions of the idea. The question presented itself again. If not pirates, then who? Why had we been told they were pirates?

"We shall bring five men aboard, but our gunmen are still ready below deck if you think of trying anything," Elias warned him.

"I understand, sir," the man replied.

The three of us and two crewmen got into the longboat as it sank into the water. The other ship lowered a rope ladder for us to climb. My concern whispered all kinds of things in my ear as I watched Elias reach for the ladder.

"Step back from the ladder and give them room to board," I heard Bram shout from our ship.

Our crew would guard against attack as we came up. I followed closely behind Elias. I tried to slow my heart and smother my feelings that something was about to go wrong.

When I reached the top of the ship, I vaulted myself over the railing. The man who had addressed us was standing before Elias, who drew his sword. The crewmen lay as still as a windless ocean. I would have thought them dead had a few of them not peered up at me every couple of seconds. It was too quiet, and I could feel the tension radiating off Elias. I waited for Absalom and the others to climb up before saying anything.

"Who are you?" I asked the man.

"My name is Barnabus, mam." He shifted as anyone would at sword point.

He looked to be in his mid-thirties, with grey hair at his temples and a round face. He also had a gut that suggested he enjoyed barley alcohol.

"Barnabus, are you a pirate?" I asked.

"No, mam."

"Are you supposed to be dressed like one?" I looked up at their false pirate flag.

"Yes, mam."

"Why?" Elias asked, pushing his blade up to the man's throat.

"I was given a sum of money to sail this ship down Hesterna and port just outside at Dalamara." He sounded sincere enough, but I still felt uneasy.

"You're a skimmer," I said with disgust.

Skimmers ran other people's ships with a new crew at every port. Any idiot that knew how to sail a vessel could wander docks and take odd jobs sailing courses or long voyages that merchants didn't want to do themselves. Either that or they were afraid of losing their men, so they sent strangers instead. Skimmers were the bottom feeders of the sailing community.

"Yes, mam."

"So, this is not your crew." I walked toward the men weaving in and out of them. "And those," I pointed at the flags. "Are not your flags?"

"No, mam."

"It's Captain Baine, Skimmer." I hurled the name out like a poisoned dart.

His face paled a little. He had no doubt heard of the Captains Baine. He looked from me to Elias and nodded.

"Somebody instructed you to dress like pirates, hoist a pirate flag, and sail a ship with one anchor downriver?" I asked, "So that I understand."

"Yes, Captain Baine."

"Were you anticipating being raided?" Elias asked.

"We were not informed of that, no," the man said, "But I'm not risking my life for some other's man's business."

"But you must have wondered," Absalom said, the curiosity in his tone evident, "why you were asked to do all these things. It should have seemed rather strange."

"Sir, in my line of work, I haven't the pleasure of turning down money because something strikes me as strange."

"Does the ship carry stolen cargo?" Elias dropped his sword as he decided the skimmer wasn't a threat.

"I believe so."

"What do you mean you believe so?" I asked, tapping my foot on the deck.

The sooner we could get the cargo and leave, the sooner I could be out of this strange situation where nothing made sense. Then we could be on our way to our treasure we had been waiting years for.

"Well, there isn't much on board worth your while, so I imagine I know what you came to get. Though the history of how it came to be on this ship, I could not tell you."

"Where is it?" Absalom ground out now impatient.

"Below deck, I'll take you. You won't harm us, will you?"

He was afraid, I realized. You couldn't always control the stories that people told about you. Some of it worked in our favor, like the rumor that we didn't leave many survivors. With countless survivors running around, it was a wonder the tale continued at all.

"If you hand over what this vessel is hiding without resisting, we won't harm you or any other person on this ship," Elias promised him and sheathed his sword. "Take us."

So, the man led Elias and me down into the belly of the ship. We left Absalom, Slope, and Will above deck in case any crew members decided to act out. It was a large ship, even more significant than ours. Once we reached the gun deck, Barnabus opened the cargo hatch door and descended even further. We walked along, passing rope and rigging to a dark corner of the ship only illuminated by the lantern the man had brought along.

"What are you hiding down here?" Elias asked as the man came to a stop in front of a small room that looked barely large enough to fit two barrels.

It had a metal slat built into it, but I could not see what was inside.

Instead of answering, he pulled out a key from his pocket and held the light up to insert it into the door. He twisted the key, and it clicked, allowing the door to be pulled open. He held the light up to shine inside the room.

"Ocean's deep!" I gasped.

Inside the tight space was a woman with auburn hair clinging to her cheeks. She looked up at us with raw hatred scored into her features.

Five

Mercy

I realized it was difficult for your eyes to adjust from complete and utter darkness to any bit of light. I thought I had known darkness. I slept in the dark and had roamed the castle corridors at night. I had even once snuck into the root cellar to steal a jar of the cook's coveted pickles. I had thought that was darkness until I had been locked up in this ship's tiny abyss; it was then I realized that I had never experienced true darkness.

It consumed everything, even sound, and it teased me into thinking things were there that weren't. It tricked my mind into thinking there was light when there was none. At first, I had rushed to the small opening when I thought I saw a lantern. It meant someone was going to bring food and a slight reprieve to the endless sea of black. Soon I realized that they brought me food so sporadically that I could not count on it. I also learned during my time there that I had never experienced true hunger. I stopped rushing to the opening altogether and now just stared at it with odium. The room was big enough for me to get up and walk a little, which I forced myself to do every so often. I had to sleep sitting on the wooden bench inside the room which wasn't long enough for me to lay on. There was a chamber pot in the room which I used with terrible difficulty while my hands were tied, I shoved it outside the slat every day to be emptied.

There was no way for me to keep track of time. Had I been there a month or a couple weeks? I couldn't be sure. If I surfaced and they told me it had been a year, I might believe it. If I was courting madness. I sang and hummed to myself to pass the time. I would pretend my maid Alita was there with me and cast myself in both conversation roles. I may have been closer to madness than I cared to admit.

When I had first heard noises, I thought it was the darkness playing its cruel tricks. I saw the faintest hint of light through the slit they used to feed me and dismissed it. Then I heard the footsteps and thought I was about to receive my small cup of salty broth and a scrap of bread. Then the clicking of the door was followed by a light that flooded into my eyes.

I had a second to decide to look away and close my eyes against the pain of the adjustment or stare at whoever was coming to see me. So, they could see the madness I felt.

"Ocean's deep!" It was a female voice, but I still couldn't see anything.

I heard a loud groan from a man and saw him bent over in pain as my vision came back. Two other people stood in the doorway. One was a woman and the other a man. They looked similar enough to be related. The woman's hair was longer and braided back in tight form, and both had the same eyes. The man was a few inches taller and looked at me with a mix of worry and regret. Even in the dim light, I could tell that he was handsome, the kind of scoundrel little girls imagined in fantastic stories. For surely, by their appearances alone, they were pirates. Though I now knew, most pirates did not resemble the dashing pirate princes that young girls tittered about over tea.

"What are you thinking, keeping her down here?" the woman who had just punched the man in the gut asked.

"I was instructed to keep her down here," he winced, standing back up.

I recognized that man's voice. I had heard him give orders to keep me locked below deck. He had also come to bring my meals a few times and had even tried to start conversations with me.

They all stared at me, but I gave nothing back but contempt. I didn't know who they were or what their plans for me involved. I was simply disgusted that they were pirates. My brother referred to them as lowly common criminals who knew only the love of fortune. I seemed destined to meet my end surrounded by the kind of people I had been raised to loathe.

"Who are you?" the young male pirate asked me.

I curled my lip at him but didn't answer. I had heard too many stories of pirate cruelty and how women were treated aboard their ships. I looked at the woman then. She was still glaring at the older man with something savoring of distaste, and he looked to be afraid of her. I had also heard of women that sailed with pirates as part of their crew. The stories painted them as perversions of nature. The woman before me looked ferocious but surprisingly lovely. She had piercings all up both ears and one gold ring through the middle of her nose.

"She says she's a Princess. She insisted upon it for the first couple of days. The girl was screaming until she went hoarse. That she's to be married to King Cyril Kosdel of Northern Ralice," the man's whose voice I recognized said, and the female punched him again.

"George, please," her counterpart said to her though there was no force behind it.

"She's obviously from Molina. The pale skin and beauty spots mark her as theirs. She's as delicate as glass coral; if she's not a princess, she's at least high born," the woman said, and I was surprised she had guessed but kept my features harsh.

"I'll kill that blasted king," the woman said, stepping back.

"I'll be there by your side, but we must get this woman up above deck if not for the sunshine alone." He stepped toward me.

"We are going to take you above deck now," he said to me carefully.

"I would rather die," I said to him, and his mouth quirked up in a half-smile before flashing back to passive.

"You will die down here," he said, "Is this how you want to meet your end?"

I had never considered how I wanted to die. It seemed a cruel thing to offer me a choice of different deaths. This man presented death in a dark hole or one no doubt waiting for me shortly after that. I thought, though, if I could see the sky once more, I would choose to delay my end a moment longer.

He must have seen the change in me as he reached out to help me up. I jerked away from him as he pulled his hand back. I would not accept the hand of a pirate. I slid my feet to the floor. They ached from being bent and cramped for so long. My hands were still bound, so I rose as gracefully as I could. I lifted my chin with disdain at them when I was ready to continue.

"She has the pretension of royalty," the woman pirate mused as I stepped out before them.

I had been blindfolded and carried down into my dark prison, so the trek back up was new to me. I had also been the most terrified I had been in my life when first coming through here, so this was a less unpleasant change.

We were at the stairs leading up to the main deck, and the sun coming down was scorching my eyes. I forced myself up the stairs without hesitating, and my eyes were assaulted with the unfiltered bright light of day. When I reached the deck, it was too much. I had to squeeze my eyes closed against it. Even that did not work, and I covered my eyes with my hands to make the adjustment slower.

"Baya consume me!" a man said, coming closer to us as I squinted my eyes open. "Please tell me..."

He must have seen the answer in the pirates' faces because he stopped talking and frowned. He was more polished than the other two and held himself with a stiffness I recognized as militant. This man was no pirate though his dress was casual.

"Who are you?" the handsome pirate asked again.

I chastised myself for thinking of him as the handsome pirate. His tone wasn't cruel, and his eyes looked kind, but such things wouldn't deceive me. I looked down at my dress which I hadn't changed since my abduction. It was disgusting and wrinkled, and I was sure my hair and complexion were much the same. With my hands tied, I couldn't even push the hair away from my face. Still, I lifted my chin and looked at him directly.

"I'm Princess Mercy Landlight, fourth born to King and Queen Landlight of Adamas." I was proud of myself as my voice didn't waver despite my appearance.

"Isn't your brother, Holt, on the throne now, Princess?" the tall man who was not a pirate asked.

"He is," I said, tone clipped.

"Absalom, we don't even know if she's the princess," the female pirate said, eyeing me with distrust.

"I think she is," he said. "I've seen Prince Holt; if they aren't siblings, I would be surprised. Also..." He trailed off.

"Also, what, Absalom?" The decidedly not handsome pirate turned to the man. "What is it that you know and haven't told us?"

"King Kosdel is to be married to a Princess of Adamas. To secure alliances between countries."

I felt a bit of relief that at least this man, Absalom, believed and knew who I was. What good it did, I wasn't sure. He may not be a pirate, but he seemed to be friends or acquaintances with these pirates. I wasn't any safer with them believing my story.

"That wasn't something you thought to share earlier?" the male pirate questioned.

"It didn't seem prevalent, Elias," Absalom said. "What care do you have if my King is to wed a Princess? You hate court politics. How was I to know she had been kidnapped or that she was the cargo we were charged with rescuing?"

"Did you know?" the female pirate's voice was quiet and accusing but held more weight than the pirate Elias' had.

Absalom looked back to her, and his tone and demeanor changed as he softened.

"Of course not," he said, "I would have told you. I wouldn't have agreed to it at all. You have to know that." She nodded as if that was enough and went back to staring at me.

"Load her onto the longboat," she demanded as two men came forward to escort me to the edge of the boat.

I took in the ship's crew lying face down on the deck. I looked upon the other ship that had pulled up alongside the one I was on. The sun glistened off a very dark wood that seemed almost black. The shock of white sails against the tone of the wood made it ominous. What caught my eye most was the woman who was carved into the helm. She had a sword outstretched in front of her, and her breasts were bared. The bottom half of her body was an octopus of some sort, and her tentacles wrapped wildly around the head of the ship. The lifeless woman looked familiar to me for reasons I could not place.

This ship must have overtaken the one I was on, but the captain of this ship didn't seem sorry to lose me to another crew. I made out that they were transferring me from one vessel to an-other, but why I could not fathom. Was it to throw off any search parties sent out looking for me? Would there be search parties?

I had a hard time picturing Holt spending any resources on my rescue. He had three other sisters to use for marriage alliances, after all.

"I demand to know where I am being taken!" I yelled as I was corralled forward. "My brother shall not stand for this, and I shall see all you degenerates hanged!"

"I'm starting to see why you had her locked up," the woman said, rolling her eyes at me. "Slope, Will, if you harm even a single hair on her head, it will come out of your wages."

"Yes, Captain," the two men replied.

I stared at the woman in a new light. Not only was she a pirate, but she was also the captain of the dark ship.

"We swore not to harm you or your crew." I heard the woman threaten the older man, "But if I even so much as glimpse your disgusting face in our life's travels, your ending will not be so fortunate as it was today."

"When our longboat is attached, you can cast off." Elias gave the man the order.

The two that had taken me to the rope ladder realized it would be difficult to get me down with my hands tied. One of them went behind me, helping navigate the unsteady ladder as I held onto what rope I could manage. They were surprisingly gentle and did not touch me more than necessary. They kept looking at the female captain worriedly. Once down, they put me on one side of the longboat and put as much distance between them and me as possible. Absalom descended, followed by the captain and then Elias.

When we got close enough to the other ship, the two men started attaching rigging to the small boat. Everyone was silent, and the three kept passing looks between themselves and looked to me occasionally. The woman captain kept pinching the bridge of her nose in anguish. I was unable to decipher what the eyes between them meant; try as I might.

The crew above had barely begun to hoist us up when the other ship's captain shouted for the anchors to be raised, and the ship slowly began to move away from us. I watched as it left, not exactly sorry to see it go. The comfort of the familiar versus the despair of the unknown hung about me. I knew nothing of this new ship, and the conditions here could be worse than they had been before. On a ship full of men, there were worse fates than being left alone in the dark.

They stopped hoisting the boat when it reached the same height as the railing of their ship, and everyone got out before me. The two men from before helped me out of the boat and then left me alone as they had earlier. I surveyed the deck and some of the crew who had come up to ogle me. The woman captain kept giving the men venomous looks, and they scattered whenever her gaze fell upon them.

"We should have Jamie look her over to make sure she is in good health," Absalom said, and Elias nodded in agreement.

"She isn't in good health; look at her," the captain said, gesturing to me. "She looks starved and pale as death, though that may be due to royal pampering."

"Who are you?" I asked the three of them as they stared from me to each other.

"I am Captain Elias, and this is my sister Captain Georgette," Elias said.

"Your Highness," Georgette said to me with a mock curtsey.

I was angry with the disregard for the status I held over them. On the last ship, I assumed it was because the crew didn't believe my story. These pirates seemed to believe me but didn't think my title worth anything.

"And I am Absalom Church, your highness." He bowed, and his tone was not mocking in the slightest.

I was suddenly exhausted. After being kidnapped from one of my brother's ships on my way to marrying a man, I didn't know. They were kidnapping me once more. It was no more apparent to me what was happening or what they wanted than it had been the last time. My nerves were frayed, and I hadn't appropriately eaten or slept in what felt like weeks.

Elias stepped over to me and pulled a knife out of his belt. He had a silver ring on almost every one of his fingers. Some were plain, and some bore words I couldn't read. One was even sculpted to look like a woman with hair covering her breasts. He touched a part of my arm with his free hand as I jerked away at the contact. He looked up into my face, and I spat directly into his eyes.

"Don't touch me, pirate."

He raised his hand, and I flinched away from him, waiting for the blow, but instead, he wiped my spit off his face. He put his knife away and stepped back from me. He looked at his sister.

"Maybe you should try," he offered, and she scowled at him.

I backed away from her as she advanced on me, pulling a knife from her belt.

"Don't!" The panic was high in my voice.

"We are trying to cut your bindings off you, stupid girl. If you spit on me, I will strike you. I don't have an ounce of shame hitting a princess," Georgette growled at me, and she gripped my hands roughly, pulling me forward.

As she had said, she cut a piece of the rope at my wrists. She unwound the rest and tossed the binding to the ground.

"Surely you have no shame at all," I murmured, "Being an immoral corruption of what the goddesses intended a female to be."

Georgette stepped back too quickly for me to do anything. She grabbed the front of my dirty dress and held the knife in her hand to my throat. My heart raced as I looked into the woman's eyes that were now alight with rage.

"Georgette," Absalom worried after her.

"Listen well, girl," she whispered, which was by far the most frightening thing about the situation. "We did not tie you up and lock you in that damned hole on that other ship. The contempt in your voice is misplaced. So far away from your tall tower with no one to protect you, Princess, I would be careful how you speak to people."

She held onto me for a moment longer so that I could look into her eyes. There were many things behind those eyes, but I knew the threat was not idle. This woman would not treat me as if I were anything but an equal or perhaps less than that. It offended me, but I also respected it. When Georgette let go, she pushed me away and spat on my boot, turning back to the others. Absalom winced at her actions but said nothing.

They started arguing amongst themselves, but I looked behind me to the ship's railing. The ship I had come off of was sailing away with such speed that we would lose sight of it relatively soon. Georgette's words had stung because she had been right. This far away from my home and anyone who cared about who I was; no one would defend me. I had never needed to protect myself against actual danger. But I wasn't a coward. I would not go complacently as a pig led to the slaughter before winter festival. I would take charge of the only part of my fate I could manage.

I looked to the three, still arguing about what to do with me, and slowly backed away from them. They didn't seem to notice; they were too caught up with each other. I reached down and swiftly removed my boots and damp stocking. I held my breath the entire time, waiting for them to realize. Still, their argument became more intense. I backed up to the railing of the ship and looked down into the water.

"Captains," a young boy was watching and pointing at me.

Elias, Absalom, and Georgette silenced at the same time and looked up to me. My legs were over the railing, and I looked at them defiantly as panic crossed each of their faces.

"Don't..." Elias called to me before I pushed off and fell.

I could choose how I wanted to die. It was my last resolute thought before the frigid water enveloped me.

Six

Georgette

I rushed to the edge of the ship, where the woman had thrown herself over. Absalom and Elias were right next to me, staring down in disbelief. I admired the defiance in the girl's eyes before she had thrown herself over. That admiration left when she had jumped, which was just foolish. I watched her below as she struggled to swim against the current, fighting to stay above water. I looked up to see Elias stripping down to his trousers, kicking his boots and socks off.

"She wants to die, we should let the foolish creature go."

"Could the current kill her?" Absalom asked; of course, he would have gone after her, but it would have been difficult for him.

"It's frigid," I answered. "She'll freeze to death before the current gets its chance."

"I'm not letting that much gold float down the river when I have the chance to catch it," Elias said with a smile as he ran to the foredeck and began tying a rope to his midsection.

"Stupid girl," I mumbled.

"Perhaps she thinks she can swim to shore." Absalom had not taken his eyes from her as we watched her losing battle.

"I think she figured she would take her chances, even if those chances included death." I turned from the railing and found Jones right behind me. It was frightening how often he knew I was going to need him.

"Captain," he said at the ready.

"Jones, get five men up on the foredeck to pull them back up when Elias is ready. Have Jamie prepare to look her over when I call for him. I need two blankets warmed on the oven and bring one to the room next to Elias' quarters. Make sure the bed is made up and have some clean drinking water brought to the room."

He eyed me warily, but of course, he said nothing. Fresh water was limited on a ship. It was precious, and no doubt he wondered why we would waste it on a prisoner. I couldn't help but feel a small amount of sympathy for the girl. She was naive and reckless, but she had been treated so poorly on her previous voyage that I knew why she had jumped to her doom. There was also the matter of her being royalty. If she were to marry Cyril and he got wind that she was mistreated aboard our ship, it would no doubt mean trouble.

I looked up again just as Elias jumped into the water. Jones shouted at some men to be up on the foredeck, ready to pull Elias and Mercy out.

I left to go to my room and scoured my things for dry clothing for the Princess to wear. She was most likely wearing a structured corset under her dress. Not to mention everything else that women traditionally wore. I grabbed my softest pair of trousers, my largest shirt, and a vest I wore only on special occasions. I added a few of my new undergarments and a thin nightdress, grumbling under my breath about having to share my new things.

I was already really disliking having another woman aboard the ship. I picked a new pair of stockings and came out of the room. I shut the door behind me and continued to complain all the way to the quartermaster's room. The room was small but not so small to seem cramped. It held a single bed, a set of drawers for clothes, and a desk. It was normally where Jones slept, but he had moved out of it for this voyage.

I kicked the chamber pot out from under the bed so it was visible. I shook the sheets and blankets out, though they had recently been prepared for Absalom and were fresh. I threw the clothes on top of the dresser and turned to leave when Jones came in with a water canister and a warm blanket.

"Captain's coming up now," he said, setting the water on the desk, and I nodded.

I moved to the door and gestured for him to put the warm blanket under the others on the bed.

I left and hurried out just in time to see Elias and Mercy raised over the ship's railing. I quickened my pace seeing the girl had turned a slight shade of blue and hung limply in Elias's arms. He laid her down on the deck, and I was up the stairs as he started trying to compress the water out of her lungs. We all stood around watching him and holding our breath. He pulled her head close to his ear and listened to her breathing.

She began to vomit river water. She was retching onto the deck, coughing and holding her throat. Elias dropped her roughly and stepped away from her.

"The next time you jump off the ship, I'll let the water take you," he said.

He met my gaze as he walked, his eyes brooding.

"Absalom and George, you meet me in my quarters," he barked, heading down the stairs.

Jones was there to hand him the blanket that he had warmed. I saw him shivering though he tried to hide it. His posture was rigid and defensive. I sighed, standing up from the crouched position I found myself in.

"I don't think I've ever seen him in such a demanding mood," Absalom said as he bent down to help Mercy up. "Are you okay, Your Highness?"

"Water cold enough to steal your breath makes him testy," I said, "Can you carry her to the room next to Elias'?"

"Your Highness, I am going to pick you up to move you to a bed where you can get warm." She was shaking, but she managed to nod as Absalom picked her up and held her against his chest.

I followed them to the room where Absalom set her on the bed as if Mercy would shatter if he moved too quickly. Soft pangs of jealousy shot through me, and I scowled at his back. I had never seen him be so gentle with a woman before, and I was not too fond of it. I shoved the feelings down into my emotional drawer, where I had all my unwanted cares locked away.

"Be kind to her," he ordered, passing me. "You may not care about her title, but she's to wed my King."

He didn't make it easy for me as feelings fought for freedom. Instead of saying anything to him, I fluttered my eyelashes and shut the door in his face. I took a deep breath and turned to see the soaking girl sitting on the bed.

"We have to get those clothes off, Princess, they are soaked, not to mention filthy." I grimaced at the dress which she had no doubt been wearing for the entire time she was down in that ship. "At least the ocean washed you off a little."

"You shall not." She had pulled her knees to her chest and was looking at me with the same fire she had right before she hurled herself off the ship.

"You cannot get warm in those clothes, and I doubt you could get them off yourself. Elias would be rather cross with me if I let him jump into that water to save you, only to allow you to catch your death in wet clothes."

She stared at me with her arms crossed over her chest. She said nothing. I knew a will of iron when I saw one. Silent defiance was often more potent than an outspoken one.

"Princess, my only plan is to get you into dry clothes. The less time I must spend in your presence, the happier we will both be. Please stand up so we can get on with this. Your childish defiance is getting old very quickly." I held out my hand to her. "Absalom will not stand for any harm to come to you. I have no loyalty or care for you, but neither my brother nor I wish to make his life difficult. We respect him and honor his wishes when we can. If you cannot trust my intentions toward you, trust my loyalty to him." I pushed a little further, stepping toward her.

"I do not know anything about either of you. You are strangers to me," she said after many seconds of silence. "Why would he care for my wellbeing at all? How am I to trust a loyalty I know nothing of?"

"If I understood Absalom, my life would be much easier. For now, I can tell you that he isn't a pirate but a military commander for King Kosdel. I have no reason or motive to lie. If we wanted you dead, we would have simply allowed you to freeze to death in the river you jumped into on your own."

The girl ignored my hand but stood up slowly and turned to give me access to the back of her dress. The river water would ruin it, so there was no use in saving it. I put a hand on her shoulder as a warning. I made a cut in the fabric with my knife and ripped it the rest of the way, letting Mercy step out of it. Under the dress was a heavy undergarment that I pulled up and over the woman's head.

"How do you function with so much fabric on you?" I asked, letting the garment fall to the floor on the growing pile of soaked clothing.

She did not respond.

I opened the drawer to get the dry nightgown that I had brought. I set it on the bed and stepped back to gesture to the princess that it was for her. Her cheeks were tinged pink, and she looked uncomfortable. I tried my best not to laugh. Modesty had never been a conviction that plagued me. I would never come out undressed in front of the crew, but that was only to avoid unwanted attention.

"You must have a lady's maid who dresses you," I mused, looking at the lacing on the corset and deciding to cut open the blasted thing.

"I do." Mercy bristled, "A little different than having some strange pirate woman cut your clothes off."

"It sounds quite scandalous when you say it like that. You'll have quite the tale to spin to your ladies in waiting when you marry King Kosdel." I laughed and cut through the top lacing of the corset. I pulled out the laces until it would be easy for her to get out of on her own.

"What do you want with me?" she whispered as I turned to give her some privacy.

"Princess," I started, "We have no want of you. I can explain more when I come back with food, but we were expecting to find something aboard that ship, not someone. Frankly, you have surprised all of us. We will discuss what we are to do with you, and I will know more later, but I have no information for you now. We mean you no harm; you have my word."

I would not divulge information to her before I had talked to my brother and Absalom. Even if that information would put her at ease.

"The word of a pirate," Mercy huffed. "I shall not be used as a bargaining chip."

"Cyril no longer has anything we want." I turned to her, now standing in the nightgown I had brought her.

"Is he not your King? You address him so casually?" she asked as I moved all the wet clothes to the door with my boot.

She was still shivering, and I pointed to the bed.

"I have no King." I reached for the door handle. "Get some rest. There is water in that canister on the desk for you to drink. When it is time for the last meal of the day, I will bring you some food. I'll lock the door on my way out; it locks from the inside."

"I'm to be kept prisoner in here? I will not stand for this." Her tone went high, and I saw the craze of exhaustion in her eyes. "I will not be subject to any manner of debauchery as your crew can come in and do whatever they please with me. You should have let me die in the water. It would have been better than what I've heard about what happens to women aboard pirate ships."

"Mercy," I said, firmly interrupting her.

I could see the panic and the fear. The fear of being defenseless was heavy, and I knew it well. It didn't help that they had locked her in a dark room with neither proper food nor sleep. Anyone would be at the end of their wits.

"No man aboard this ship will dare enter your room or come near you without your permission. If they did, they would forfeit their life by my hand. I'll come back at dinner, and we can discuss it further but for now, get some sleep." I opened the door, latched the lock, moved the clothes outside, and shut it behind me.

I picked up the clothes frowning as they dripped onto my boots. I went to the edge of the ship and dropped the whole lot into the water with pleasure. They were too disgusting to be saved. I made my way back to Elias' quarters, where I assumed he and Absalom would be. While I had been in the princess' room, the ship had started to sail once again. I heard the crew shouting at each other and saw Jones at the wheel.

I knocked on Elias's door and heard laughter inside. I was glad that at least Elias wasn't still in a bad mood. He opened the door and gave me a grin, stepping aside so I could enter. His hair was still damp, and he had pushed it behind his ears.

"Glad to see the water didn't chill your temper for too long," I mused, sitting in his plain wooden chair.

Elias and I may have been twins, but our living quarters couldn't have been more different. Elias was tidy and had truly little around his room. A bed was secured in the corner, a simple desk with several drawers and one chair. He had a few things hanging on a coat rack in the corner, but even those looked meticulously placed. My room was strewn with clothing, and my bed was never made. I cluttered every surface with books and things I found on our voyages.

We were calm and chaotic.

"Did you get our new crewmember settled?" Elias asked.

"Yes, she'll be ready to pull the sail in the morning." I rolled my eyes at him.

"Is it too much to hope that this has derailed the plan of mystical treasure?" Absalom asked from where he was leaning against a wall.

"You've never been much of an optimist Absalom; no need to start now." I ran my fingers over the grain of the desk.

"We can't take her with us," I said, looking at Elias, hoping he agreed.

I didn't like the woman, but I would not stand for her to be tied up or locked in a room on board while we searched for treasure.

"No, we will have to write the King asking him to send men to take her as soon as possible. I don't want her aboard longer than she has to be." The tension lined Elias's voice again, and I wondered what it was that was bothering him.

"I will most likely escort her home, and the King will send a company," Absalom said.

"Perhaps Absalom should write him and say he fears for her safety aboard the ship," I said, "It would be believable, and he may be more inclined to let us unload her early."

"I'll write my father," Absalom volunteered. "I think he had a vague inclination of the princess being aboard that ship. He gave me more warnings than usual of the dangers of getting entangled with you two. He said if I let myself be carried away by your recklessness, the King would have my head. Though I assumed it was something worth a considerable sum, not the next countess of the country."

"How many wives does Cyril have already?" I asked as my blood started to boil.

Countess was a nice name for a woman who married a King after he already had a queen. You were primarily a political pawn or pretty thing to warm the King's bed when he got bored of his other wives. The girl that we had just taken aboard our ship looked to be thirty years younger than King Kosdel. I shivered, thinking of her fate.

"She will make four," Absalom said, taking in my disgust. "All kings take multiple wives, George. Only King Dalion hasn't, and that's because he's only been on the throne for a year."

"I'm sure it is not for lack of trying," I grumbled. What did I care if this woman was to marry a man with three other wives? It was no business of mine.

"I didn't know you held such conservative views on marriage," Absalom said from his corner.

"Oh yes, George has grand romantic ideas," Elias agreed.

I blushed slightly, trying to control the fear that rose in me. I hadn't told anyone of my ideas of marriage or life outside this one. Though I knew that they were only teasing, I felt vulnerable. They were too close to the truth for me to be at ease.

"Though she keeps a wide range of company in her bed ... Tell us, George, do these gentlemen romance you before they delight you?" Elias asked.

He meant no harm by it, but I felt Absalom's mood sour. A glance over at him confirmed a deep frown had settled into his face. I wished Elias had something lying about that I could throw at him.

"I have given up on romance for myself," I answered.

I brushed it off as if I hadn't noticed Absalom was bothered. I watched Elias look at the other man with a mischievous grin and then look back at me. I shook my head slowly at him in a warning, and he nodded with understanding in his eyes.

"Pirates," Absalom cursed under his breath.

"So, we keep her aboard in the room ..." Elias went on.

"We cannot force her to stay in that room," Absalom argued.

"We can't have her wandering about the ship," Elias countered.

"I am not going to have her go back to the King and report that I stood by while she was kept prisoner in a room."

"Would there be no way to frame it as if it were for her safety?" Elias asked.

I let them continue the conversation. I would side with Absalom when they bothered to ask me. No person should be locked up. Though the room we gave her was much bigger than the closet she had come out of, it would still feel wrong. I also felt responsible for providing the girl some sort of freedom, as it was unlikely any would be afforded in her future.

"She isn't a criminal or some possession you can lock away," Absalom said.

"King Kosdel seems to think she is, and who am I to argue with the great King himself?" Elias threw his hands up for dramatics.

"Elias, she can't be kept in there," I interrupted, and Absalom looked to me gratefully.

"Oh, of course. I only wished to see if Absalom thought I would force her to."

"Bastard." Absalom loosed a sigh that turned into a chuckle.

"Though I'll warn you, I'm not responsible for her. If she jumps overboard again, you'll have to get her, mate. George wanted to let her go the first time, so I doubt she'll volunteer either."

"We'll need to port at Liven," I decided.

"Why?" Elias asked, bothered.

It was true that I preferred to port more often than a ship needed. I tried to be as low maintenance as I could be. I did washings in small hand baths aboard the ship. I kept my hair braided back tightly most of the time to avoid having to jump into the ocean. The men bathed this way between ports.

"She'll need to bathe, and also, she needs her own clothes."

"Are you trying to convince her that all pirates aren't the savages she thinks they are? I don't think any number of freshwater baths or new clothing will do that. I thought you would be against treating her like a princess." Elias stood up.

"We'll treat her as a living creature who deserves the same rights and luxuries we do. I will not bow or lace her into a corset, but she deserves to be treated like a lady. I would expect as much, and we will treat her with as much decency as we can afford. We do not handle others as equals for their benefit but for ours." I stayed seated with my arms crossed in a challenge.

"It's humorous how faithful and proper you turn when you are defending something that would benefit you. Not long ago, you told me to let her drown. Now that you will gain something by claiming we need to extend human decency, you have become a devout believer in propriety."

"Liven, Elias," I said, smiling as he saw right through my pious speech.

"Hypocrite," he accused, and opening the door to his quarters, walked out.

"What's in Liven?" Absalom asked, looking after him.

I stood up, almost giddy now. The thought of Liven being only a day away and an excuse to go into town was exciting indeed. While Elias didn't care for the river port, it was one of my favorites. We didn't often go because of the location. It was easier to sail through Hesterna than to port along the river.

"You've never been?"

"I have never been anywhere in Hestiege."

"Truly?" I asked, surprised.

Though I knew I shouldn't be. My lifestyle offered me a view of Marecult that others weren't afforded. I reveled in the cultures and differences of all the places I had been to.

"I'm not, nor do I believe I ever shall be, as well-traveled as you." He offered me a genuine smile, and it was a glorious thing to behold.

"You'll love it. I'll show you all my favorite things. Perhaps we can convince Elias to stay two nights, though that's unlikely."

I walked up to him. Taking his arm in mine, I escorted him out of the room. We were a comical sight as he towered over me.

"I shall play the wide-eyed storybook lad being whisked off to exotic places by a charming pirate woman." He tugged on one of my braids.

"I'll corrupt you yet, Absalom Church. I swear it."

Seven

Mercy

I woke to a knock at the door. I looked nervously at the lock that seemed to still be engaged. I stayed awake with worry and panic, staring at the door for a long time. Georgette's promise of my safety meant nothing to me, and I ended up shoving the wooden chair underneath the door handle for extra protection. I had taken a long drink of water and had fallen into the warm bed. I hadn't intended on drifting to sleep, but exhaustion had overtaken.

I sat up and looked around. There was a small window in the room, and it looked to be morning, but I wasn't sure. The water was so strange to me. Though the boat's rocking was soothing, I hated to admit how well I slept.

The knock came again, and I pulled the sheets and blanket up around my chest as if they could protect me. I was relieved that no one had attempted to come into my room that night. At least it seemed Georgette hadn't lied yet.

"Who is it?" I called out.

"Captain Georgette," she responded. "I come bearing food."

My stomach grumbled in reply. I stepped out of bed and regretted it as the air was brisk around me, and the night had chilled the floor as well. I moved the chair away from the door and slid it back to the desk. I unlatched the lock on the door and opened it slightly, seeing Georgette with a large tray of food on the other side.

She was wearing her hair in the same two braids but was wearing a tricorn hat over them now. She had a brown leather vest over a plain linen shirt and some black trousers. I was slightly jealous of the comfort and ease I imagined the clothes afforded her. She didn't look any less feminine, only more comfortable. The pants seemed to be tailored to fit her and would be rather provocative if worn in high court.

"Am I allowed in, or will you continue to stare at me for the remainder of the morning?"

"It's morning?" I asked.

I hesitated but eventually stepped away from the door so she could come in. She set the tray down on the desk, and I closed the door and locked it behind her. Georgette handed me a mug with something steaming in it, and I took it, retreating to the bed. Ignoring the food as my stomach rioted.

"I came last night and knocked, but there was no answer. I figured you didn't want food, or you were sleeping. Here." She hopped up on the desk and sat next to the tray of food.

She took the cloth off the tray to reveal it was filled with dried meat, slices of fruit, and bread with some spread on it. She reached out and handed it to me.

"You've got to be starving."

I eyed it and then looked up into her eyes. She shook it a bit, urging me to take it, and then sighed as if I were the most tiring creature in the world. I finally reached out and took it. Resting it in my lap, I gingerly picked up a piece of dried meat. I bit into it as my stomach rumbled again. I looked up at Georgette, embarrassed, but she looked out the small window and seemed not to notice.

"So, what are your questions?" Georgette asked.

"I don't understand what is going on," I admitted.

"Well, I'm not sure how much light I can shed on that," she said, leaning back against the wall where she sat. "We were charged by King Kosdel to rescue what we thought was an item of great value. He didn't extend the courtesy of informing us you were a person."

"Pirates ... working for The King of Northern Ralice?" I tried to keep the disbelief out of my voice because the last thing I wanted to do was anger my captors.

"Indeed," Georgette mused as if she thought it strange as well, "Though he may deny it when asked. I don't think he would be proud to claim us. We were sent to overtake a pirate ship that had stolen from King Kosdel, and you turned out to be what was stolen. We are now traveling back to a port where Absalom, and some other of the King's men, will take you back to Urorah."

I could not imagine any sort of King colluding with savage sea thieves. While I didn't know King Kosdel well, it seemed to go against everything my family and tutors had taught me. I had conversed with him by letter three times, and my brother had assured me of his great character. Though I didn't think it would have mattered if he had flawed character, I still would have been shipped off to him.

"Who were the men that kidnapped me first?" I asked.

"We don't know the answer to that. Was it the same skimmer that handed you over to us on the last ship?"

"What is a skimmer?"

"The man, the captain of the last ship where we found you."

"No," I said. "The men that took me from my brother's ship had been waiting for us. They were rough and cruel, and I think they slaughtered many of my brother's men. They threw me into the bottom of their ship in that hole you found me in. From the time they took me to when you came, I stayed in that damned hole for who knows how long."

"Weeks," she answered. "You were down there for weeks."

Georgette took a few breaths looking out the small window of the room as she finished an apple. Now that I had gotten some sleep and felt slightly refreshed, I took the female pirate in. She looked young but held herself as if she were noble. Her features seemed quite friendly. It felt strange to think of a pirate as warm, but her eyes were bright and happy as if she were used to laughing. The grey of them contrasted against her sun-bronzed skin.

"It is most likely that another crew kidnapped you and handed the ship off to the skimmer crew. I couldn't say who took you in the first place or why they took you for that matter."

It didn't seem as if she wanted any more input from me, so I sat silently, trying the bread and finding the spread to be a sweet fruit jam. I devoured the whole slice as Georgette continued to stare out the window. She took off her hat and rubbed both her hands over her face.

"Who exactly is Absalom?" I asked finally.

"He's a commander in King Kosdel's army. He doesn't sail with us; he was only sent for this rescue. The King insisted on one of his men coming along. Absalom's father, who is one of his King's highest-ranking Generals, thought it would be a good idea for Absalom to be the one to accompany us."

"He's friends with you both." I didn't phrase it as a question, but there were indeed many questions to be asked.

"We've been friends since childhood. His father and our father were friends, and we grew up together. As much as you can grow up with someone while you live on a ship."

"You took the ship over from your parents? You look barely older than me," I asked.

"We'll be nineteen in a month or so," Georgette answered. "Our parents never kept track of the actual day but always marked it mid-spring."

So, they were only months younger than me. I had recently turned nineteen in the cold dead of winter.

"You seem a little young to be married off to a King. Is that traditional in Adamas?"

I flinched away from the question. It was a crushing reminder of the fate that still awaited me. I wondered, not for the first time, if death would have been so bad compared to being married to a man I didn't know. I had to admit that I felt less desperation after food, water, and sleep than I had the day before.

I reminded myself of my duty to my country and how I could endure much to honor my father's memory. If Adamas needed me to marry this King, I would attempt to be the best Countess the country had seen. It wasn't a life I would have chosen, but I hadn't been born free to choose.

"My brother has the authority to marry me off whenever my country needs it most," I said defensively. "As is his right."

"Is it?" she asked but said nothing else about it. "We port at the end of the day. We will take you to get some clothing and anything else you require. I have put some of my clothes in these drawers for you. They won't fit you because you are taller and thinner than I. We can't have you on deck in a nightgown, so they will have to do for now."

"You're letting me out?" I asked, surprised.

She didn't answer. Instead, she pulled a delicate metal comb out of her pocket and a small length of leather cord.

"Turn so I can braid your hair back. You won't want it in your face."

I had a hard time associating her with the stories I had heard of female pirates. Rampant promiscuity and dark magic were the stories spun. Tales that spoke of women that murdered children in the streets for pleasure. Georgette seemed rather ordinary in comparison. She may have had gold hoops dripping from her ears and tailored clothing intended for men, but she didn't seem like a child-killing dark magic user. Though maybe it was an illusion to trick one into thinking that she did not swim in darkness.

She ran the comb through my hair and was very gentle at removing the knots caused by the seawater. If I wasn't so on edge, it might have been comforting. Something you would imagine a sister or a mother doing. My three sisters hardly ever spoke to me, and my mother was as far from nurturing as you could imagine someone to be. I closed my eyes as I felt her weaving my hair into a tight single braid. She tied it at the base of my neck, letting the rest of it hang loose.

"Undergarments, trousers, a shirt, and a vest are all in the drawers. Your boots are the only thing I saved and are outside your door. Get dressed and meet me on deck," she said, grabbing the tray off the desk. "I'll be sure to show you the best points to jump from where we wouldn't be able to save you if you still wish for death."

I shot her a look, but she was already halfway out the door chuckling to herself. I stood up, locking the door once more but leaving the chair where it was. I opened the drawers to survey the clothing. I started with simple undergarments that were much more lightweight than I was used to. They had not been made to alter the appearance of my figure and were less restricting. I pulled on the trousers, and they were loose in the thighs and waist and much too short but manageable. I tucked the shirt into them and put the vest on over the top. Though I would guess they were traditionally men's, someone tailored them to fit a woman's shape. It was apparent that Georgette was gifted with proportions different than my own but I found that I liked the weight of them. I did not care, however, for how thin the trousers were and felt almost naked without layers of skirts.

I stepped out of the room and pulled my black boots on, which seemed rather formal than the rest of the attire. I closed the door and ventured out to the deck where the sun had risen and men milled around doing all sorts of things. I met a few of their gazes, and they nodded at me but passed without comment.

I heard Georgette before I saw her. She was above the main deck, talking to Absalom and Captain Elias.

"Good morning, Princess," Absalom greeted as they all three looked down on me.

I felt somewhat uncomfortable in new clothing being scrutinized by people I didn't know. I didn't answer but instead located the stairs and walked up to them. The morning was cool, but I was glad to be in the sun. I looked around to see water on either side of us without a shore in sight.

"Absalom Church, at your service." He stepped toward me and bowed low. "Commander of King Kosdel's ninety-eighth company. The pleasure is mine, Princess."

I heard Georgette snort, and I looked over to find the woman rolling her eyes. Elias was behind the wheel of the ship. His eyebrows were raised, but aside from that, he seemed disinterested. I tried not to make eye contact with him or remember how I clung to him when he had rescued me from a watery doom.

"A single gentleman aboard, I see," I said, smiling at him. "The honor is mine, Commander. I'm glad to have found some good company."

"If you need anything, I am at your disposal," he continued.

I was glad to know he seemed bound to convention. It brought me a slight sense of comfort.

"I'm glad of it. Though I am interested to know how you became caught up with such a crowd."

"Believe me, lady, I ask myself that quite often."

"Says the woman wearing trousers," Georgette interrupted. "Elias, are you going to show her around the ship?"

I looked at him then, the pirate captain who had saved my life. I recalled the moment I accepted my death and stopped fighting the current. I had taken one last deep breath and closed my eyes. My limbs had gone numb in the cold water, and I felt heavy as I let myself start to sink. It was almost like falling asleep when you were too exhausted to even crawl under the covers. Then someone woke me up. Someone was talking in my ear. Not shouting but persistent and steadily pulling me back from the frozen sleep. 'Come back, Princess,' I heard over and over as I drifted in and out of consciousness. But then, when I had woken up fully, he had dropped me on the deck of his ship like a sack of fish.

He looked at me too, and his unimpressed expression held fast. He perused me over from the tip of my ridiculous boots up, directly into my eyes, and pursed his lips. I'm sure it was merely seconds, but it felt longer.

"I'm sure she would prefer Absalom's company," he said, mouth changing to a smile. "Being the only gentlemen aboard, he may cater to her feminine sensibilities."

"What feminine sensibilities might those be?" I challenged him indignantly over his obvious dispassion for my station.

"I have not met a noblewoman that thinks herself below or even the equal of any. You think yourselves so far above common riffraff. Do you claim to be different?" he asked, and I couldn't argue.

"My breeding and station in life are superior to yours as well as everyone else aboard this ship. I have every right to feel superior to a common thief." My tone was harsher, and his grin split his face as if I he had expected nothing less.

"Such arrogance from the princess of the most discriminatory country in Marecult. Even the common thief thinks you all too stuck up to steal from. The longer I am in your presence, the more I think not even Adamasian royalty is worth the effort."

Georgette cackled, and Absalom frowned but said nothing. My cheeks were hot with anger, but his grin never faltered. His grey eyes darkened, and I avoided admiring his features that I had initially thought rather dashing. I now saw the malicious pirate lurking beneath.

"Elias," Absalom finally warned from where he stood.

"Absalom would love to show you the ship. He's at your disposal, after all," Elias said, waving to the commander.

It was not a feeling I was used to experiencing. As a princess, I had only met people that were overly kind and accommodating of me. Even if someone did not particularly enjoy my company, they would never dare say it. This rakish pirate captain treated me as if he would rather jump back into the river than talk to me. I felt at a loss as no one came to my defense. No one was there to punish him for speaking to me in such a way. I was free to decide how to respond. I could form a response that spoke of who I was instead of where I was from.

"I'd rather you show me," I answered after a pause. "Unless the reason you are refusing is that you feel intimidated. In which case, I'm sure Commander Church will rise to the occasion quite well."

"That must be it," Georgette answered, and I found her slight smile and taunting tone directed at her brother humorous. "Are you intimidated by our fair princess?"

I watched as Elias shot his sister a sideways look. He stepped out from behind the wheel and towards me. Elias bowed, surprising me with both his grace and perfect form. Standing back up, he offered me his arm as if he were a polite nobleman asking to escort me around the garden.

"Your Worship," he said as I took his arm in mine. "Allow me to show you our most humble of vessels. Though nothing in comparison to the mighty warships of Adamas, I hope you will find it charming."

His tone had gone proper. If he hadn't been dressed like a pirate, I might not have been able to tell him apart from a true gentleman. His casual seaborn accent disappeared, replaced by delicate flattery, and it made me somewhat uncomfortable. He wasn't smiling, but Absalom and Georgette were, and both looked to be holding back laughter.

"I don't appreciate being ridiculed," I said to him through clenched teeth as he led me down the stairs.

"And I don't appreciate being talked down to, Princess."

Eight

Mercy

The more time I spent with Elias, the pirate captain, the more my irritation for him grew. It seemed somehow, even the very breath he breathed was mocking me. I quickly realized the more I rose to his derision, the more it encouraged him. I eventually stopped responding with anything more than dirty looks. Mostly I gave them to his turned back but suspected he knew anyway.

Like Georgette, he held himself very nobly, as if he were more than a pirate. Either that or he didn't care if it was an undignified position. They both acted entitled and slightly arrogant. I wasn't the authority on pirate culture, and perhaps they were a sort of royalty in their own respect. I made a mental note to ask Absalom about it.

I had been on very few ships. I couldn't say with much certainty what was customary and what wasn't. Though, in my limited knowledge, I thought Elias and Georgette ran their ship rather well. When I pictured pirate ships, I pictured chaos. When Elias brought me to each new room of the ship, what I saw was ordered. More than that, the crew respected him and even seemed to like him. He seemed proud as he took his time explaining everything to me, a man showing off his prized pigs. His tone never grew bored, though I was sure it wasn't riveting for him to explain things like the rigging that hoisted sails.

No one had ever shown me something that wasn't related to my duties as a princess in such detail. My attention focused on being a good daughter and sister to my father and brothers. Some of my training was on being an amenable wife once my brothers secured a profitable marriage. I enjoyed gardening and keeping flowers, but even that was used as a skill to make me a more desirable female for political use. They had bred me to sell at a high price.

No one had bothered to tell me anything about ships or military actions before. Once when I was fifteen, I had insisted on going to war and strategy meetings with my brothers, but they had laughed me out of the room. My oldest brother Holt, who had always treated me as a pet, had handed me a piece of wrapped candy and patted me on the head, sending me away. I had been much too old to be given sweets in exchange for obedience. However, I had given into it after fighting very little. It seemed futile to be seen and used as anything more than the sex and duty I was born to.

After my tour, I invited Absalom to take tea with me that evening. I also made the mistake of asking in front of Georgette. She had laughed as if she had never heard anything funnier in her life. Absalom had shot her a look and told her to stop cackling like a savage. It had only caused her to laugh harder. He had agreed to come to sit with me for the evening meal, telling me privately he had brought his own tea aboard. He said it to me as if it were a bond we shared, and perhaps I might understand where the others would not. I did, in fact, and having a good cup of tea would be a great comfort.

I spent a good amount of the day observing how everything worked together. I was intrigued by both the similarities and differences of the two pirate captains. I found out they were twins; if their looks were not obvious enough. Georgette smiled often and laughed even more. They each took pleasure in making fun of each other and the people around them. They would bark short orders or criticism at a shipmate one second and be back to poking fun of each other the next. It was the dance of familiarity.

I wondered what it was like to have such affection between your sibling; I certainly didn't know. My relationships with my siblings were tense and often full of false pleasantries. Looking at the twin captain's unmistakable warmth toward each other made me ache for something I wasn't sure I would ever have.

Absalom joined in their banter occasionally. At times he seemed to find it ridiculous and spent silent periods observing as I did. Both captains also seemed rather fond of the Commander, and I noted Georgette smiled over at him often.

All three responded to my questions when I had them. However, some things went unanswered in evasive wording. The twins seemed well versed in half-truths. Whenever I asked a question, Elias looked rather pleased that I was taking an interest. The satisfied smirk he gave me was enough to cause my blood to boil.

Georgette had shown me a small library aboard the ship that housed everything from novels to ship history. I picked up a familiar childhood adventure and a book on piracy. The title was _Limited History of Piracy_, though the book was quite large and did not seem limited. Georgette had raised an eyebrow at the choice but said nothing.

I asked to return to my room, and Georgette obliged. She stopped first in her quarters to get me a fresh pair of undergarments. I blushed crimson when she handed them to me outside the door, but Georgette seemed unfazed. Neither of the captain's rooms had been included in the tour, but I got a glimpse of Georgette's as she shut the door. It was cluttered and messy, and the smell of cinnamon and sweet almond oil drifted out. The clothes she had given me carried the same fragrance. It was spicy and feminine, not at all what I would have assumed a pirate to smell of.

"You can go anywhere you wish to on the ship," Georgette said. "Don't cause trouble and stay out of the way of the crew, but you may wander as you like." Georgette stopped in front of the door.

"Thank you," I said because it seemed that she was extending kindness.

"We will arrive at the port this evening, and I'll take you into town to get some clothes of your own tomorrow."

"Will I be required to wear pants?" I asked, which elicited a slip of laughter from her.

"Mercy, you are not required to do anything. If you want to wear boned and laced corsets under seven skirts, I don't wish to stop you. However, it will be hard for you to get into them yourself, and I certainly won't help you, though Elias might be willing. Would you like me to enquire for you?"

I let out an affronted gasp and threw open the door to my room, scurrying inside. I heard the endless sound of Georgette's laugh as I slammed the door. I set the books on the dresser and sat down heavily on the bed, and cried.

It hadn't been Georgette's suggestive comment that started the spiral. It was the weight of everything else that had happened in the last couple of days: being shipped off only three months after my father died, unknown villains kidnapping me, and I was now on a foreign vessel. That and it seemed as if my future of an arranged marriage still hung before me. If I was honest, it was that these people aboard this ship had treated me more like a person and less like some royal pawn than anyone ever had. I was scared and alone, with no real idea of what was to become of me.

I cried and let my tears dry. I pulled myself together, feeling slightly less burdened. I wasn't sure why, but sometimes a good cry was necessary to move on with life and not feel sorry for myself. I got off my bed, opened the book on piracy and began to devour it with enthusiasm at the small desk in the room.

It was as much about pirate history as it was about different ports around all Marecult. I felt as entranced as a child reading of all the famous pirates and their conquests. I was surprised to find a handful of female pirate captains talked about in the book, and they seemed even more ruthless than the men. I was engrossed in an account of a female pirate, Captain Helena Snipe, when there was a knock at the door.

"Come in." I realized then I hadn't even enquired after who it was and was shocked at my sense of ease.

Absalom opened the door slowly, carrying a tray and a teapot. I got up and grabbed the teapot from him as he reached outside the door and pulled in an extra chair he had brought. He set the tray down on the dresser and situated the chair against the door facing me as it was the only place in the small room to put it.

"I'm glad you agreed to take tea with me," I said, a little guarded.

I closed the book I was reading and uncovered the tray to reveal two small crude clay cups with no handles and three small white bags tied up with twine.

"I am glad you asked, Princess," he responded, giving me a warm smile that I imagined won many hearts.

When I observed him earlier, he seemed to not express many emotions, in stark contrast to his two friends. He was quieter than they were, and at that moment, I was glad for a reprieve from the assault of words and laughter.

"I was surprised there is a small burning stove aboard," I said as he poured some tea into one of the mugs.

"Yes, Princess. It comes with its risks and rewards. Though you should see the looks I just got when I asked for some hot water for tea."

"Do the sailors not drink tea?" I took the cup he offered me.

"I think they find it a waste of freshwater. Drinking water aboard a ship is limited. Mostly the sailors drink spiced wine or grog."

I took a sip of the tea, finding it floral and delicate. I had never tasted anything quite like it and enjoyed the flavor it left behind. It was naturally sweet with a slightly bitter finish. I looked up, and Absalom was looking beyond me out the window, completely content sitting in silence.

"This is very pleasant," I said.

"It's one of my father's favorites," he said, "A little floral for my taste, but many teas in Northern Ralice have the same flavor. It's a native flower that grows in plenty, so we put it in everything."

"I shall have to get used to it then." I took another sip. "What else have you brought?"

"Some of my favorite treats from our country." He beamed and unwrapped the packages. "I snuck them aboard worried about what manner of food I would be subjected to."

I smiled as laughter played at the back of my throat. Absalom handed me a small red candy out of one bag. It was perfectly round and wrapped in a bit of transparent paper. I set the wrapper aside and popped it into my mouth. It tasted of fresh apples and a hint of some other fruit I couldn't name.

"I thought I would bring you some things from Northern Ralice and answer questions for you if you had any," he said, "Not that I would assume to be able to answer all your questions. I just thought you might be a bit more comfortable asking me than Elias or George."

"Very kind of you, Commander."

"You may call me Absalom if it suits you, Princess," he said, reaching into the second bag.

"I do have a question for you." I smiled. "How does a commander of a king's army come to be acquaintances with two pirate captains?"

"Ah, the question that is posed to me most frequently." He handed me a thin cream-colored roll unwrapped.

"I think my brother's men might be hanged if they associated with pirates," I said and realized it sounded rather rude. "Not that I'm suggesting it is a punishable offense, of course. It just seems strange to me."

"It is certainly that." He smiled, and I was glad he took no offense.

He crunched down on his treat and looked up at the ceiling as if wondering where he might begin. It was so strange a thing to me. I tried to imagine one of my guards taking meals or spending a free day with pirates. Their lifestyle was so hated, and I had been raised to loath them so wholly that I was still rather shocked that Absalom, who seemed an upstanding military man, was friends with two notorious pirates.

"We have been friends since childhood, infancy really. I saw them infrequently only when they ported at Odie, as that is where my mother and father lived."

"Surely your lifestyles have clashed?" I questioned, "When you became a commander, that is."

"I've never had any trouble separating my friendship with them from my service," he said. "Until now."

"This is the first time you have been on a voyage with them?"

"Yes, Princess."

"I shall not be a princess for very much longer." I took a bite of the gift and found it was crunchy pastry covered with some nut cream. "Will I be called Countess as your King's fourth wife?"

"Countess, yes," he answered, reaching in the last of the bags. "Countess Landlight or Countess Mercy, whichever you please. Simply Lady if Countess doesn't suit you."

"Is it as strange a position in your country as it is in mine?" I asked, and he looked carefully over at me. "You needn't hold back the truth on my account Absalom. I know what my fate is to be."

"I suppose there would be some that might look down upon the role."

"But not you?"

"If I had an opinion on it, Princess, I wouldn't express it. It isn't my place," he said, and I understood that he was as bound to his duty as I was. "Though you are the friendliest of the King's wives. But I should not say that either."

"Perhaps marriage to him corrupts their good humor."

He said nothing, but his face expressed that it very well may have been. He handed me two small tea cookies, half covered in white chocolate. I watched him dip them in his tea and swallow one bite, and so I did the same thing. The cookie was flavored with the same fragrant flower that the tea was. It melted in my mouth, leaving flowers and white chocolate on my tongue.

"What is my betrothed like?" I dipped the next cookie.

He thought for a long time and let out several breaths. He was a slow sort of gentleman, and I could tell by the way that he spoke that he was patient. I assumed he would have to be, to be friends with Elias and Georgette. He looked back out the window for a few seconds finishing off his last cookie, leaving me in silence.

"I think you should ask Georgette," he said finally.

"Why is that?"

"I believe you deserve to know, and she is in a position to be as honest with you as she wishes. I am not."

"Do you think she will answer or just mock me?" I set my mug on the desk.

"Most likely both."

"Do they truly answer to no higher power?" I asked, trying to hide the amazement from my voice. "No government of any kind?"

"They do not. They answer to their own consciences. They are subject to each other, and they answer to the crew. They recognize no government heads as authorities over them. The arrangement they have with the king is more of a partnership from their point of view."

"I'm sure he doesn't view it that way." I leaned back in the chair.

I was reminded again how unrestrictive the clothes I was wearing were. I decided then that I would not go back to skirts and corsets. At least not for the duration of this voyage.

"I think you are right."

"You're more than childhood acquaintances with them." I did not want to make him uncomfortable, but I was genuinely curious.

"We are friends," he said.

"More than that, you love them."

"My mother used to say my soul strings are tied to theirs," he agreed, and his tone tinged with something dark.

"Your father is a military man as well?"

"Yes, a general. Master Church is his title, a general of generals."

"Does he approve of your friendship with them?"

"Not in the least," he laughed. "When we say our fathers were friends, it's a half-truth. Captain Nathan and my father were business partners. My father turned a blind eye to Nathan pirating in the waters of Northern Ralice in exchange for a percentage of their spoils being given to the King. Neither of them approved of the bond that we formed."

"Yet the friendship remains."

"They aren't a bad pair," he said. "A little obstreperous at times but not bad. I admire them for many things. In many ways, they were as much born to the duty of their lives as we were. I cannot fault them for filling roles that they were brought up for any more than they can fault me for doing the same. I don't always agree with their methods, Baya knows."

"Their parents handed the vessel down to them?" I asked, and he frowned as if I had caught him in something.

"That is their story to tell."

"Not a story they like told," I guessed.

"Some know it. Though from what I have gathered, piracy requires a certain amount of secrecy and larger-than-life tales. Some are true, and some are stretched until unrecognizable." He offered me another small cookie which I accepted.

"How shall I know the truths from the lies?" I asked.

"Time, Princess."

"That is a luxury I don't have. Soon I shall be back in a palace where I belong, and this pirate nonsense will be behind me."

"That is one thing I envy them. Something I'll never quite have." He poured himself another cup of tea.

"What's that?" I held my empty cup out.

"Their freedom to choose where they wish to belong."

Nine

Georgette

"She sleeps in longer than any person ought," I grumbled to Absalom.

I had just finished knocking on Mercy's door for the second time that morning. I was impatient to get off the ship to a nice warm bath and fresh food. Liven was one of my favorite places, and this girl had now kept me waiting almost thirty minutes.

"Well, she is a princess, George," Absalom responded.

"As if that has anything to do with anything."

"It has a lot to do with everything. You and Elias refusing to live in reality doesn't make it not so." He bit the words out at me, and I looked at him sideways.

"Morning, Captain." I nodded to Elias, who walked up to us.

"Morning, Captain... Absalom."

"Perhaps I should come with you in case anything is to happen," Absalom said, and I rolled my eyes. "Liven is a large city..."

"I can take care of myself." I brushed him off before he had a chance to finish.

"I know you can take care of yourself; it's that I don't trust you to take care of the future wife of my King."

"I'm wounded, Absalom." I stared at the princess's door, willing her to come out of the room.

"Mate, you wouldn't want to go where they are going," Elias said, "I feel it would offend your sensibilities."

"Oh, shut it, Elias, you're just trying to cause trouble now." I narrowed my eyes at him, and he grinned wide.

"I thought you said you were going to take her to bathe and get new clothes?" Absalom now looked much more worried.

"I am."

"Where are you taking her exactly? Hopefully, a reputable public bathing house," he insisted, and I cast a dark look at Elias, who was enjoying the chaos he had unleashed.

"I am usually not welcome in reputable bathhouses. I do not make it a habit of going to places where I am despised."

"You can't take her to one of those questionable back-alley bathhouses. She's a princess, for Baya's sake!" His alarm increased.

"We aren't going to a bathhouse at all," I assured him.

"Then where...," he trailed off, looking into my eyes, his face paling.

His face transformed from concern to incredulous offense and anger.

"No," he said flatly.

"I wasn't asking." I defied him by stepping back and giving him a look of indifference.

"You cannot take her to one of those places. It's not proper!" he spoke. "I know you care nothing of propriety, but what would possess you to think to take her there?"

"She needs a proper bath; I can't take her to an established bathhouse, and she will need as much privacy as I can afford her. I thought you would be pleased that I am not going to parade her around at some public bathhouse."

"Oh, Baya, consume me!" He dragged his fingers across his forehead and pinched the bridge of his nose. "My father's going to kill me. The King is going to kill me."

"No one is going to find out. I doubt the princess will want to reveal that she bathed in a whore house."

"Oh, Absalom, don't be so worried. Maybe she'll learn a thing or two about how to please your future king," Elias said as he walked by him, and Absalom reached out and hit him across the back of the head. "You should take Absalom as well so he can release some of that pent-up frustration."

Absalom advanced on him, and Elias held his hands up in surrender.

"Finally!" I shouted as the door to Mercy's room opened, and the girl emerged wearing the same clothes from yesterday.

They looked less unnatural as if she weren't as uncomfortable as the first time. She was approaching us with no sense of hurry. The silent defiance lingered in her eyes as she looked at us. Though her gaze softened, and she smiled at Absalom, which sat a little uncomfortably with me.

"I thought I was going to have to get a bucket of water," I said to her, and she looked on silently. "I have been waiting since the sun rose."

"That is of no concern to me. You don't acknowledge my status as a princess; then, I shall not recognize your status as a captain. I shall not be ordered about by you or anyone aboard this ship."

Absalom coughed to cover up a laugh and my mouth quirked up in a challenging grin. I preferred this princess to the other of the last two days. A woman with a spirit was always preferable to a complacent puppet. When I met Mercy's eyes, the girl did not back down from my gaze.

"Very well," I conceded. "Shall we go then?"

"Yes." Mercy walked toward the stairs that had been mounted to walk down to the dock.

"I rather wish I was coming along," Elias said. "Absalom and I have to go post a letter. It will be nowhere near as fun as watching your morning unfold." I turned and flashed him a rude gesture before waltzing off after the princess.

Liven was magic in the morning. All the shops were open, and wares were for sale along with a giant marketplace that spanned a quarter of the city. You could smell the spices of Hestiege, which were rich and pungent. The fragrance of roasted meat and sugar-covered sweets hung in the air. Voices greeting and haggling filled every space and blended into a market song. It was a kind of simple beauty that I loved.

Though Mercy had found a bit of defiance, she was now relying on my benevolence. The girl had obviously never been beyond the walls of the castle borders, and it showed as she took in the sights, sounds, and smells. She looked like a small child seeing a street performer for the first time. I walked a little slower to let her enjoy it.

"It's incredible," Mercy said, catching up to me where I was buying fried dough covered in sugar and a local spice.

I thanked the street vendor and handed one dough-filled paper cone to Mercy. She looked at me as I popped one in my mouth and enjoyed the warmth of the freshly fried dough.

"We will order you some clothes first and have them delivered to us," I said, weaving in and out of booths and stalls and dodging desperate sellers yelling about sales and deals of a lifetime.

"I...," Mercy said, trying to keep up with me, "don't have any money on me. What I had was taken from me..."

"Your intended will reimburse us for the cost of clothing," I said, stepping into a brightly colored alley draped with beautiful satins and silks. Embroidered fabric hung from every stall and whispered of their creator's talent.

"Well, that's very kind," Mercy said, "I suppose."

"I want my clothes back. I wouldn't call it kindness," I said, stopping as I felt something at my waist.

I whirled around and caught the wrist of a tiny hand.

A girl around the age of seven looked up at me with midnight eyes. She had a head of wild black curls and deep brown skin. The people born in Hestiege had light to dark brown skin and eyes that glittered with dark magic. The girl looked afraid as I glared at her. She squinted and turned her cheek, waiting for a slap across the face. Her clothes were riddled with holes, and her nailbeds dirty and broken. She was barefoot and looked almost starved.

"Hasn't your mother ever told you not to pick the pockets of a pirate?" I asked as I gently moved the girl's chin so she was looking into my eyes.

"She might have if she wasn't dead," the girl said, putting on a face as if she hoped the softness and innocence of her features would grant her leniency.

"You'll get no sympathy from me for having a dead mother after trying to rob me, girl," I said, and the girl jerked her chin out of my grasp.

"What will you buy with the money you've stolen from me?" I glanced at Mercy, who was staring at the girl with a face full of pity.

"I would buy food. For my brothers," the girl said, and though shame laced her words, her voice was firm.

"How many brothers do you have?"

"Just two, Miss."

"Are you the oldest?"

"Yes, Miss."

"What pains brothers are," I said, winking at her.

I motioned for her to follow me. Though she looked skittish, she stepped behind me and shook out her hands. I stepped to the nearest booth, and the owner perked up instantly, going into a bit about the finest silks she owned. I held up a hand to stop her.

"This girl needs two complete traditional work outfits. Make sure they are from quality fabric and don't short her, or you'll answer to me. She'll need a pair of shoes as well and a few sets of underthings." The woman looked at the girl with obvious disgust but nodded at me with respect.

"Yes, Madam," she said as she turned and stepped back into the recesses of her shop to gather some premade clothing that would fit the girl.

"If you keep stealing money for a single day's worth of food, you'll never be anything more than you are right now, a poor thief." I squatted down so I was at her height.

The girl said nothing, but her eyes filled with tears as she looked back at the woman gathering clothes for her. She nodded at me in understanding but said nothing. I reached into a pocket of my pants, pulled out a few coins, and handed them to the girl.

"You take your clothes and wash yourself up. Go to the upper west side of the city and find a man called Hestelle Noden. He runs a few tea houses around the city. You ask to speak with him and tell him Captain Baine sent you and that he owes me a favor. He'll give you a job." I smiled at the girl who was nodding profusely, now trying to blink away tears.

"Seven blaks." The shop owner's tone was now relatively short, realizing that she wouldn't sell us silk or embroidered dress-es.

I stood up and pulled out the coin for the woman, handing them over as I stared at the pile of clothing she had collected.

I sorted through, making sure she hadn't shorted us. I then asked the woman to wrap the clothing in the shop paper. The woman rolled her eyes but complied for an extra copper. Once the girl had her garments and some extra coins to feed her family, she looked to me and bowed.

"Thank you, Mam. I shall never forget your goodness toward me and will thank Jilor for you every day." She clutched the package to her chest.

Jilor was one of two goddesses in Hestiege.

"Put in a good word. Be on your way, and if I come across you picking pockets again, you'll be sorry to have met me today."

"Yes, lady, thank you, lady." She ran off with her new clothes and money faster than I thought anyone capable of.

I turned and headed further down the alley with Mercy in tow. She was silent, saying nothing until I slowed. I was looking for a small green and gold door set into one of the brick walls. I peered between the stalls, as they often changed, but the green door never did.

"I think they cut off the fingers of pickpockets in my country," Mercy said quietly.

"I'm sure they do here as well. It's a widely used punishment," I said, squinting as I walked a few more paces.

"She was just a child," Mercy answered, "Trying to feed her brothers."

"Some children grow up faster than others. Some hungry children pick the wrong person's pocket and end up with one less finger."

"Such coldness after you were so generous with one such child," Mercy bristled.

"I saved that girl's fingers, but I have neither the means nor the time to save them all. I cannot lay awake at night worried about the things I did not do. I can only be content with what I had the means and opportunity to change." I spotted the door and moved toward it.

"I'm slightly surprised that you helped her at all, let alone to that extent," Mercy went on.

"Because I'm a pirate." Not a question, and I turned to look at her before I reached to open the door.

"Yes."

"Pirates are about as diverse in character as any other profession. To assume I am callous toward those in need is simple ignorance."

"A lot like you and your brother making assumptions about me for being born a princess." Mercy lifted her eyebrows.

"Well... I suppose you are right." I opened the door and stepped over the threshold of the small shop. "Though we have met our fair share of nobles. How many pirates are you acquainted with?"

"Welcome!" the old woman greeted us before she saw me. "Oh, Captain! What a pleasure to see you."

"The pleasure is mine, Shelita." I threw my arms around the grey-haired woman with a cane.

My mother had come to this shop for clothing, and it remained one of my favorites. Whether it was the quality or that, it reminded me of my mother, blurred together in an emotional tangle.

"You've brought a friend." The woman smiled at Mercy.

"Yes, I am requesting some of your fine craft for her. She needs three or four full sets of clothing, undergarments included. A pair of boots and a hat to keep the sun off her fair skin. If you have them in stock, if not, we can go find some in the market."

"I think I have some that will fit her," the woman said, now eyeing Mercy carefully, determining her size.

"We need premade items, Shelita. I know you hate that, but Elias will insist on leaving tomorrow morning."

The woman tsked but said nothing else, grabbing a measuring tape. She began measuring Mercy with fierce determination, and Mercy had the good sense to look startled. However, she got over it quickly and lifted her arms at the appropriate times for her. I thumbed through some beautiful fabric as I waited. The small shop was covered from floor to ceiling with meticulously folded fabric and delicate hats and ladies' shoes.

"Will you want to wear pants as well? I won't have anything as tailored as what Captain Baine wears, but I could find something fit for a smaller man, I'm sure." She looked up at Mercy, and I smiled, anticipating the answer.

"I have been enjoying the comfortability of the pants; however, I feel completely exposed," Mercy admitted, "Much too used to skirts, I think."

"Shelita, don't some of your young men here wear the pant that drops lower but still cuffs at each ankle?" I asked, recalling the billowy pants that looked much like skirts.

"Yes, among noble or highborn men normally," The woman answered, "I have a few pairs, but the colors are rather ostentatious. I don't sell them to the working-class." She rubbed her chin in thought.

"Mercy can order whatever she pleases, but she may prefer the feel of those." I pulled a bolt of beautiful silk off a shelf. It was hand-embroidered with flowers of golden thread and emerald green crystals.

"I'll bring out a pair, and you may try them on to see if they are to your liking." Shelita scurried into a back room.

"Perhaps Cyril will allow you to wear pants," I chuckled absently.

"What is he like?" Mercy asked bluntly, causing me to look up. "I asked Absalom, but he insisted I ask you."

"No one could say that he hasn't any sense." I set the fabric on a table. "Cyril certainly isn't the worst noble we've encountered. Awfully selfish, but that comes with the territory. He taxes his people too much to fund his obsessive need to protect the borders of his land. He's old and stuck in his ways. His wives are treacherous, and you should be wary of them."

"How old is he?"

"Older than you." I felt a slight pang of sympathy. "Older by twice your age and a half, maybe more. Though he carries it well, he's handsome enough for his years. He's vain as anything and puts a dark powder on his hair to appear younger."

Mercy nodded, looking around. She didn't seem upset by the information but rather resigned to the facts. I watched her out of the corner of my eye as she thumbed some delicate fabric. She looked much better, though she had only been in our company for two days. She looked less tired as the dark circles under her eyes had lessened. There was a warm pink tinge on her flawless skin. It shone through under the scattered freckles across the bridge of her nose and cheeks. She also moved much more comfortably, and I noticed a natural elegance to her steps. No doubt it had been bred into her just as the perfect posture and restrained smiles had been.

I hated to admit it, but she looked regal. Her copper hair contrasted against sharp eyes as clear blue as any sky after a summer storm. She was long and slender, making that natural elegance look effortless. If I imagined an Adamasian princess, something close to her likeness would appear in my mind.

"Here." Shelita came from the back.

She carried a pile of clothing and ordered Mercy to go in the back and try on a pair of beautiful pants in a shade of violet. While she was in the back, I brought the red silk to Shelita and asked her to create a formal dress for me out of it.

"In what style?" she asked.

"Whatever you like. I trust your work. I don't keep many dresses, but a few to have on hand is always useful, and I can't pass up this detail. You can have it sent to my address in Odie." I exchanged money for the dress as well as Mercy's clothing.

I used Absalom's home in Odie as a place to receive posts and packages. I ordered things from all over Marecult, and he housed them for me until I returned to get them. Some of my items still sat in his home. I had a closet there with things that weren't practical to bring aboard The Siren.

"How do they look?" Mercy asked, coming out.

"Brightly colored," I answered.

I preferred a more muted color palette of browns, blacks, and tans, but the bright colors suited her. The pants emulated a skirt just enough to be feminine but with the maneuverability of trousers.

"You wear them well, Lady," Shelita answered. "I have a green pair as well as a blue I will send you with, and some simple shirts. I have a vest I recently created that will look lovely with these. A little more feminine than anything the captain orders, but I think it will suit you well."

"Perfect, Shelita, I knew you were the woman to see. Will you have her things sent to The Charmed Flower?"

"Of course."

"With that, we must depart, though I look forward to visiting a touch longer next time." I hugged her again.

Mercy changed back into my trousers, and we left. We walked into the street, which had gotten substantially busier since we had left it to go into the shop. It was louder now, and many more voices added to the market cacophony.

"You didn't call me princess in there, and you only referred to me as Mercy," she said behind me as we made our way back out the way we had come.

"Just because we wish you no harm doesn't mean no one does. It's better if no one knows of your title."

She said nothing more as I led her through the streets to The Charmed Flower. I didn't warn her because I couldn't think of the right way to do it. So instead, I walked into the establishment with Mercy behind me. I half dreaded the scene that would unfold.

"Ladies, Welcome!" The Madam that greeted us was dressed brightly with her cleavage dangerously exposed.

"Thank you," I said. "We need two rooms and all-day service.

"All day rates are more," the woman sang happily.

"I am aware."

"Georgette." I heard Mercy whisper my name in panic behind me.

"Yes."

"Is this..." She looked around the visually obtrusive room and cringed as two women dressed in little came out of the back and smiled at us.

"It is a whore house," I confirmed.

"Are you mad?" Her eyes blazed, but she still tried to keep her voice down. "If anyone hears that, I've been seen here..."

"No one even knows who you are; how likely do you think that is?" I nodded at the two girls who had come to fetch us.

"I don't know what game you are trying to play with me, but I am not that sort of woman." Her fists clenched, knuckles white.

"What sort of woman is that? The morally perverse kind?" I recalled Mercy's words said to me.

"Exactly." Her cheeks, once been tinged pink, had gone fully inflamed.

"Perhaps this is one of those instances of you judging others before you know the whole truth." I walked to the Madam, who was behind a desk waiting for me with a saccharine smile.

I set payment on the desk.

"I won't," she defied from where she stood.

"You will." I turned on her then, voice going stern, "I told Absalom I would return you unharmed, and if you keep throwing a tantrum, I will have to break that promise."

"How dare you threaten me."

Instead of commenting, I splayed my arm out to invite Mercy into the back. My face was stone that dared her to make more of a scene. Mercy took a moment but eventually stalked forward, huffing as she passed. We followed the two girls into the back of the establishment.

"Immoral creature," she spat.

Ten

Mercy

"Madam, would you like help washing your hair?" the girl called from around the partition between us.

"That would be lovely thank you, Lydian."

Georgette could have told me that we were simply using the rooms here for bathing. There had been plenty of opportunities for her to lessen the horror that I had felt upon our entry. I decided that she lived for the chaos of it all. She enjoyed watching me squawk and fight. I had wanted to slap her when we had gotten to the rooms, and she had explained to the two women that we did not require their regular services. She paid them for the entire day and let them know they could do whatever they liked with it after we bathed.

I had watched her satisfied smirk spread over her face as the realization dawned on me.

I heard the door open and close, and I was alone for a moment. I glanced at the large tray of salts and oils for the bath next to me and began opening each one to smell them individually. I had requested rose oil for my bath and was well pleased with the delicate smell. It reminded me of the gardens at home. I inhaled an oil of deep amber that I liked very well, and I set it to the side.

When Lydian came back, she brought with her a large bucket of water. I peeked around the divider that separated the bath from the bedroom and smiled. I wondered how old she was because she seemed so much younger than me. I was used to an audience when bathing, as I had at least one lady around me most times in my chamber. While this situation was vastly different, I wasn't uncomfortable.

Lydian said nothing but came behind me and pulled my hair away from the nape of my neck. She pulled a few things off the tray of jars and began rinsing my hair in the fresh water. She lathered it with soap and then ran a few more things through it before rinsing it clean.

The bath was nowhere near as large as mine at home, but something was comforting about it. The girl, Lydian, would have made an excellent ladies' maid. She was gentle and significantly more intuitive than most maids I knew. I missed my ladies' maid. Alita had been more sister to me than anyone. Holt had not permitted me to bring her to Urorah. He'd insisted that I would have a plethora of ladies' maids when I was the Countess. And so, she had been put in the service of my sister Prudence.

"You aren't a pirate, like the other woman," she said to me while she dried my hair.

"What gives it away?" I smirked, thinking of a litany of differences.

The girl walked behind the partition so I could get out of the bath and dry off. I stepped out onto a soft rug and took a sheet the girl had provided. I grabbed the bottle that smelled of amber and rubbed some of the oil onto my skin.

"Your hands are soft without callouses," the girl answered my question from over the divider. "Also, you looked uncomfortable coming here."

"I meant no offense," I said, suddenly feeling sheepish for the judgment I initially cast.

I still felt less than comfortable and stood by my convictions about this type of establishment. However, I was pleasantly surprised by the kindness shown by Lydian. The room was also very well kept and delicate. In the last couple of days, I found myself confronted with the inaccuracies of many assumptions and teachings I had accepted.

I did not like the constant feeling of being confronted with how naive I was. It was something Elias and Georgette had pointed out a heinous number of times in the last two days. I had lived a relatively sheltered life, but I didn't enjoy thinking of myself as ignorant. It was becoming more apparent by the second that I might be.

"Not at all, Miss," Lydian went on. "I've dealt with much worse than someone being offended by my lifestyle."

"How old are you?" I asked, unable to contain my curiosity.

"Not yet sixteen," she answered, and my heart broke.

She was even younger than my twin sisters. I had so many more questions for her, but they all seemed too personal. So, I took in a deep breath and allowed my sadness to wash over me.

"A tailor's boy delivered your clothing. Would you like me to fetch them for you?" Lydian smiled.

"Yes, thank you." I wrapped the sheet around me and ran my fingers through my damp hair.

Before the girl could step to the door, there was a forceful knock, and without waiting for an answer, Georgette burst into the room. I rolled my eyes as the pirate smiled at us. Her hair was loose, and a slight wave was forming as it air-dried. She looked refreshed, and I wasn't sure that was a good thing. She carried many paper-wrapped packages, which I assumed held my clothes.

"How was your bath?" she asked, setting the package on the bed.

"Quite excellent," I said, smiling intentionally at Lydian, hoping it came as a compliment. "I'll have to get some of this amber oil for my personal use. I quite like it."

"They have the best here in Liven," Georgette agreed, opening a package carefully, revealing clothing that was neatly folded and individually tied.

"We must get dressed to meet Elias and Absalom for a meal. I'll show you as much of the city as I can before we have to return to the ship." She started pulling out clothes.

The first was the pair of green pants that Shelita had found for me. She tossed me a white cotton shirt and dug around for another package. She opened it and pulled out a brown leather vest. Unlike the vests that Georgette wore, they had a collar and gold buttons. I got closer to it and realized that the edges had been trimmed in gold thread.

"I'm afraid to admit I'm a bit jealous." Georgette smiled and set it on my pile of things.

"You don't have to show me around the city." I looked at her.

"It may be your only opportunity to experience a new place," she said casually. "You'll most likely be locked up as tight as you were locked up before."

"I'm not living in discontent. I'm quite satisfied with the prospect of my life," I frowned, picking up some of the clothes.

"Are you sure, Mercy?"

"Yes." It came much less sure than I meant it.

"Don't you want a little adventure? Just a little?" She held up her fingers to signify a tiny amount.

Instead of answering, I turned and went behind the curtain to change. I was afraid if I stood there any longer that Georgette would be able to see the truth. I did want an adventure. My soul ached for experience outside of any castle walls. I wanted to participate in at least one grand adventure before I spent the rest of my life being someone's pawn. I wanted to wear pants and wander a pirate ship doing controversial things with questionable company. I smiled, realizing that I was already far into my very first adventure.

After buttoning my vest, I came out and realized she had my boots in her outstretched hand. They looked sturdier than the feminine boots I had worn before and a great deal more practical. I took them gently and pulled them on over the stockings I had put on. I shifted from foot to foot, getting used to the feel of them.

"You look rather lovely," Lydian said.

I saw she had wrapped up the rest of the clothes back in the paper. She set a brown leather hat on top of the package. It wasn't like the three-pointed one that Georgette wore but resembled a man's hat with a slightly wider brim.

A spotty mirror was leaning against the wall in the corner. I admired the way the pants resembled a skirt to my mid-calf before being tucked into the boots. I would have to get the tailor's address and order some things from her when I settled in Northern Ralice. I turned back to Georgette and nodded.

"Where are we going now?" I asked, and she looked much too pleased.

"Can you have these delivered to The Siren on West dock, Siv?" she asked Lydian playing with one of the hoops in her ear.

"Of course."

We walked out into the hallway, and Georgette gave the girls a few extra coins. They said we were welcome back anytime, making me wonder how much money she had given them. I never stopped to wonder how lucrative a life of a pirate might be.

"Thank you," I said as Georgette looked up and down the walkway.

"For what?" she asked, raising an eyebrow at me.

"The clothes and the bath."

"I told you your future husband would repay me for the clothes, and the bath was a favor to everyone aboard."

There was a loud whistle from across the busy street, and both of our heads snapped to the sound. Through the sea of people, I saw Elias and Absalom standing in front of a shop. Absalom smiled and waved, and Georgette started across the road, dodging people walking and horse-drawn carriages.

As we got closer, I noticed both men together with their height differences. Absalom was very tall, and Elias was rather average. He was most likely only a few inches taller than me. Absalom was clean-shaven and had his blond hair pulled back to the nape of his neck. Elias had pushed his temple-length brown hair back haphazardly, and he had a day's growth on his face. The commander stood at attention, and while his face looked relaxed, his posture was stiff as if he were expecting an attack. The pirate's posture was relaxed, and his smile, lazy.

"We've been waiting," Elias said as we came up.

"I don't recall asking you to wait," Georgette smiled.

Elias shook his head at his sister and turned his attention to me. He made no move to hide that he was blatantly observing. I was uncomfortable but refused to look away from him. Georgette said something to Absalom, but I was too focused on the hot embarrassment that coursed through me to pay attention.

"You look like a pirate," Elias smiled.

"Is that a problem?" I asked.

"Depends on how you define a problem." His lips transformed into a wicked grin." I don't think it's a problem."

I shook my head at him, offended by his forwardness. His challenging smile let me know that he was teasing and expected a sharp response. I knew I would do well not to rise to the occasion, but something about him made it impossible for me to practice the princess-like manners I had known my whole life.

"The next time I am deciding what to wear, I'll be sure to take your opinion into consideration."

"I would be flattered to be thought of first thing in the morning by a Princess."

A hand came out of nowhere and hit him on the back of the head. I turned and smiled at Absalom, who was now frowning at him with disapproval. I laughed. It startled them as the sound bubbled out of me. The longer I laughed, the funnier the situation became. I stopped after a while wiping tears from my eyes. They were all staring.

"I'm sorry for him, Princess," Absalom said, directing the statement at Elias.

"I need to eat." Elias ignored Absalom's disapproval and grabbed the Commander's shoulder. "We are half-starved waiting for you ladies to finish your primping."

Elias and Georgette went back and forth about where they wanted to eat. They left Absalom and me out of the conversation due to our lack of experience in the area. Finally, when the twins agreed on a location, they headed in a direction with confidence. They both walked very determinedly with their heads up. People moved aside for them as much as they did for me at home. Many people stared at them, obviously aware of what they were. Georgette got the most attention due to her clothing, but she didn't seem to notice or care.

We ended up walking down a small alley covered in all manner of trinkets. Baubles and shiny things were being sold all along the walls. Georgette led us to the end of the passage that dumped out into a courtyard littered with plush velvet couches in various colors. People were scattered about them, eating and chatting. On one side was a large garden that was only partially visible behind a stone fence.

I got up on my tiptoes to see if I could see inside. It looked beautiful and thriving for a place that seemed to be mostly desert-ed. I longed to walk around in it and see what flowers and plants this country had to offer. Instead, I followed my party to a group of couches. Absalom sat first, and Georgette sat next to him. I was surprised by how close she sat so that they were almost touching. I also noted that Absalom was undoubtedly aware and was looking at Georgette with a voracity that I felt he hadn't intended anyone to see.

I sat delicately on a couch next to Elias but made sure there was a proper distance between us. He seemed to notice and winked, catching my eye. I flushed, turning away from him, pretending to be interested in the outdoor sitting room.

"This is lovely," I said to no one in particular.

"Isn't it?" Georgette answered, "I came upon it one visit here, and it's become one of my favorites."

"We should leave by this evening. I've informed the men to be ready in two hours," Elias cut in, and Georgette groaned.

"Elias, we just got here." She sat up from her previously relaxed position.

"We arrived to a letter waiting for us," Elias said, "Almost as soon as you left, a post boy came by and delivered it to the ship."

"Who from?" she asked, and I saw the concern etched into her features.

"My father," Absalom said, "Giving us particular instructions on which path to take to transport the princess. King Kosdel will have men at the Skirttown Port to transport her the rest of the way by land."

"He knew," Georgette said, looking sideways at Absalom.

I had nearly no idea what they were talking about, so I watched their interactions to glean what I could from their body language. Georgette seemed to be a little sad, but not for herself. Elias was irritated, and Absalom was doing his best to look indifferent. While a brief lull fell over the group, a woman came by with a tray of flowered pastries and a pitcher of something cool to drink.

"Bastard," Georgette said, biting into one of the pastries.

"He has his loyalty, George; we cannot fault him for serving his King well," Elias reminded her.

He poured some of the light blue liquid from the pitcher into a cup and handed it to me.

"Serving his King at the cost of his family. He knew she was aboard that ship, and he didn't tell you." The pirate captain pushed her hair behind her ears and sat back with a huff.

"Not everyone esteems family above all," Absalom smiled, and I realized Georgette was upset on his behalf.

"It will work out just fine," Elias said. "Absalom will escort her after Skirttown so that he isn't complicit in any more pirate nonsense."

"Yes, that would be preferable," Absalom agreed.

I was confronted again with their closeness. I tried to recall if I had ever communicated things with someone by simply looking at them. My lady's maid and I were relatively close, but we were separated by class. There was always an underlying tension. I started to question if I had ever really had a true friend. In the company of three, I felt a huge deficiency.

"Fine, but I want to go to the spice district before we go," Georgette said, grabbing another pastry off the table and tossing it to Absalom. "I'll take Absalom, and you can take Mercy through the desert garden."

"Oh, that's quite alright..." I argued.

I did not want to be left alone with Elias. His eyes were too clever, and his half-smiles were too knowing.

"I've seen you eyeing it since we came in," Georgette said, standing up, followed by Absalom. "Elias will enjoy it almost as much as you. He adores flowers."

"Strange trait for a pirate." I looked over at him, and he shrugged.

"Don't you have one tattooed on you?" Absalom joined in the teasing, and I let an easy grin slip onto my face.

"Go on," he shooed them with his hands, "Be gone from me. You best be back to the ship on time, George."

They were both still chuckling when they walked away. I sipped the liquid, which tasted of cool honey water with a hint of fruit. I stood up from the green velvet couch, grabbing one of the last pastries on the tray. I ignored Elias's gaze as he put the payment on the table and stood up.

"We will have to walk back out and around to get to the garden," he spoke.

"Is it as lovely as it looks?"

"It's one of the major draws of the city. There is a natural spring in the middle of the garden, and no one can explain why it's there, but the water feeds some of the most beautiful flora I've seen." He started walking back toward the alley.

He waved to the woman who served them, and she gave him a flirtatious wave and a smile back.

"I have a small garden I keep at home," I said, walking behind him, "Though we often have very harsh winters in Molina and every spring, I must begin from nothing."

"I cannot keep a plant alive aboard the ship, despite my best efforts," he said, "The temperature in Urorah is rather temperate. It will be very conducive to a garden if you plant one."

I didn't respond to that, but I supposed I should be glad about it. The thought of being the fourth wife of a man much older than me overshadowed any prospects of a garden. I distracted myself from the idea by browsing wares in that alley that were being sold.

Elias walked more slowly than Georgette did as if he didn't have anywhere pressing to be. He stopped with me as I browsed the stalls and didn't seem irritated by it. I fingered delicate jewelry and detailed knives. People tried to sell me shiny stones for healing and potions for true love. I sidestepped a few, thanking and declining profusely. Elias stood by, watching casually.

"Surely, such a lovely young lady needs something to adorn her beautiful head." A man stepped into my path. "To catch the eye of a lover perhaps or to keep yours' eyes on you alone." He nodded to Elias.

"I've no need for either," I smiled, charmed by his large grin and friendly face.

"With a head of hair that beautiful," he continued, "It would be a shame to leave it plain."

I turned to his booth and saw he was selling crowns and circlets. Polished gold and silver winked back at me. Gemstones of every color shone in the sun casting colorful patterns all around. The crown I wore at home for special occasions was rather ornate, fixed with silver and emeralds. My mother favored the green stone due to the stars that I had been born underneath. Supposedly emeralds were to bring me good luck. I stepped toward the booth to admire the craftsmanship.

"They are lovely, but I do not need such a thing." I felt Elias step up behind me.

"That one," he said, pointing to something in the corner I had not noticed.

"Ah, a man with such excellent taste." The man stepped back into his booth and pulled out a silver circlet.

The silver was bent and twisted to represent branches and forged into delicate flowers and leaves. I laughed a little seeing a tiny emerald in the center of each flower. The man handed it to Elias, who shifted so he was in front of me.

His hands brushed my temples as he put it on and situated it on my head. His fingers were warm and surprisingly gentle against my skin. He moved my hair a bit and stepped back, satisfied.

"Clothes of a pirate but the face of a queen," he smiled.

"I'm not a queen," I said, eyeing the man who didn't seem to think anything of the comment.

Before I could protest, Elias pressed money into the man's hands and thanked him. He continued down the alley, and I followed him.

"Captain, this is completely inappropriate."

"It reminds me of the garden blooms," he said simply.

"I will neither be a queen nor a princess when I arrive in Northern Ralice," I reminded him.

"You are what you decide to be." He stopped his swift pace so he could look at me. "No one gets to tell you who you are. Stop living as if you are here to serve someone else's end. If you think of yourself as a princess, then you are. Demand the respect that a princess demands, and you will have it."

"Not from you or your sister." I smiled to cover up the vulnerability that surfaced.

"Show us you deserve the respect you think you were born to receive." His voice got lower as if he were telling me a secret. "We may not recognize respect that comes with a title, but we do recognize the respect due to someone with pride and exceptional character. You have the potential to be more than what they told you that you are."

"You don't know anything about me." He had offended me now, a pirate, telling me how to be a princess as if I hadn't lived my whole life training for it.

"Do you know anything about you?" he asked, looking into my eyes for a brief second before walking off.

Leaving me with a question I wasn't sure I wanted to answer.

Eleven

Georgette

"Whenever I smell cinnamon, I think of you," Absalom said, bringing the bundles of cinnamon that I had handed him to his nose.

"It's the only thing that keeps my clothes fresh between washings," I said.

His eyes closed against the smell, and I admired the way the sun hit his face. I smiled at the thought of him thinking of me every so often. I perused the large open carts with barrels and bags of spices while picturing him thinking of me. I hoped it was during strategy meetings or other equally inopportune occasions.

The spice market was one of my favorite places in Marecult. I would bring some spice back I had never heard of before and have the cook find a place for it in the food. A ritual that I went through every time I visited. This desert land was known for its spices, despite Hestiege being one of the poorest countries of Marecult. I had yet to see a market that rivaled it in both color and diversity. People were friendly, and there was always a bargain to be struck.

I smiled at a man who held out a piece of chocolate coated in some brown spice. I sampled it and was surprised by its earthy sweetness. I gestured for him to bag a half bag of it up for me.

"It's rather inconvenient at times," Absalom rambled. "I mind my own business when suddenly a cup of tea or a slice of sweet bread crosses my path...."

"Are you saying the thought of me is inconvenient?" I masked a smile with a bag of whole peppercorns.

He looked at me sideways but didn't answer. His arms were full of things that I had handed him, and he carried them without complaint. He pursed his lips when I added something new but refused to say anything. We went further down the line of carts, sampling and laughing with the vendors. I had noticed the longer we stayed, the more absent Absalom seemed. He was mostly silent. It was almost as if he was avoiding my gaze or any unnecessary conversation.

Whenever we ported The Siren at Odie, we spent most of the time together. I never got tired of his company, though a lot of his beliefs drove me to the edge of insanity. I knew I had a way of tearing his patience to shreds, and yet he always seemed content around me as well. We were the best of friends. However, this trip was different. It had been different from the day I saw him at Odie before we learned Cyril's plans for us.

I had tried to single him out several times on the ship, but he maneuvered his way out of it every time. He would either have some pressing question for Elias or Jones or would talk to me for mere moments before drifting off to something else. My frustration was starting to get the better of me. However, I had too much pride to ask him outright.

"Do you want to talk about your father?" I asked, walking beside him, and watched as he stiffened slightly.

"There isn't anything to talk about," he shrugged. "His loyalty is to our King, not to me. It isn't as if I don't know that."

"He knew we were going to find a princess in the bottom of that ship, and he didn't even tell you," I said and regretted it instantly as I saw a brief wince cross his face.

"If my King asked me to withhold information from my family...," he said thoughtfully, "I would have to comply."

There was no use trying to talk him out of his loyalty. It was something that we bickered about constantly, and neither of us changed our position. He would never abandon his commitment to King Kosdel because he felt it was his duty as a military son. As far as I knew, King Cyril Kosdel had never done anything to inspire loyalty on his own. It was something he inherited from his father and his father before him.

I never met any king that could inspire that kind of loyalty from me, and I swore there never would be. Kings were too powerful to be trusted with one's devotion.

"You think I'm foolish," he said.

"No," I said firmly. "Never. I disagree with you, of course, you know that, but I have never thought you a fool Absalom. Your father is the fool. I've never met someone more trustworthy than you."

I linked arms with him and watched him smile down at me and relax a little. We walked through the market with our arms together, and it felt a little closer to our standard. He stopped at a cart of pastries and small treats and had the man bag several up.

"Are these for your afternoon teas with the princess?" I asked, smiling at the delicate bundles that he took from the man.

"Is that a hint of jealousy I hear in your tone?" he asked.

"Please," I said, "she isn't even the sort of female that you would be attracted to."

"She's a princess," he reminded me. "A beautiful princess… what isn't there to be attracted to?"

"She's too…" I waved a hand up in the air, looking for the word, "Controlled."

"I see," he laughed. "I can only be attracted to reckless pirates that throw all caution to the wind?"

Here we were at the line again, dancing on it.

"Well, aren't you?" I challenged him.

"Oh, George," he sighed.

He hadn't said it romantically or endearingly. He said it tiredly, and the sadness laced in his tone caused me to pause and stare at him.

"I have to tell you something about when I return home," he said sternly, changing the entire tone of the conversation.

"Okay…" I felt as if I needed to throw my guard up.

"When I get back home, that is to say, my father…" he stumbled. "No, I won't defer this to him. I have decided…"

"Captain Georgette Baine?" an enquiring voice came from behind us. Absalom stopped talking immediately and turned.

I turned after him to find two men standing behind me. They were both dressed in military wear of deep blue and gold. I focused on the one who seemed to have spoken. I was taken aback at first by his general loveliness. He was well built, but there was something dark and beautiful about him. A light dusting of freckles highlighted a sharp nose and high cheekbones. A single livid scar marred his perfect face. It bolted across his mouth, starting right under his nose, and stopped short of his left jawline. He had dark hair that he had half pulled back into a bun on the top of his head. He was slightly shorter than Absalom. However, his stance and gaze signaled that he thought himself superior to both of us.

The other had his same coloring with his hair all bound behind his head, though he was broader and rougher. He was eyeing Absalom warily as if expecting him to attack. His hand was resting lightly on a sword at his side. In his other hand, I saw that he held a reward bounty poster. I knew it well enough to know a likeness of me was sketched on one side, heralding me a pirate. The only places where bounties were offered for pirates were Coranthia and Southern Ralice. I tried to look at the poster to gauge where they had gotten it, but I could not see much from where I was situated.

"Are you Captain Georgette Baine?" the first spoke clearly as if he already knew that I was the one he sought.

"I'm afraid you have the wrong person," I said, meeting his dark eyes.

Absalom had turned and stepped slightly in front of me. I thought he may have done it subconsciously and wasn't bothered that he was trying to protect me. I let him stay there as I put my hand on my weapon and gave the second man a look that let him know I wouldn't hesitate to draw my sword.

"Do I?" the man asked and smiled. "You aren't Georgette Baine, sister of Elias Baine, daughter to Hazel and Nathaniel Baine, Captain of the Pirate ship The Siren, the ship with a stolen princess aboard?"

"A female pirate captain with a stolen princess aboard her ship? Sounds like the stuff of fairytales," I said more shakily than I would have liked.

My pulse was deafening in my ears, and my stomach twisted painfully. I tried to slow my breathing to appear calm. I looked up at Absalom, who was much better at keeping a stoic face, but his eyes had gone slightly wide.

"My mistake." The smile that never wavered from his face was unnerving.

"Not a problem Sir. Enjoy the market," I said, keeping my hand on the hilt of my sword.

I felt Absalom slip his hand into mine and give it a slight tug. We both turned and started moving more quickly than we had before, almost running. As far as I could tell, the men weren't pursuing us. I didn't make an outstanding effort to look behind me. Absalom said nothing, following as we made our way back to the center of the city. I stopped when we reached the main cross street. My breathing was labored as I decided if Elias would have returned to the ship already or be back at the garden where I sent him.

"Those men were wearing Southern Ralice military uniform," Absalom said. "What would they want with a bounty on you?"

"I don't think it's the bounty they're after," I said, heading back to the garden. "That bounty poster doesn't have mine or Elias's first names on them. Let alone any of that other information he was spouting off so arrogantly."

"What do you mean?" he asked, following me as I started back up at a quick pace.

"I'll tell you when we get back to the ship."

He didn't question further as we made our way to the alley that led into the garden behind where we had eaten. I signaled for him to stop as I noticed a woman selling headscarves across the street. He waited while I went over to her.

I bought four at the cart and threw too much money at the shop owner. I wrapped one around my head and gave one to Absalom so he could do the same. It was common for people to wear them here to keep the sun from their faces. It would obscure our identities without seeming suspicious.

We were hardly five steps from the cart when we saw Mercy and Elias coming out of the alley that led back to the garden. I pulled my shawl down and caught Elias's gaze. I made a gesture in the general direction of the ship, and he looked around worriedly but nodded at me. I walked toward them, threw the remaining two shawls at him, and led the way as we all headed back to the harbor.

We walked in silence and only saw more men in Southern Ralice uniform when we reached the docks. Though I counted about a dozen, it felt as if they were closing in. We attempted to walk as casually as possible not to attract attention. When we got to the ship, I stayed back as the rest of them stepped aboard.

"I'll stay here until anchors are raised," I said.

Elias nodded and began barking orders. I looked down the pier and saw Will and Jamie walking casually toward the ship.

"Move it, boys!" I shouted. Their heads snapped up as they picked up their pace.

"What is it, Captain?" Will asked, shoving Jamie up the loading plank.

"Are there any more crew out in the city?" I asked, ignoring his question.

"Not that I know of, Captain," Will answered.

I looked up and saw the same beautiful man in military wear that had cornered us in the spice market. He squinted at me, trying to gauge who I was under the headwrap. I turned, but it was too late, and I watched him draw his sword as he charged toward us.

"Get up to the ship and pull up the loading board," I demanded, drawing my sword from its sheath.

"Are you sure, Captain?" Will asked. I gave him a stern look.

He scrambled up, and he and Jamie began pulling the board as I heard the anchors start to rise out of the water. With no time to spare, I threw the scarf off my head and turned to catch the man's blade with my own. I noticed he had tattoos on both sets of knuckles that flashed dark against his pale complexion. He held me there with him and made no move to step back or engage further. He stared at me with a curiosity I found offensive.

"Has anyone told you that you are too lovely to be a pirate?" His eyes sparkled with mischief.

"Has anyone ever told you that you might sound better without a tongue?" I stepped back and advanced on him as he blocked my blade quickly.

"You would be the first." He blocked several more advances. "Hand over the princess, Captain Baine, and this doesn't have to continue. You can go on with your life; stealing and raiding without any interference from the King of Southern Ralice."

"I'll have to decline that very generous offer." I advanced again, getting irritated at how casually he blocked me as if it took no more energy than fighting a child.

"I must warn you this may be the last time I can offer clemency. The next time we meet, I will be forced to kill you." We had come together again, and his voice was commanding as if I were to be afraid of him.

I saw the ship start to move, and I advanced on him and attacked. I kept attacking, hoping to distract him from the ship. He blocked me and almost looked bored by my attempts. He talked and even fought with superiority. My blood sang in outrage at his air of condescension.

"You have the advantage of knowing my name, but I don't know yours," I said.

"What will you give me for my name?"

"Not a princess," I said, blocking an advance as he started pushing me toward the end of the pier. "That hardly seems a fair trade."

"It's a very good name," he countered.

"It would have to be very good indeed."

"How about a kiss?" he suggested instead, and a sharp bark of laughter escaped my lips.

"Do you often hand out threats of murder followed by requests for kisses?"

"Since I have sworn to kill you next time I see you, this may be my only opportunity to kiss a pirate."

He advanced, and I defended until I was at the very edge of the pier. I watched as his attention turned toward the ship, which had nearly cleared the dock now. He lowered his sword and sheathed it. He didn't call for any men but looked at me as I sheathed my sword also.

"Give your king my regards," I said.

"Until we meet again," he assured.

"I doubt we will."

I dove back into the water behind, reveling in the coolness of it against the sweat of my skin. I swam quickly, only coming up for air when I reached the side of the ship. The crew had lowered a rope ladder for me, and I started climbing. I stopped midway, pushing my wet hair out of my face. I looked back at the pier and saw my opponent and the other man he had been with earlier standing on the edge of the dock. The second man was looking at the first sternly, but the man paid him no heed. He held my gaze instead.

I gave him as graceful a bow as I could manage and blew him a kiss. I watched as he held his hand up in a gesture to catch it. I laughed at him before climbing up the rest of the way. I threw myself over the railing and onto the deck of the ship. I closed my eyes and laid there as the sun warmed me.

"George!" I heard Absalom yell, and I opened my eyes to see him standing over me, and I smiled at him.

"Fancy a swim Absalom?" I asked.

I heard Elias chuckle from somewhere. Absalom shook his head, irritated, and held his hand out to help me up. I took out my sword and handed it to Jones to be cleaned and dried. I started wringing seawater from my hair, muttering about how I had just taken a bath and now my hair would be destroyed. I looked up and saw Mercy staring at me. Her head shawl had fallen on her shoulders, and I saw she was wearing a silver circlet on her brow.

"There's our princess," I smiled, and the girl colored a little and touched the circlet as if to take it off.

"You shouldn't," I said. "It suits you."

I walked to the back of the ship, followed by Elias, and looked back at the pier where the two men were growing smaller but still standing.

"Who are they?" he asked me.

"Absalom said they wear Southern Ralice military colors, and the one I dueled with confirmed they are here on behalf of King Dalion."

"What does he want with us?" Elias asked.

"They wanted Mercy. He asked me to hand her over," I explained, running through scenarios in my head.

"How do they even know that we have her?" he asked, confused. "I thought King Kosdel and the King of Southern Ralice were on good terms. He's supposed to grant us safe passage through his waters."

"Maybe Cyril thinks they are, but if my theory is correct, I think King Dalion of Southern Ralice is the one that had Mercy kidnapped in the first place."

"Politics," Elias sighed.

I had to agree with him.

$Twelve$

Mercy

"What if they catch up to us?" I asked, still rattled that someone was tracking them on my account. My worry crept up my chest and tightened, making it hard to breathe. I cursed myself for wishing for any kind of adventure and suddenly wanted to be back home where everything was comfortable and familiar.

"They won't catch us," Absalom said, but his assurance did little to put me at ease.

"How can you be so confident?"

I ran my fingers along the spines of some books packed into shelves in the cramped room. I hoped it was giving the illusion that I was calmer than I was. I pulled out a volume bound in maroon-dyed leather. It was well-loved, and a glance at the title revealed it to be *Quick Botanical Poisons and Antidotes*. I flipped through the pages waiting for an answer to my question. The two captains stood across from each other with their arms braced against a table covered in maps and large volumes of books. The candlesticks on the table were so covered in melted wax they were now permanently attached.

"Because no one catches The Siren," Absalom said with a slight shrug as if this were common knowledge.

I looked over at him, clutching the book in my hand, knuckles going white. He stared at me, and his eyes held the same confidence that his words had. He was entirely sure of the ship's ability to outrun our pursuers. I had too many questions that I couldn't voice. There were too many concerns building in my head. I wondered if his loyalty was his fault. It seemed unlikely to me that there was no ship in all Marecult capable of overtaking this one.

"They don't have George or Elias," he said, seeing the doubt plain on my face. "I've never known captains, or a crew, do what they can; pirate or otherwise."

I could appreciate that his tone remained as confident as it had been. I still looked at the ship's captains with blatant disbelief, unconcerned if they saw it or not. Perhaps they had earned his trust and confidence, but they had not earned mine.

"Borders between Northern and Southern Ralice have always been tumultuous," Absalom continued to explain to us all in the navigation room.

I thought of what history I knew of the countries. Northern and Southern Ralice had once been a single country of Ralice. Two and a half centuries prior, there was a split among the royal family. The bastard son of the King of Ralice challenged his legitimate brother for the throne once their father had died. The country had split into two, and there was a civil war that was said to be one of the most horrific Marecult had seen. Eventually, the brothers arranged to split the country. All citizens were counted and divided as families were forced to relocate for the sake of peace. Each country had seen four or five rulers since then, but they were still distantly related.

As Absalom talked, I began to feel a bit cramped in the room. Though it seemed a rather cozy place, it was not meant for four people to have a discussion.

"The man on the pier confirmed they were working for the King of Southern Ralice," Georgette said. "He said his King had sent them to find the princess we kidnapped and us as well."

"The kings of Southern Ralice are a treacherous and malicious breed." Absalom spit. "It would not surprise me to find that they were behind the kidnapping of Princess Mercy."

Absalom may not have been surprised by the information, but I was. I thought my brother had at least some ties that were peaceful with the country. If I was honest, I didn't know much about my country's politics. I searched my mind for any helpful information that may be of use.

"Why doesn't that surprise you?" George asked him.

I was astounded by her resilience. She had been in a sword-fight a moment ago but looked no worse for wear. If anything, the encounter had given her a bright pinkness to her cheeks. She had braided her hair back in her typical fashion that I assumed she always wore and was now pulling at the end of one in thought. A half-smile played on her face reminding me of a mischievous sprite from a book of children's fantasy.

"King Dalion is always trying to break through our southern border along the Lapulous Lakes. There are violent skirmishes between his army and ours. We constantly have to drive them back into their territory. It doesn't surprise me that he would try something."

"Why?" Elias asked, scratching the back of his head as if it was getting to be rather obnoxious to talk about.

"King Dalion Senior recently died," I recalled suddenly. "He was said to be a cruel man... his only son took the throne a year ago and has his father's same reputation for wickedness," I spoke it in excitement. Not that it was exciting, I was simply happy to have remembered something of value.

I tried in vain to remember the son's name. Was it Clifton? or Caspian... I closed my eyes. The information was of no value to them, but it was beginning to dawn on me just how foolish I was not to know of any of this. I couldn't even remember the name of a King of a country, for Loripta's sake.

"But what would he gain from interrupting Mercy's delivery to Northern Ralice or kidnapping her in the first place?" Georgette asked.

"War," Absalom decided. "They've been itching for it, and he would have either killed her or used her to spark another war between countries."

"I'm sorry I cannot offer more insight," I said, finally casting my eyes away from them. "I thought my brother and the King of Southern Ralice had at least neutral alliances, but I can't say with much certainty. I am kept out of many things."

"You need not apologize," Elias said. "No one can be blamed for not knowing about war or a King's mind; both are impossible."

"His men all but confirmed it on the pier, and Absalom recognized their military colors. I think it is safe to say that even if your brother had peaceful relations with them, that time has passed," Georgette said.

"But if he had her...," Absalom mainly wondered to himself.

His brow furrowed as if trying to piece together something that didn't quite fit. I doubted he was asking any of us about politics. I was only slightly more helpful than the pirate captains. They seemed disgusted by it all as if they wished they would never have to discuss another King again in their lives.

"Why hand her off to another crew that was intentionally trying to be captured?" Absalom was rubbing the bridge of his nose with his eyes closed.

"Who can know the mind of a king?" Elias repeated to his friend.

I supposed he meant it to soothe Absalom's nerves, but it only made the commander look more distraught.

I did not know the mind of a king. I didn't know the mind of my brother, this King in the Dalion line, and I certainly didn't know the mind of the King I was to wed. The closest I had been to truly understanding the mind of a king was my father. However, I supposed that I knew more about his heart than his mind.

"I think I'm going to get some air." I smiled at them as the room had suddenly gone small.

The smell of books that had started charming, was now cloying, and I felt as if I couldn't breathe. With my thoughts now turning to my late father, I had to leave before displaying some sort of weakness. Georgette nodded and dismissed me as she seemed more interested in following Absalom's line of questioning. It was only Elias who caught my eye as I left. I cursed silently, thinking that he would see the tears threatening to spill over.

I made my way to the foredeck, where I had noticed that the crew hardly was. I leaned against the railing and looked out over the river. Though Georgette said we would hit the ocean soon enough, I had responded by saying I couldn't tell the difference. I couldn't see land from where we were now. Georgette had said I would know once we were out on the open sea. She said you could feel the wild deep beneath you.

I closed my eyes and tried to imagine what wild deep might feel like. I wanted to let it overtake the memories of my father that flooded me. Though the manifestation of a feeling I never had, struggled to block out the loss I felt. My father's ashen face was painted on the back of my eyelids, and it refused to leave. It was the last time I had seen his body, and without his soul, he had looked so wrong.

"The three of us are enough to drive anyone from a room." Elias's voice came from behind me.

I waited for him to come up next to me. He leaned back against the railing so he could look at my face easily. I was glad the breeze had dried my quick tears. He pushed his nutbrown hair out of his face and waited. It didn't feel as if he were rushing me or even that he expected a reply.

"I wouldn't lump the commander in with you and your sister," I said dryly.

"I suppose you're right. Absalom has too much virtue for us."

"I think most people would assume that the average person has more virtue than a pirate," I thought aloud.

"And you?" he asked, meeting my eyes.

I didn't like it when he met my gaze. His eyes were too perceptive for my taste.

"Perhaps I would have said the same thing only days ago." I looked out over the water as the sun drifted lower.

"What are days past in the face of today?" he asked. "What would you say today?"

I thought about it. I didn't know what I would say. I had assumed that pirates had kidnapped me from my brother's ship, but maybe they hadn't been pirates after all. Or perhaps they had been pirates, but they seemed a different sort to me than Elias or Georgette. These thoughts didn't even touch on how I had begun to feel about these pirates. With their lack of government and made-up code. A beautiful pirate captain who seemed more assured of herself than most royalty I knew. Then there was the man in front of me. A captain as handsome as one out of a story meant for young maidens. He had embarrassed me, irritated me, and assumed to know things about me after only three days of my company. Yet, I didn't hate him as I had been taught to.

"You aren't as... despicable as I had imagined." I kept my eyes steady on the water.

It was so beautiful out there; the light when it hit the river and sparkling a different color every moment of every day. It constantly surprised me, and I wondered if I could ever get tired of the sight. I thought that it could be the first and last time in my life I would see the ocean. Something deep in my chest ached at the thought.

"Quite the compliment," Elias said, chuckling.

"What I meant was…"

"It's quite all right, Princess," Elias interrupted me. "You aren't as despicable as I thought all princesses to be. Perhaps we could both do with less assuming."

"No, most princesses are terrible. I have three sisters, and I find them insufferable."

He picked his head up to meet my eyes again and began to laugh. He didn't laugh as often as Georgette did, but it was a rather pleasant sound. It made me happy, and I wished to hear it again. That laugh, paired with the dusky orange water, was as close to contentment as I could remember feeling.

"I'll remember if I ever have the misfortune of running into them," he said, finally pushing his unruly hair back once more. "What are their names?"

"Prudence, Temperance, and Charity."

"Such ethical names," he nodded.

"Yes, my mother thought that if you gave a young woman a holy name, she would grow into a holy woman."

"And your brothers?" he asked.

"Holt is the oldest and my King now, Tobias the second oldest, and then Langston, I'm fourth born, Prudence and Temperance are twins, Herold is the youngest boy, and Charity is the baby, she's eleven."

"Eleven, and you already find her insufferable?" There was more laughter behind his words. I could hear it hesitating there.

"Oh, she's the worst of them all," I informed him as he laughed again.

"And your parents? Are they as terrible as the majority of their children?"

"No." My tone was clipped as he had asked a question too close to my aching heart.

"No?" he answered calmly, even in the face of my demeanor change.

I didn't know what to say. I felt the words rise to spill over, but this wasn't a man I could open up to about such things. Though he and Georgette had a way of talking to me where I forgot who they were and where I was. It was unnerving the way they spoke, as if they had been well-bred and educated. It made me feel as if I was currently talking to a charming gentleman instead of a charming pirate. Aside from the casual use of slang and the frequent vulgar jokes, it was like talking to nobles.

"I can barely handle one sister," he finally continued. "How would I manage six more siblings?"

"I've never seen siblings like you before." I looked at him, grateful he had changed the subject for me. "You... rely on each other. It's as if you know what the other is thinking. You are breathing in time with one another, though it sounds silly when I say it out loud."

"George is dearest to me in the world." I was surprised that he wasn't ashamed to say it because my brothers would think affection a weakness. "I suppose it has to do with how we were thrown together with only each other against the world. It bred closeness. We know no other way."

"I envy you," I admitted, allowing him to see a little bit into what I had been thinking the last couple of days.

"You can borrow her if you like," he smiled. "I would like her back eventually. Much easier to operate a ship with two captains, you see. More people should do it."

"I meant more of your closeness. I don't know that I could manage her." I turned around because I was sure that I heard Georgette's voice coming toward us.

Perhaps we had summoned her by speaking her name.

"No one can," Elias said. "I pity anyone who tries to manage her."

I smiled because I heard Absalom arguing with Georgette as if to prove Elias's point. The two were getting closer, going back and forth, and Elias looked at me pointedly. He stood up and seemed to be preparing himself for their arrival.

"Absolutely not," Absalom said, coming up the stairs to join us.

He talked down to Georgette, who was right behind him and their first mate, Jones.

"Don't think of me as a woman then," Georgette argued, and I smiled as Absalom looked at her like it was an impossible request.

"She's practically not a woman at all," Elias chimed in, and Georgette gave him a dark look.

"Elias, get Absalom to agree to a swordplay contest," Georgette requested.

"If you can't get him to agree, how shall I?"

"He's worried about my feminine sensibilities." She elbowed the tall commander in his stomach.

"Is he to count as part of the crew for the bet?" Elias asked.

"Yes, Captain," Jones said.

"And what are the stakes this go around?" Elias asked, and I saw a shift in him.

It seemed as if feral competitiveness excited him.

"Twenty silvers from each man's pocket," Jones went on, and I sucked in a breath.

Twenty pieces of silver was no small amount. I marveled how every pirate on the ship could have twenty silvers that they could afford to gamble away. It gave me some indication of what kind of income a pirate made. Still, I had counted at least twenty-five men aboard the ship.

"And twenty silvers for each crewman if the captains lose," Jones said with a smile.

"That's pretty rich, mate," Elias said, but even I could see the eagerness on his face, and there was no mistaking that he would agree despite his protest.

"'Oh, come on, Elias, when is the last time we lost?" Georgette pleaded, "It will be a good distraction from less than pleasant circumstances."

"Very well!" Elias shouted, and the crew that had been listening for his decision below cried with excitement.

He and Georgette walked to the railing overlooking the main deck.

"Tomorrow, after we are well on our way, we shall begin the duels! Sort amongst yourselves who you will pair together. At the end of two days, you shall present to us your two champions. One will duel Captain Georgette, and one will duel me. If either of them beats either of us, you shall be named the victors. Twenty pieces of silver shall be awarded to every crewman, but if you lose, twenty pieces of silver shall come out of every crew's pocket." Elias shouted over the deck and was met with a bellow of voices in agreement. It seemed most of the crew had gathered, and their excitement was also a hum among them.

"I didn't agree to this," Absalom said, standing next to me, still looking somewhat hesitant.

"Oh, if you make it to the end, Mate, I'll fight you. You needn't go up against George." Elias smirked at him, eliciting an eye roll from Absalom.

"May I participate?" I asked, and the four of them went dead silent.

Georgette and Elias looked rather impressed that I had asked. Absalom looked horrified, and Jones stood behind them all, sizing me up. I tried to hide a smile behind a look of stupid innocence that they no doubt expected.

"Anyone aboard may participate; you'll have to borrow a sword," Georgette said.

"No, she will not." Absalom's tone had turned to stone. "She could be injured, and then what do I tell my father and the King?"

I bristled slightly at his tone as it reminded me of Holt. It drew me back to his stern manner, telling me that I couldn't do something and using my safety as his excuse. Though as I looked up at the commander, my anger dissipated. While Holt used protectiveness as an excuse to control me, I could see the genuine concern etched on Absalom's face.

"Tell them she was injured gambling?" Georgette suggested and suppressed a laugh for Absalom's sake.

"She should have the right to choose," Elias said. "Mercy, you may join in the game if you like."

"Oh, Baya, consume me!" Absalom was back to rubbing the bridge of his nose.

"It isn't as if anyone has gotten seriously injured," Georgette said. "Not in recent times, at least…"

"I'll be fine, Commander," I said to assure him. "I most likely won't get very far at all, and that will be that."

"Very well," Absalom agreed, "But if any harm comes to her…" He pointed to both captains, "I'll take more than twenty silvers from both your hides."

"I say!" Georgette said with her hand to her chest. "Elias, did you hear him threaten us?"

"Is it always the crew against you in these bets?" I asked, walking to Elias, who was still looking out over the main deck.

"Yes," Elias said. "We haven't lost one since we were thirteen when my parents were still aboard this ship. We did it secretly then as they didn't approve of such things."

"That's a long time to be undefeated," I smiled. "And between the two of you, which is a better swordsman?"

"Elias is," Georgette said.

"Barely," Elias argued, "and only when sparring. We are equals when fighting. She cannot muster the passion unless in imminent danger."

"Seems about right." I looked at Georgette, who shrugged as if she couldn't deny it.

"I've never been more stressed in my life, and you two look as if you are looking forward to a fine meal on holiday," Absalom grumbled.

"I think it would help if you loosened your cravat," Georgette mentioned, and I covered my smile with my hand.

"Perhaps you could take it off completely and use it to wipe your brow, old friend," Elias mocked. "The thought of using your blade for dueling instead of ceremonial pomp is causing you to sweat."

"I hate pirates." Absalom shook his head and walked down the stairs to be rid of them.

Thirteen

Georgette

"So, we are to drop Mercy and Absalom off at Skirttown instead of bringing her back to Odie?" I asked, reading the letter that Elias had handed me.

The first chance Elias had gotten, after the chaos, he had brought me a letter that had been waiting for us at Liven. Gerald had given explicit details on where he expected correspondence checks. He had also blamed mysterious complications for the change in where we were to pass off the cargo. I bristled that he was still referring to her as cargo though he knew she was a person, and a princess no less.

"That's what the letter says." Elias was lying on my bed with his eyes closed.

He had knocked on my quarter doors as I had been getting ready for bed. I was now reading the letter in one of my chairs in a nightdress with my knees tucked up under me, which made me feel like a child. I chewed at my lip as I reread the letter

slipping into the comfortable silence that I could only find with my brother.

"Is it a good idea to drop them off in a country that we know is after her?" I asked finally.

"I don't think that's our problem," he said, eyes still closed, though I noticed his boot-clad feet were tapping, a sign he was not wholly at ease with the idea himself. "We made a deal to do what that bastard asked, and it isn't our business what he does."

"But Absalom is our friend," I said. "Shouldn't we be a little concerned if we are dropping him off into a siren den? I don't have a deep affection for Mercy, but I certainly don't wish her harm."

"Absalom can take care of himself. He will do what his King asks. You would have a harder time convincing him to stray from Kosdel's orders than anyone. As for Mercy..."

He left the sentence unfinished in the way he did when his feeling ran deep. I tried not to think about what it implied. I knew he would do what was right for the ship no matter what. That was something I had complete faith in. His feet were twitching about in the silence of his broken thought.

"She has her duty to her country," he finished. "It isn't our concern. We do not get involved in

royal or political affairs. If father and mother even knew that we had made a deal with a King, I cringe to think of what they would say."

"They aren't here," I reminded him as he often reminded me. "This is our ship, and we are doing this our way. They had their vision, and we have ours. This was how we were going to get to the island."

We took turns being the reasonable one in our relationship. Elias took up the mantle much more often than I did, but occasionally it fell to me. It was nice to know we didn't always have to be collected. There was someone that would be calm for the other when our minds trailed to places they shouldn't.

"There isn't any guarantee that Dalion's men will stop following us once we release Mercy and Absalom. We could be hunted in their waters. More than likely, the friendly ties that King Kosdel has with him are on more uncertain ground than he knows. We could be in danger if we attempt to get to the island now," he said.

"What are you saying?" I realized that he was right and tried to keep the disappointment from my voice.

"I don't know what I'm saying, George," he sighed. "That's why I'm here. I'm upset that we've

made this bargain with this selfish cod of a man. It may now have turned out to be completely fruitless for us. We have now gotten involved in something we don't want to be enmeshed in. We have placed ourselves in the middle of a great political struggle that has brought more questions than answers. We went against the pirate code, and now there is a King who has men after us."

"Well, we've had that happen before."

"Yes, but not for such a personal and specific reason. We may have been chased for being pirates but, we've never been hunted for running a King's errand. I don't like it, and something feels off."

"What feels off?" I asked.

When Elias was in one of these moods, it was best to ask leading questions until he had talked out everything that was keeping him up. I would ask until his feet stilled, and he smiled at me, saying that we had no reason to worry. I was most comfortable with that because when he was on edge, I was on edge.

"The first people that took Mercy, why was she handed off to a skimmer crew? Why was that crew prepared for us to board and take her? If it was Dalion that had her in the beginning, why allow Kosdel to have her back? That man in Liven, how did he know so much about us? How did someone

know that we were working for King Kosdel to begin with?"

I made a noise to let him know I was listening but didn't interrupt his thoughts. He sat up, finally running his hands through his hair, looking over at me. It was more than a bit of nervousness that plagued him. I saw it on his face, making his vitality seem dampened. I was worried about all the same things he was. I would most likely walk the ship in the early morning hours thinking of the same, but it was my time to be the composed one.

"What if something happens to the ship," he continued. "What if something happens to you. Oh, oceans deep!"

"Nothing is going to happen to me, or you, or the ship, Elias. Nothing that we can't handle at least," I assured. "We will take Absalom and Mercy to the port Gerald and Cyril have requested. Absalom will not allow anything to happen to Mercy; he's too loyal to the crown. At our next port, we will write to Gerald and tell him about Dalion's men. If we cannot safely get to the island in Southern Ralice's waters, we will develop another plan like we always do. This is merely an inconvenience, nothing to get worked up about."

"You're right," he sighed. "I'm acting like you."

"There's only room for one worrying captain aboard," I agreed, "and I do it so much better than you. I don't come sobbing to you every time I get a little upset. I have to coddle your every anxiety when you're like this."

"Hey, ease off," he chuckled, standing up off my bed.

"Want to play a game of Gorshelt?" he asked, rubbing the back of his neck.

The tension had left his tone. He seemed more relaxed and seeing it made my shoulders less tight.

"One game." I got up and pulled out a deck of star cards.

"A couple at least," he said, inviting himself to a decanter of alcohol in a corner cabinet.

He drank it straight from the bottle, and I sighed. I went to another drawer where I had two crystal glasses wrapped in clothing so they wouldn't break. I slapped the deck of cards into his open hand and yanked the decanter out of the other. I pointed to the table in the corner as I poured us both a drink.

"How do you think with this mess?" he asked, just staring uncomfortably at the table.

It held a pile of everything from spices from Liven to dejected clothing. I swept it all on the floor, his fingers twitched as his frown deepened.

"You invited yourself in here; just remember that," I said, sitting in my chair, and he sat across from me.

"What shall you do with your share of the treasure?" I dealt the cards as he sipped his drink.

While the situation had derailed our plans, I wanted to keep the excitement of our original voyage alive. We had been waiting years for this opportunity, and until we were confident that it was an impossibility, I wouldn't let it go.

"Store it all with the rest of our wealth," he smiled. "What else am I to do with it?"

"That's rather boring, Elias." I picked up my hand of cards and smiled over them.

"Would you have me cover our Lady Siren in bronze and gold?" He frowned at my obvious glee at the hand I had been dealt. "Finding the treasure is less about the wealth and more about the title we will gain from finding it. Wealth holds no appeal to me."

"Typical." I shook my head at him.

"What are you planning on doing with your share, George?"

I could have told him then. Told him about the house I wanted to buy that would lead to a larger conversation. A conversation I was still too scared to have.

"Perhaps I shall buy a ship of my own, so I don't have to share this one with you," I said finally, and he snorted.

We played at least fifteen rounds of our game and emptied my entire decanter. We laughed, and all stress between us and around us dissipated as we enjoyed the straightforward company. It reminded me of when we were little and would play cards by lamplight into the early hours of the morning, sharing sweets bought at port.

I hadn't remembered falling asleep, but when I woke, my head was resting back against the wall. Elias sat across from me, sleeping as well. His mouth open and a terrible snoring sound was coming from him. I was glad I didn't share a room with him anymore. The memory of being woken by the noise made me cringe.

I grabbed a blanket off my bed and draped it over him. I put on suitable clothing and looked for a coat as I blew out the lamps that lit the room. I stepped out as quietly as I could manage and put on

the coat against the cold air. The sun would rise in less than an hour, and the promise of it dimly lit the horizon.

I made my way to the ship wheel, where Bram was sitting against the ship railing, sleeping. I smiled, standing behind the wheel, and looked up. I was surprised to see Mercy across the ship on the foredeck with her back to me. I made no move to join or disrupt her. In my experience, when a person woke up before the sun to look at the stars, they wanted to be left alone.

I hummed a tune the crew sang sometimes. It was a rather nasty song about a captain's wife being passed from sailor to sailor until she was so worn that no one wanted her anymore. In the song, the captain fed her to some hungry mermen who made her their queen. In the end, the woman came back and murdered the whole ship crew as revenge. It was dismal and focused on the evil vengeance of women like most sailor songs did, but was rather apt to get stuck in one's head.

My humming woke Bram, who stood up faster than I'd ever seen him. He looked mortified that I'd caught him sleeping, and I resisted the urge to laugh at him. I accepted his profuse apologies with a solemn nod. We had left Bram and Jones to run the wheel the night before to sail as far as we could without stopping. Bram was lucky I caught him

sleeping instead of Jones. Our quartermaster was much less forgiving than most.

"Best be keeping a better watch next time, sailor," I warned, still trying to keep my voice even.

"Yes, Captain, Sorry, Captain."

"Go get yourself some breakfast, Bram. First day of the wagered games. You're one of the best swordsmen the crew has." I winked at him, and he gave me a hint of a smile before heading down the stairs.

I continued to hum, watching as Mercy turned and saw me and made her way over. We would reach the ocean if we didn't have to stop for supplies before the end of the day. Though we would have to take inventory of what we had since our last porting was cut short. We would also have to change the way we were sailing. The journey would not be so casual now.

We would hit smaller ports and run the ship through the night until we reached Skirttown. Elias and I had agreed that we needed to tell Gerald that Dalion's men were aware of our presence and coming after the princess. We might need to port and let her and Absalom off early. Meanwhile, the plans of going to our island hung in the balance.

"Good morning Georgette," Mercy said to me, coming up the stairs.

"Good morning, Mercy."

I noticed she was still wearing her circlet, and she walked a little taller than she had a few days prior. She looked a splendid sight in her bright purple pants and cotton shirt and vest. A true pirate princess if there ever was such a thing.

"Did you sleep well?" she asked.

"No, terribly." I smiled, and she opened her mouth to respond but shut it as footsteps came up the stairs.

"Morning, Captain."

"Morning, Captain, please tell me your head hurts as badly as mine does," Elias said, trudging up in a more crumpled state than usual.

"My head doesn't hurt; you've just got a weak stomach." This was a lie, as the front of my head pounded with the effects of too much to drink and then sleeping in a stiff chair.

"I swear," he gave me a sideways look, "for how small you are, you can outdrink any man I know."

"It's all that vinegar in her blood," Mercy offered.

"That must be it." Elias put his head out on the railing overlooking the river.

"We'll reach Hesterna's mouth today," I said. "Are we to port somewhere in Paix or wait?"

"Paix is too central," he said to me, still holding his head down, and I snickered.

"So, off the finger of Hesterna then?"

I just received a groan in response. I let go of the wheel and walked over to him, thumping his back soundly.

"There, there. Let me go get you some food." I walked down to the stairs to go below the deck.

The crewmen were milling around, and there was a sort of peculiar energy crackling in the air as I hit the second deck of the ship. A few acknowledged me as I passed to go to the kitchen. I nodded, trying not to see too much of them all getting dressed for the day. I reached the kitchen door and walked in.

"We should have the fair one go first and get her out of the way so she doesn't waste our time," I heard Bram's voice say.

They were in the back. About ten crewmen, including Will and Goose, were huddled about. None of them even looked my way, no doubt

assuming I was one of them. I grabbed three biscuits off the small stove and a couple of pieces of fruit, listening to them casually.

"Who shall we pair her off with, though?" a man named Foghat asked.

He was a long and stringy sailor who looked to be about fifty years old with hardly any teeth. Though he was quiet and hardworking, he had never gotten underfoot as long as he had been aboard. I was surprised by his voice in the crowd.

"Jamie the gentle doctor," Bram said with a tone of mockery, and the group laughed.

"I wonder if he's ever held a sword," one said.

"A soft petite lady and our gentle doctor," Goose cackled, and a spark of irritation burned in my chest.

"She may be able to best him; he just stopped nursing on his mother's breast," Will said.

"You lot would do best not to judge people by their sex or age," I spoke up, heading toward the door, and the bunch of them went dead silent.

They all turned to me, and their faces went pale with fear and surprise. I looked at every one of them in the eyes, willing them to contradict me. None of them did, and most had the good sense to look

ashamed. Some had brief flashes of anger on their faces. I made a note of those. Men did not often take kindly to being reprimanded by a female so young. The ones that had the most adverse reactions to it were the ones I monitored more closely.

"Sorry, Captain," Bram spoke for a lot of them.

"Am I to assume you look down on me for my age and my sex?" I asked, drawing out the discomfort in the room.

"No, Captain," a few of them chimed in at that.

"Good, because if the past wagers are anything to go by, none of you do very well at these things, excluding Bram, of course. Instead of running your mouths, perhaps you could use your time practicing."

A few mumbles of reluctant agreement came to me.

"It's first light, and there is work to be done before you go counting your victories," I said, holding the door open for them as they all muddled out with their heads down.

I felt like a mother who had just scolded her young children. However, most of these men were more than twice my age. There was a litany of 'sorry captains' as they left.

I made my way back through the crew quarters and saw Jamie putting his boots on, sitting on the edge of one of the gun boxes. I told myself to leave him and continue on my way, but I found myself detouring anyway. He looked up and smiled half-heartedly.

"How goes it, Doc Jamie?" I asked.

"Fairly well, Captain Georgette, thanks."

He looked so young to me. I couldn't help the nagging concern in my gut. However, I knew hardships when I was his age and had gotten through them fine enough. I reminded myself that he didn't need me taking care of him. I was much too apt to have a soft heart for the down and out. It wasn't a trait that helped me in a life of piracy.

"You ever held a sword, Jamie?" I asked in a whisper as not to embarrass him.

"No, Captain." He shrugged one shoulder as if apologizing.

What need would an apprentice doctor have of a sword? I thought of telling him that he needn't participate. The crew would give him a more challenging time for not participating than they would if he fought and lost, so I kept it to myself.

"You tell Bram or Jones to give you a three- quarter sword to fight with. If you've never held a

sword before, a full-size one may throw you off. They don't have the reach that a longsword does but better to wield a blade you can manage than try and look accomplished with a sword you can't."

"Thank you, Captain."

"I prefer a longsword, but Elias prefers a cutlass, nothing to be ashamed of. You need to use the tool that works for you."

He nodded profusely, but he still had a look of dread on his face. I wondered how badly the crew had harassed him about his evident inexperience. It would toughen him up a little, so I took a deep breath and stepped away from him.

"Try not to look so nervous. Convince yourself of your confidence, and you will look less foolish. Be a good sport when you lose, and they will respect you for it."

"Yes, Captain. Thank you," he said again and finished putting his boots on as I made my way up to the top deck.

The men were in a hurry to get their duties done that morning, and they shuffled about with their heads down. Twenty silvers was no small amount for them to wager from their own pockets. I wondered who they were ultimately betting on. Bram and Jones were the obvious choices, but I

wondered if they had a trick up their sleeves. Though perhaps boredom had caused them to dip so deep in their troves.

Elias had disappeared, no doubt to find some more spiced wine to cure his aching head. Mercy and Jones were on the opposite side of the deck, and neither noticed me as I walked up. Jones offered her a delicate sword in a simple leather sheath. It must have been a spoil of some raid as I had never seen it before.

My own sword was named Silva. I hadn't named it; the previous owner had bragged of it when I found him drinking in a bar. It was a longsword, not traditional for a pirate to carry, but I found it comfortable. The blade itself had been inscribed with a prayer of protection from a religion I didn't know: *By my holy intent, may my aim be true.* I had often wondered if my unholy purpose hindered the prayer. The handguard was relatively unadorned with a brown leather grip. It was the hilt that had initially caught my attention. A rose was engraved on the top of it in such detail I found it magnificent. Once the previous owner had passed out drunk, I bought his next round of drinks and left my sword to replace his.

I went to walk over to Mercy to offer her food when she gripped the sword given to her with familiarity. She swung it around to face me in a few

practice thrusts. I went wide-eyed, realizing she had perfect form and an excellent stance. She met my gaze, and her cheeks colored slightly.

"Nobody bothered to ask if I had been trained in the sword." She stood up and brought the blade back to her side in a graceful motion.

"We certainly didn't," I grinned. "Our mistake."

Fourteen

Mercy

I am not sure why I received so much pleasure by surprising them. Perhaps it was because I thought the two pirate captains needed a bit of knocking down. They were much too sure of themselves and what they knew to be true. Perhaps it was the way Elias smiled a bit under his astonishment. To my horror, I found myself preening under his approval. I wanted him to be amazed. And he was, they all were.

It took me a few minutes to get used to the delicate cutlass that Jones had given me. It was broader on the end than a fencing sword and a great deal lighter than the dull practice swords I used at home. I found I quite liked the feel of it. If I swung it properly, it sang through the air like a bird.

Luckily, the first round of sparring was with Jamie, the youngest surgeon I had ever encountered. To his credit, he held his sword with determination, but there was no denying that it was the first swordfight he had ever been in. Though when I overtook him and he admitted defeat, he looked almost relieved. I assured him that I would be of absolutely no use if someone came to me with a life-threatening wound, and he gave me a small smile.

I think the crew wrote off my first win as some sort of fluke or blamed Jamie's inexperience. Though after they paired me with several more crew members, and I beat them with almost as much ease, the tone shifted. While Elias and Georgette looked on with approval, the crew became tense and irritated. They were being beaten by a woman and a woman who seemed to have no pirate-like qualities at that. I was also pleased by their vexation.

I knew my good humor showed as I was sparring with more flare than necessary. Most of them had little to no formal training, and their moves were crude and shortsighted. We took many breaks in between for water and food, and at the end of the first day, I collapsed onto my bed without dinner and fully clothed. I was sore from head to toe, but I went to bed smiling. I wasn't sure when the last time I had done that had been.

The second day I was set to spar against Jones. Absalom would be paired with Bram as they were the two best swordsmen on the ship, aside from the captains. The matches wouldn't be until later in the day to give us a little more of a rest. I was glad for it. My shoulder ached, though I did my best not to show it.

I was eating a midday meal with Absalom, who had brought out something he purchased at Liven's market to share with me. We talked about wedding ceremonies and the differences in our country's traditions. I took a tough bit of ginger candy and chewed it thoughtfully as we looked out over the water.

Georgette had been right about the ocean. As soon as the ship left the river to sail on open seawater, I had felt the shift almost instantly. It wasn't a wildness under my feet but an air about it. It was as if the ocean was claiming me as its own, telling me I belonged to it. It was both serene and frightening.

"You mean to tell me that all the brides in Northern Ralice wear the same color to their weddings?" I asked in disbelief.

"There are some variations, but they tend to range from cream to a very light dusty rose color." Absalom nodded at me.

In Adamas, a bride could choose whatever color or style of dress she liked. I tried to think of the female outrage if there was a decree to wear a particular color over all the realm. I chuckled a bit, thinking of women storming the castle in satin ribbon and oversized bustles demanding to speak with my brother.

"I had thought to wear a green gown," I mused.

"It would suit your complexion. I would never assume to tell you what you can and can't wear on your wedding day, my lady. I was just making conversation."

"What is the reasoning?" I asked.

"Our goddess Baya is depicted in those colors, so dressing in the same is considered an offering to her. In return, she is to bless your marriage."

"I see."

I thought of the gods of my home. Each Kingdom of Marecult had its religions as diverse and different as they could get. I had, of course, studied them all for countless hours and therefore knew Baya was the goddess of both eternal love, death, and the ocean. It had always struck me as odd. I struggled to remember my studies and found it difficult to recall a picture of her.

"Remind me of how her likeness is painted. I know much of your religions, but I forget how Baya is depicted." I closed my eyes, trying to draw up a memory from a dusty schoolbook.

"She is depicted in many ways," he said. "Though in some of my favorite illustrations, she looks much like Georgette. Bronzed skin, flowing hair, and fearless."

He said it absently as if he had for a moment forgotten that I was there at all. He looked up to the deck where Elias sat to Georgette's left, and she stood behind the wheel. She had placed her tricorn hat securely on her head, and she leaned against the wheel, watching her brother carve something into a bit of wood. I had to admit that the pirate captain looked formidable. When I turned back to Absalom, he looked up at her as if perhaps she was the goddess herself.

"Well..." I cleared my throat and smiled at him as he colored. "She'd certainly be lovely then. I don't think I've met a more temerarious female."

"I might be afraid of such a woman if you had." Some pink of his embarrassment was still visible. "I'm extremely impressed by your sword skills. I suppose that goes without saying. Are all royals taught in Adamas regardless of gender?"

"I took an interest when I was younger. I only have one sister that trains with me. The others have no interest, and it isn't forced upon us if we don't wish it. Though it is either swordplay or horse riding, and I've never taken to the latter."

"No? Why is that, Princess?"

"I'm slightly frightened of the creatures," I admitted. "I'm told that they can sense nervousness, so I've never become proficient."

"Swordsmanship seems more useful in any case," he assured.

"Unless one is presented with a horse to ride instead of a sword to swing." I smiled, and he nodded, giving me a look as if he understood my point. "Will I see much of you when I am in Urorah?"

"It's not likely," he said, shaking his head. "My father perhaps, but I am of little importance in the King's army. Not notable enough to have frequent visits to the palace."

"That is a shame; I shall miss our tea and sweets."

"I'll send them by way of my father for you, Princess," he said, leaning back on his arms behind him.

"So, your father is higher up in the King's army, and you are an exemplary commander. Your mother has her hands full with two military men," I smiled.

I immediately saw the pain that crossed his face and regretted my choice of words. His previously relaxed look now held a sorrow that made my chest ache. He took a long breath and closed his eyes. I searched for the proper words to undo what I had said, but I found there were none, so I simply sat in his silence until he spoke.

"My mother died," he said finally. "Years ago, now."

"I'm sorry."

I saw on his face the same suffering I felt when I thought of my father's passing. A pain one could only feel when you had a deep love or affection for the one who was no longer with you. It was the look of someone who never got to say goodbye. I had never been any good at comforting people. Even though I felt an acute empathy for his loss, I wasn't sure if I should reach out and touch his hand or sit by and wait for him to offer more.

"She drowned." His words were short as if he were forcing them out of his mouth.

"You needn't tell me if you don't wish to; I didn't mean to pry," I assured.

"That is to say she drowned herself in the ocean," he said, and I sat back in horror as he forged ahead.

"She was... well she... My mother often heard things in her head that other people couldn't hear. Voices, other people's voices, or maybe her own," he said, sitting back up straight as he started playing with a button on his vest. "She was often unwell and unhappy."

"I'm sorry," I said and cringed at the line that I had repeated now with nothing else to say.

"It's alright." He looked at me and smiled a little. "My mother, she loved deeply, but I think sometimes it was too much for her. I like to think that she doesn't suffer now; because she suffered so much here.

"Elias and George were there for me, as much as they could be. Their life doesn't always allow them to be present for those of us bound to the land. My father... well, he was overwhelmed with grief in his way and left me to fend for myself."

I couldn't bear the thought of telling him I was sorry again, but I couldn't think of anything worthwhile to say either. I remained silent, watching him as he looked down at the button that he had all but twisted off his vest. He seemed forlorn but not swept away by his grief. Some of that would be the passing of time, but I knew that when people believed their loved ones to be in a better place, it brought peace that transcended death.

I wondered if that's why my own father's death was too hard for me to let go. I wasn't sure what he believed, or what I believed for that matter. I envied Absalom of his faith and the peace it afforded him. He was looking past me now as if he were thinking of something else for a moment before he stretched his legs out and stood up. He was a towering presence at his full height, and he smiled down on me, holding his hand out.

"Princess, I do believe we have a bet to win."

"Indeed," I smiled, allowing him to help me up.

⸻ ⸻

Jones had sorted the matches before either of us had any say in the matter. I did my best to ignore my shoulder. The pain had faded to a dull ache of muscle exertion. I stood at the top of the foredeck watching as Absalom faced Bram first. They were both talented, but Absalom was better; anyone could see that. Bram made him work for it, but the match was over, with both men panting, and Absalom proclaimed the victor.

After some cheering and grumbling, Jones nodded up to me. I grabbed the sword he had given me the previous day and headed down to meet him. We started with blades touching, and he recited what I supposed was the pirate dueling tradition.

"To yield, and no more."

"Aye," I winked, using the casual phrase which elicited a few chuckles from the crew around us.

I looked to Elias and Georgette, who had come down from their perch to view the matches better. Elias leaned back casually against a railing, talking to Absalom, who had come to stand beside him. Georgette sat on a barrel with one leg tucked up under her and the other dangling down as she popped a handful of something into her mouth. It was so unladylike that I almost laughed. I glanced back to Elias and found he was staring at me now. Our eyes met, and I yanked mine away as warm embarrassment crept up my cheeks.

Jones advanced first, and I blocked him quickly. I slipped into the assessment part of how I fought. I blocked as Jones attacked. I could almost guarantee that after a minute or so, you could glean all you needed to know about your opponent. Jones was a skilled swordsman, but I noted almost immediately that he favored one of his legs, protecting the other subconsciously.

I advanced for the first time and struck at his right side. He deflected it easily but stepped back quickly. I moved again, mercilessly attacking the same side. As he tried to keep up, I could tell that it wore on him, and he became slower, barely catching my blade with his own. I stopped putting so much force behind my advances as not to hurt him.

I loved to fence. It made me feel strong and capable. At home, it was about the only time I felt that way. When I was using a blade as an extension of my arm, the world went quiet, and I focused on the dance that was swordplay. My mind drifted to our training room and sparring with my sister Temperance, who was superior in skill to myself.

"I yield!" Jones said as my blade came down on his and the force of it dropped him to a knee.

I gasped, dropping the blade. I had been distracted and forgot to hold back on the blow. I knelt next to Jones.

"Forgive me, Master Jones; I did not mean to strike at you so hard."

"Lady Mercy," he grunted as he stood up, and I stood next to him as the crew's surprise bubbled from them in a multitude of sounds. "If you beat one of the captains and make me twenty silvers richer, I shall not complain. It makes no difference to me how we win."

I smiled as he winked at me and walked away. I winced as I saw him limp slightly. I picked up the sword that I had dropped carelessly on the deck and looked up to the ship captains, who were both staring at me. Elias's expression was guarded, and he almost looked upset, though why I could not guess. Georgette had the biggest grin on her face I had ever seen. She looked like a child about to run through a mud puddle after their mother had told them not to.

"I am very impressed," Absalom said, coming up to me.

"You flatter me," I said, dabbing at the sweat on my forehead.

"I could certainly flatter you if I so chose, though I am sincere when I compliment you now."

"Will we face off against them today?" I asked, hoping the answer was no. My shoulder screamed at me after re-exerting the muscles there.

"I think not. If I know the twins well enough, and I like to think that I do, there will be a celebration."

"A celebration?" A burst of laughter came from me. "A celebration of what? No one has won yet."

"If there is anything you should know about pirates," Elias said, having walked up without my notice, "it's that we enjoy a good party. We celebrate our crew's champions. We celebrate a life of freedom, and we celebrate riches and food and good company. Why must we have a reason to celebrate?"

"Perhaps it's just the spiced wine you like," I fired back. "Though if yesterday morning was anything to judge by, you seem to hold your alcohol as well as my youngest sister."

"The longer she's here, the more I like her," Georgette said, joining us, and she threw her arm around my shoulder, squeezing me to her.

It was such an effortless touch of friendship that I found myself more than a little surprised. I was taken aback by the gesture, but more surprised by the easy smile that slipped onto my face and the spark of happiness I found blooming inside me. The arm around my shoulder felt like a comfortable acceptance. I found myself leaning into it. I pulled back and away from Georgette suddenly, scolding myself. She did not seem to mind as she turned toward her room.

"If you wish to wash up before tonight, Mercy, I shall have some water sent to your room," she said to me, completely unaware of my bewilderment.

"Certainly, thank you." I curtseyed out of habit, and she laughed to her room.

When I turned back, Absalom had stepped away to talk to Jones. Elias was standing before me with his same look from earlier. I decided it was a displeased look, and I stayed silent, avoiding his direct gaze.

Elias was only a couple of inches taller than me, which meant that I was near enough to notice something new about him every time we were close. What I saw then was how his ears stuck out slightly from his head. He had a small thick gold hoop in either earlobe, and his temple-length hair curled at the tips of them. I always thought it such a waste when men had such beautiful hair that women would covet. He and Georgette also had a small matching freckle under one of their eyes.

"You have a very unnerving way of looking at me without looking at me, Princess," Elias noted.

I met his silver eyes. Around his eyes looked young today; some days, they looked older, more tired. I might have told him that I did recall my title, and yes, that looking directly into those vacillating eyes of his made me squirm.

"Perhaps you are too comfortable with being looked at," I suggested, trying not to let the heat rise to my cheeks, having been caught staring.

"I'm afraid that comes with the lifestyle. We draw a certain kind of attention wherever we go."

"People must be curious what it's like to be a pirate."

"I think," he smiled, never looking away from me, and my eyes slipped to him again. "People are less curious and more horrified."

I didn't respond but knew he was right. When we had been at Liven, I had noticed the stares that they attracted. I wasn't sure what set them apart as pirates or how people could know what they were. Their gazes followed them all the same, as if they were fated to stand out wherever they went.

"I shall see you tonight. Will you save me a dance? My father once told me that ladies in higher court keep cards to keep track of which men wish to dance with them. Is that true? Shall we provide you with one?" His eyes smiled.

"There will be dancing?" I asked, raising an eyebrow, unsure if he was toying with me.

"We have a few men aboard that play, and normally Georgette entertains a few of them with a dance and even manages to rope me into a few as well."

"Oh," I could think of nothing more clever to say.

Thinking it sounded rather like a pirate ball. I started thinking of the men dressed in their most acceptable cotton shirts and Georgette whirling about in her captain's coat. I thought of pirates lining up to sign my dancing card with bows and curtseys. I started laughing at the thought, and Elias's smile reached his eyes.

"I shall save you a dance, Captain," I assured, stepping away to give my shoulder rest before I was required to dance and drink in the company I had started to admire.

Fifteen

Georgette

I dabbed some sweet almond oil behind my ears and wrists, sorting through some of my clothes to find the least disheveled. I growled my irritation as I picked up another tousled cotton shirt too creased to wear. I didn't usually mind the mess of my room, but when I couldn't find a single item of clothing without wrinkles, I cursed myself. I would have to bring some of my clothes down to be rinsed and pressed.

I went to a large trunk and opened the lid. It held clothing I wore less often, skirts, dresses, and more formal wear. They were a necessary evil, and I sometimes donned them for meetings and things when the situation called for it. You could typically seduce a man easier in a dress than in pants and lace-up calf boots. I had yet to understand why. I pulled out a white cotton dress with off-the-shoulder sleeves and tugged it over my undergarments. I slipped my arms into my black leather vest and laced up the front. I put on stockings and boots and headed out the door.

The crew knew better than to say anything about my dress, but it didn't stop them from staring from the corners of their eyes. I ignored them all, surveying the deck, which they transformed into a pirate's carousal. It was a sight that I loved and a pity more people did not see it.

Lanterns hung from masts, decorating the deck in soft glowing light. There looked to be hundreds, though I knew there weren't that many. They sparkled on the dark water below, and the full moon and stars lit the sky above. A small band of men picked at their instruments to make sure they were in tune. Someone had pushed barrels together to makeshift tables with the last of our food placed on them. We would port tomorrow, so there was no food spared this evening. I had never been to a gala or a ball, but I couldn't imagine how it could compare.

I walked to a nearby barrel with a spigot screwed into it and grabbed a metal cup from the top. I poured myself a generous cup of spiced wine and sipped it as I allowed my mind to wander to another world. The ship's deck was transformed to a ballroom floor with handsome couples parading about, cheeks colored with wine. Lively, music played, and stringed lanterns lit the room. Women were streaming down grand staircases, gauzy dresses flowing behind them. Men were looking at ladies as if they were the stars over a vast ocean. I pictured tables of pastries, roasted meat, fruit piled high, and punch served out of crystal glasses. In my vision, a man stepped to my side to ask me to dance.

"You're wearing a dress." Mercy's voice interrupted my thought. I turned to look at my imaginary suitor, and his face disappeared before I could see it.

"Indeed," I smiled. "I do own a few. I just find them abhorrently inconvenient most of the time."

"You look enchanting," Mercy said. "Though you look lovely in pants as well, I suppose I should say you look more delicate than normal."

"I hardly take that as a compliment." I turned to her, but the small smile she wore told me she had already known that I wouldn't.

"Your stature is so petite..." She went on despite my scowl. "You hardly reach five foot five if I were to wager. You have a friendly soft sort of face, doe eyes, and feminine curves. I am sorry to inform you, Captain, but you would be the paragon of desire at court. My court, in any case."

"I've never been more offended in all my life." I shook my head as she laughed silently at me.

"What a backwards world it is aboard this ship," she decided finally.

I had just been dreaming of a court ballroom, so I chose not to taunt her for the statement or risk feeling hypocritical.

"While we are paying compliments, you also look beautiful. Do they instruct you how to do that in Princess training?" I joked, but her face soured as if I touched a nerve.

"They do indeed. My mother and governesses were always rather vexed with my lean figure, always referring to it as boyish. I think they would rather I look like you, more appealing to men, I suppose," she said it distantly, like it no longer bothered her.

"What a stupid thing to assume," I said as irritation on her behalf flared up in me. "That all men would find one figure attractive. You don't look boyish. You look graceful."

She was wearing her loose green pants and a cotton shirt with her decorated leather vest. Her new boots laced and polished with that silver circlet in her coppery hair. I had a sneaking suspicion it had been a gift from my brother, which only reinforced my hunch about his lingering glances her way. Perhaps, I was not the only one that needed a warning on less than profitable affections.

She smiled her thanks but didn't say anything. We sat in silence as I offered her a cup of wine which she took with eager fingers and drained the entire glass in seconds. She coughed a little, and as I looked on in surprise, she poured herself another full glass. Her cheeks warmed as I watched her take another long drink from her cup.

"I'm not...," she tried to explain to me as I did my best not to laugh, "very comfortable at things like this."

"Surely you have large balls and masquerades at home, celebrations at least?" I asked.

"Certainly," she agreed. "Since the young age of fourteen, I rely on the alcohol-laced punch to help me endure them."

"I hope you find ours less insufferable," I smiled. "Though help yourself to as much wine as you please, gods know we will. You also needn't participate in any way you don't wish. We will not require any princess-like duty from you."

"I think this is the first time in my life that courtesy has ever been extended to me," she said and then pursed her mouth as if she wished she hadn't.

"It is a luxury to be able to do as you wish," I nodded. "As long as you are aboard our ship, you will be afforded that freedom."

"Thank you." She looked into the dark red liquid in her cup.

"A dress?" another voice called to me as Elias came toward us.

The crew may not mention my attire, but my brother certainly would. I scowled at him and challenged him with scowling eyes.

"A dress?" Absalom called as I drained my cup of wine, extending my glare his way.

Mercy coughed to cover up a laugh.

"For someone who made fun of my very fashionable green vest the first day aboard this ship, I find you to look much too embellished for the occasion," Absalom forged on despite my frown.

He was wearing the same vest now and a grey cravat to complement the deep green of it. He had brushed his hair back and away from his bright eyes. He looked terribly handsome against the backdrop of a lantern-lit ocean. His face had been shaved clean of the days' growth he had worn earlier, and he seemed to have nicked the corner of his chin in the process.

"I'm surprised you didn't don your red and gold commander's coat," I smiled.

"There's only so much harassment I can take." He reached for the cup of wine Elias handed him.

Before I could think of anything to say back, the music began to play and swept across the deck like a welcome breeze. It was slow at first as the men gained their confidence and became louder and faster by the second. I had always loved music and the way it could elicit a range of emotions. I loved to dance. My mother had taught me many dances from all over Marecult, and I had taken very well to it. Elias had been less fond of it but would still dance occasionally.

"My lady," Absalom offered Mercy his hand. She looked so wholly scared I wanted to laugh but held it in.

They set their wine down, and Absalom led her to the middle of the dancefloor as the men playing took the cue and started another cheerful song. Soon Mercy was laughing at something Absalom was saying, and they were tapping away together. I wasn't sure why Mercy had been worried; she danced very well. Her graceful limbs were falling into time as if she was born for it. Maybe it was the wine, but there was a glow to her cheeks. I knew it was not the ocean air doing her good and shook my head at my brother, where he stood staring at her.

I turned down two offers to dance as I made my way to the food. I was ravenous. I had pulled rope all morning after we replaced the sail on the back mast of the ship. My arms were sore, and hunger struck, causing the wine to gurgle in my stomach. I positioned myself by a plate of hard cheeses and some grapes. I picked through them to get the best of the bunch and popped them in my mouth, watching as some men gathered to do a jig of sorts after the previous song had ended.

Elias wandered over to me. The thing about my brother was that he never ended up somewhere he hadn't been intentionally going. If he came over to my end of the buffet, he had meant to. I knew by the look in his eye he wished to speak with me.

"You seem to be doing well." He nodded when he finally placed himself next to me as not to block my view of the dancing.

"What do you mean?" I asked, shoving a bit of hard bread in my mouth.

"I mean, you and Absalom seem to be... doing fine," he continued awkwardly.

"I don't know why you continue to poke around in things that don't concern you, Elias," I said as harshly as I could around the rockish bread.

"I just...," he sighed. "Want to make sure that you're okay, that you're getting what you want. That you are happy...."

I looked over at him, swallowing, trying to decode his facial expression. My first reaction was to snap back to his concern with sarcasm. As far as immediate happiness, I was stuffing myself with food under the light of a perfect evening. I was listening to music, and I would get to dance. I was with Elias and Absalom, two of my favorite people in the world. While something was amiss with Absalom, I had no doubt it would work itself out, and we would be back to normal within the week.

As for my overarching happiness, I was doing what my parents had trained me to do, what I had always imagined myself doing. I was doing it successfully. I was captaining alongside someone that I knew would always have my back. What wasn't there to be happy about? A small voice in the back of my mind told me if I was happy, I wouldn't be dreaming about a life on land, of ballrooms and dresses and children and a husband. I silenced that voice and shoved it back where it belonged.

"Of course, I'm happy; why wouldn't I be? What a strange question." I dismissed him but watched closely as his gaze followed the princess talking with Absalom on the other side of our ship.

"Elias," I said, a tone of warning in my voice.

"Yes."

"She's a princess, Elias." He turned to me, and I could tell the irritation he was about to direct at me was to cover up something else.

It was something that I had sensed over the last couple of days. It had started the day that he had first seen Mercy in ship wear, then there was the circlet and the lingering looks. The way he looked at her like she was an unattainable prize, and the way she looked at him like he was some rakish adventure.

"You don't have to remind me," he said darkly instead of pretending he didn't take my meaning.

I supposed it was the end of the conversation because he left to walk over to Mercy and bowed in front of her, holding his hand out for a dance. I wish I could have called him back and said something different, told him that he deserved her, and more. It wasn't that I thought she was above him, only that we had a job to do, and his attraction to her was as much in the way of our goal as my history with Absalom. It wasn't that he was a pirate, and she was a princess. It was that he was a pirate, and she was someone else's wife-to-be. And not just anybody's wife, but a King's. A King who we now both worked for and owed a debt. We had his gold, and he did not have his princess.

I grabbed some seeded crackers, eating them and turning out to look over the water, so I didn't have to look at my brother another second. I stepped to the railing to look out into the depthless ocean. When I was younger, I would look out on the dark water and imagine mermaids or sirens coming up out of the water and giving me deep-sea treasures. I imagined pink pearls, lost crowns covered in stones, pretty rocks, and pieces of orange coral. It hadn't helped that my father told us tales of mermen stealing princess brides and sirens falling in love with sailors before bed every night. My mother thought it silly nonsense, but it was one of my most cherished memories of my father.

"You have yet to dance. I figured you would be four partners in by now," Absalom said from behind me.

I flicked my last cracker into the ocean and turned back to him and the music beyond. His hand was held out toward me, causing something in my heart to constrict. I took it as he led me out to our main deck turned ballroom. He bowed to me, and the men played a soft song that reminded me of springtime and wildflowers. He assumed a formal dance position that was native to his country. One of his hands was on my waist and his other hand in mine.

"My favorite dancing partner was preoccupied. Perhaps I was feeling rebuffed." I smiled.

"I have never known a single man to keep you from doing what you want, so I doubt that." He narrowed his eyes at me. "Also, I can count on two hands the number of times we have danced together. How have I earned the honor of being your favorite dance partner?"

"I was speaking of Goose," I said with a mock-serious tone as Absalom's eyes wandered to the crewman, who was already stumbling drunk and half asleep on the stairs.

Absalom let out a genuine laugh accompanied by the sparkle that lit his eyes when he was joyful. I started thinking about Elias's question again. I had a sinking feeling it was going to plague me much longer than I wished.

"Would you say that you were happy?" I asked Absalom, who looked slightly startled.

"In what way?" he asked, dipping me down to a sway in the song.

"In whatever way you like to answer, I suppose."

He was silent for a long time, and I was comforted to know that I wasn't the only one taken off guard by the question. I looked to my left and saw Jones and Mercy dancing. She smiled at me, and I smiled back. She didn't look as if she wished to be in the corner of the ship tucked away from everyone else.

"I suppose I am. Here, with you and Elias. I am happy. I feel less weight here, as if I don't have to worry about my responsibilities at home. It's easier to be myself with you both, where my father isn't constantly pushing me to be less like my mother and more like him. Though Baya knows you and Elias give me more than my weight in anxiety, I feel untroubled. When I arrive back at Odie, I will be...." His voice dropped lower. "...satisfied."

"Satisfied and happy sounds terribly different."

"I think they are." His arm tightened around me, "You both have always encouraged all parts of me, and it's not a freedom often found in the world."

"We like you any way you come, Commander Church." I smiled up at him. "Always."

He held up his right hand, showing off the fleshy part of the bottom; a deep rough scar in the shape of an X stared back at me. I held up my palm with the matching scar. The music had switched to a faster-paced tune, but Absalom had stopped dancing and pressed his palm to mine. His fingers were warm and comforting as I looked at the vast difference in our hands. His were lighter in color but with just as many callouses as my own.

I thought of the night he, Elias, and I made a vow of friendship to each other under the light of a full moon on a sandy beach.

His father had not been pleased and had punished him for it. Our parents hadn't been happy either, but they understood. We all three bore the scars proudly, as a vow of friendship unto death.

"Captain, bless us with a song!" Bram called to me, breaking me out of the trance.

"This early in the night?" I smiled over to him as the crew thundered their approval of the idea.

"Yes, George, let's have a song!" Elias called out where he stood by Mercy.

"Very well." I pulled away from Absalom, aware that we had been frozen in a spectacle of a moment.

I went over to the lads who played for us and thought of a tune that would be easy for them. I hopped up to sit on a barrel close to them and gave them the title as they began. The fast-paced and joyful melody roused a yell from the crew.

"I'll dedicate this to our graceful champion," I hollered over at Mercy, who looked like she might want to hide after all.

I laughed and started to sing the words out.

Oh, Lad I know the tides are rough and the waters bitter cold
But the sea she sings me secrets that the land could never know
When I was just a little babe on me mother's knee
The water called to me and said many a treasure you'll see
Join a ship, join a ship to plunder, bed, and steal
Join a ship, join a ship the reasons I'll reveal
Oh, Lad you will see a lady a plenty with loose and wily knees
But be sure it's not the captain's daughter for he will not be pleased
Bed a lady, take her out for wine and fancy fare
But check your sash, she'll rob you blind for the pleasure you found there
Join a ship, join a ship to plunder, bed, and steal

Join a ship, join a ship the reasons I'll reveal
Oh, Lad you've heard of silver n' gold but of riches, you know
not
'Till you see a haul of pirate treasure stolen or fair got
You'll bathe in rubies, drink up emeralds and clean your teeth
with coin
Now you see the ship life is the life that you should join
Join a ship, join a ship to plunder, bed, and steal
Join a ship, join a ship the reasons I've revealed
Join a ship, join a ship to plunder, bed, and steal
Join a ship, join a ship the reasons I've revealed

When the song ended, I looked to Mercy, who shook her head with feigned disapproval, but a traitorous smile spread wide over her face.

Sixteen

Mercy

I made my way up to the upper deck to watch the others enjoy the night. It was by far the least abhorrent celebration I had attended. I had danced with several crewmen, and most of the songs had been quick and happy. No drawn-out tunes that seemed to go on like a midweek lecture. The only songs that seemed to take longer were the ones I danced to with Elias. I was aware of every place his skin touched mine. I was more aware of his self-satisfied smile as he realized I was enjoying the night.

The men were having almost as much fun as Georgette, who looked to be in her element. She only seemed to gain more energy as the night went on. With every song, she smiled wider and laughed more. The wine had colored her cheeks, and she had taken her hair down, so as she spun, her dark brown waves whipped to and fro. Absalom was either dancing with her or smiling after her in admiration.

When I reached the upper deck, I realized Elias had also retreated there. He was sitting against a wall to the side, so I hadn't seen him. A glass of wine sat next to him, and he had a bit of wood and a knife that he always carried. He looked up and gave me half a smile before going back to his whittling. I realized he was giving me the option to speak or remain silent. I took the second option for a bit. I turned my back on him and watched the moon and stars and the crew of pirates beneath them.

Georgette pulled Absalom in for another dance. It was a fast-paced sort of jig, and they moved parallel to each other with Georgette's arm on Absalom's back, and his arm draped over her shoulder. I watched as his smile radiated at her, or for her, and her alone. She beamed back at him with rosy cheeks and merriment. They were familiar with one another and moved as if anticipating the others' next change.

"I'm not sure why it's taken me so long to see it," I said, aloud though only loud enough so Elias could hear me.

"Hm?" He made the sound casually.

"They're in love," I said, feeling stupid to have not seen it before.

I looked behind me over to him after there was a silence. He was biting on his lip, as I had noticed Georgette sometimes did. He turned the wood he was working into a tree over in his hands, running his thumb over the shaped branches.

"I think something akin to love, yes."

"What is akin to love that isn't love?" I turned and leaned back against the half wall to confront him with ease.

"I couldn't say for certain." He looked past me as if he could see the couple through the wood. "Though there has been something between them for years. I don't think they are in love. Affection, perhaps, or friendship mixed with a certain amount of attraction. Or perhaps a certain amount of familiarity and the fear of things not being as they are forever."

"He seems to love her," I said, turning slightly to see Georgette laughing at Absalom, who was shaking his head.

"Oh, I'm not saying they don't love each other. Certainly, we all share a bond stronger than that of most people. Perhaps for Absalom, it is that life-altering, reckless sacrificial love. Ocean knows he's had plenty of opportunities to marry and had rejected many a maid."

I turned back to him and raised an eyebrow. The two pirate captains hadn't offered me so much as a kernel of intimate truth while I had been aboard. Every word they spoke was either covered in sarcastic humor or haughty command, but what Elias shared savored of truth. It sounded like a truth that he had been sitting on for a long time.

"Why don't you suppose it to be love, Captain? Have you had much experience?"

"Firsthand? None at all. Though I have had the pleasure of seeing many great love stories in my life." He went from looking at me to picking at his wooden tree. "Absalom and George's lives are as different as the sun and moon, and neither is willing to sacrifice their identity for the other. So, they remain conflicted. Their closeness sometimes causes a greater divide between them. So no, I do not think that to be the love that you are speaking about. A love perhaps but not *the* love. The love that people search for, that books are written on, and the love for which dragons are slain."

It should have sounded silly. Like a boy talking of love as if it were a wondrous magical thing that existed out there and was to be yours if only you believed sturdily enough. I should have laughed. I did not believe in that kind of love. I was taught to be married, not to be loved. I had been taught to be quiet and subservient to my future partner but not to be loved. It was the love of fairytales and knights slaying dragons. It was not the love of reality.

"Were your parents in love?" I asked, and his eyes snapped to mine.

"They were."

"They were in the magical sort of love that you claim to have seen?" I tried to keep the disbelief from my voice.

"I never said magical; I said dragon slaying. My parents were two tempests set on a course for each other. My father's will was iron and absolute, and I am convinced the only person in the world who was more stubborn than he was my mother."

"How then could you know it to be love?"

"Something...," he faltered and looked up to me again, wholly vulnerable. "It was something about the way they apologized to each other and touched foreheads after they fought. The way they refused to disparage the other and how they danced. Something in their determination to outdo one another in showing their love to the other. I cannot quite put words to it. I know that when I see it, I know it to be the love."

I tried to think if I had ever encountered love like that. It seemed almost impossible. Though the way Elias's words carried the explanation was a soft promise that it was real. That could be something I dreamed about for the rest of my life as I shared an old king's bed with several others. I imagined his soft and assured voice coming to me on nights I felt most alone, promising me that there was some magic left in the world after all.

"If the sun and the moon cannot be in love for their differences, are all opposites to suffer the same fate?" I asked, shifting the tone of the conversation to be slightly lighter. "Day and night might be doomed as well?"

"Oh no, certainly not." He got up and came to stand next to me, looking out over the deck. "While the sun does not let the moon shine in its presence and they never do quite meet, day and night are quite a different story."

"Oh, do tell, oh tale weaver." I smiled over at him.

"Day and night allow each other to stand out separately and independently. Both beautiful and useful, but when they meet, that's how you know they are most assuredly in true love."

"How is that?"

"Sunrise, sunset, dusk, and dawn are the loveliest times of the day. They are beautiful apart, but together they are magnificent." He was looking at me again.

The draw to see what he was thinking was too strong. As I met his eyes, I saw something alive in them. It was part humor, part truth. However, there was something else there, too, something more profound. He was waiting for me to accept something that he was offering. He was waiting to see if I was worthy of whatever he had just given me. I had a feeling he didn't extend it freely, and I wanted so badly for it to be mine.

I found myself again in his company as if he were gentlemen and I was a lady. As if we were discussing love, friends staring out over a balcony, and neither of us had a duty to our futures. For the first time in my life, I wished that I didn't have a commitment to my country. I had never resented it until then. Instead, I wished I was just a lady talking with a gentleman or even a pirate talking to a pirate. Though, the reality was that I was a princess talking to a pirate. A pirate who was working for the king I was to wed.

I couldn't bear to dismiss his offer, and my nagging conscience wouldn't let me accept what he was gifting. So, I gave him a small smile instead and turned so I looked over the revelry below. I glanced at his hand so close to mine resting on the railing. I had the overwhelming urge to set mine on his, but I drew away from him altogether. I tried not to look as if I was bothered.

"I think I shall retire; you pirates are used to much more excitement than I. I'm afraid I'm exhausted."

"You had better get your rest for your spar with Georgette in the morning; she won't go as easily as the other crew that you sheared through." He seemed to understand why I was pulling away and was going to let me go.

"Goodnight, Captain Elias," I said, reminding myself.

"Princess Mercy," he nodded, and I wondered then if he had been reminding himself earlier and again just now.

I fell asleep to the sound of music coming softly through the door of my room. The Siren rocked soothingly on the water, and the moon shone in the window. I slept soundly, just as I had all the other nights. My dreams wandered to dancing beneath the starlight with the deck of a pirate ship beneath my feet.

I woke up with an ache in my shoulder, though the rest had helped it slightly. The sun had just barely started to come up, and I heard the shuffling of the crew outside. The past six days, I had almost always been the last one to wake up. I pulled on my clothes, thinking it a wonder that I had only been on the ship six days. It felt both longer and shorter than that. In six days, I had been rescued by the Captains Baine, been brought to a den of iniquity, found out they were being pursued, taken part in a pirate's wager, and attended a pirate revel.

It was almost too much to take in, but it didn't feel overwhelming either. I found I liked the fast-paced change of the ship. I also found I enjoyed the company of Absalom, Georgette, and Elias more and more every day. I was now looking forward to the days' worth of banter and information. Today I would spar with Georgette, and we would reach the port of Quizit. I was rather excited to experience another place I hadn't been to.

I stepped out of my room and almost ran into Elias, who was coming from his quarters. I had left my circlet in one of my drawers that morning on purpose. When I looked at it, I started wishing for things I could never have, so I had left it and covered it with a shirt. I wore instead the hat Georgette had ordered for me back in Liven and braided my hair back from my face in a single plait.

We walked together out onto the open deck, and I shivered against the chill of the morning, though I knew that it would warm up soon. Georgette waved to us from where she was talking with two sailors I hadn't met. She made her way over and met us halfway.

"I've spoken with Absalom, and the matches this morning are set. Absalom against myself, and Mercy against you, Elias," she beamed, but it wasn't in her smile; it was in her whole demeanor.

"Absalom agreed to that?" Elias asked incredulously.

I looked around for the commander but didn't see him on the upper deck. I felt as surprised as Elias. I imagined the commander flat-out refusing to take on Georgette as an opponent.

"Why?" I asked her.

"Because I think you can beat my brother, and I'd like to see it firsthand."

"You do realize that the roughly five hundred-forty silvers will come from each of us, do you not?" Elias laughed but sounded more amused than anything. "Whose side are you on?"

"I would gladly the boon alone, to see you bested by a princess Elias." She smiled at him as if it were a certainty, but the way that Absalom talked about their sword skills, I had expected to lose.

"Not only do you want to see me fail, but you are counting on it? What kind of sister are you?" he asked.

"The kind who is tired of never seeing her brother bested." She smiled and walked away with joy in her step.

"It seems we are to be opponents today then," he said, bowing to me.

"It appears so." I shook my head.

"I suppose we will start soon since we are to reach port today and will have to prepare for that." We went our separate ways, him below deck and me up to the rear deck.

I walked up the steps and looked out to see Absalom emerge carrying a tray of tea. He saw me and nodded, making his way up to stand beside me. He had prepared the tea for us, and I offered him thanks as we began to drink. The sun rose quickly, and I had the pleasure of watching a sunrise over the ocean for the second time. I sipped the floral tea, letting the perfume of it fill my nose.

"How did Georgette get you to agree to let me fight Elias?" I asked.

He did not respond and didn't even look as if he intended to. Instead, he looked across the ship to the woman in question. He then went back to drinking his tea. He could not or would not tell me, and I would not push the issue. His sword hung from his hip, and he touched the hilt of it absently. Though shortly after I had asked, the crew all started to gather around in anticipation.

Georgette waved to Absalom, who nodded, setting his cup on the tray, and made his way down to the circle of pirates. Elias had just come from below deck and made his way up to me to watch by my side. He picked up Absalom's discarded cup and tasted the remaining tea. He made a disgusted face and set it back down quickly.

"To yield and no more," Georgette said as they both drew their blades and touched them together.

Georgette hadn't so much as advanced when Absalom completely withdrew from her. He sheathed his sword as Georgette looked on in what seemed to be disbelief. Her shock soon turned to thinly veiled anger as a murmur of disapproval ran through the surrounding crowd of men. Though when I looked at Absalom, he stared directly at Georgette with no regret for his action.

"What is he doing?" I whispered to Elias.

"Don't do it, mate," he whispered back, but he wasn't talking to me; he was talking to Absalom.

"Yield." His voice rang out clear and steadfast despite the blatant fury on his opponent's face.

"Won't the crew be upset?" I asked in a hushed tone as the whole ship had gone silent.

"If I were him, it wouldn't be the crew I would be worried about," Elias said, gaze focused on the scene below.

Georgette still held her sword in front of her. Anger seemed to pour out of every surface of her, just like her joy had earlier. It appeared whatever emotion she was having exploded from her without a means of containment. She looked as if she might strike at him still with his sword put away. He stood before her as if he would take it if she did. I watched as she drew in a breath and sheathed her sword.

"I accept your yield, Commander Church." From where I stood, I could hear the wrath of her words and almost felt sorry for Absalom.

"Why would he do it?" I asked.

"To protect her in case a blade should slip, and she gets harmed," Elias said, "Though he has suggested now that he thinks she is weak in front of the whole crew."

"How long will she be upset?" I wondered how much of our voyage we would feel the tension of the commander's decision.

"They've certainly fought before... but this? I'm not sure," he said, still staring down at his sister, who had taken a seat on a barrel. She stared daggers at Absalom, who moved away from the crowd.

"Shall we take our positions then?" I suggested. "Perhaps it will lessen the stress of it."

"My sister will not be placated by anything, though I suppose we can hope to soothe the crew." He nodded to me, and we both made our way down to the circle as the men parted so we could take our place among them.

Georgette looked at us, interested but with the displeasure still clearly visible on her face. Absalom seemed to have disappeared, which I thought was clever of him. Finally, I spotted him up on the quarter-deck looking down on us, keeping an eye on me no doubt, but staying out of Georgette's way. I shook my head and focused on the fight in front of me. Elias had his sword outstretched to meet mine. I drew my weapon and met him while the crowd around us hummed with anticipation.

"To yield and no more," he recited, and I nodded as we both stepped away.

He didn't wait for me as he made the first move, and I blocked it effortlessly. I started studying him as he made advances, and I defended. We moved along the deck, and the crowd moved with us. Absalom and Georgette remained at their posts. I hardly noticed anyone but Elias attacking me with mocking ease.

A few minutes in, my arm started to get tired from blocking, and I began to get flustered. When I thought I spotted a weakness or some flaw in Elias' swordplay, he would change his style entirely and throw me off again. I finally looked up to meet his gaze, and he grinned wide. He had guessed my game by watching me spar the previous days. He was changing his styles on purpose so that I couldn't read a weakness. So, there was only one thing to be done; attack and see which one of us was better.

I attacked for the first time. A fire ignited in his eyes as if I was finally doing what he had wanted all along. That fire was contagious, and it illuminated something inside of me. It wasn't anger but more of a flirtatious competition. If he thought he would grin through this whole fight and take it from me freely, he was wrong. I attacked again harder, and his grin turned into something like determination as he blocked.

We danced this way for what felt like a lifetime, but I knew it to be only a minute or two. I could feel it in my hands, shoulder, and even knees from the constant starting and stopping. I forced him up the rear deck stairs, and as I landed on the last step, he came at me once more. Back and forth it went until both of us were sweating and gasping for breath. His step faltered, and I struck out at his leg, a blow he barely caught. I pulled my last bit of energy and struck him, pushing him against the railing of his ship. I knocked his sword from his hand and pressed my blade to his throat as he braced his arms on the wood behind him.

"Yield, Captain Baine," I demanded of him, a smile of satisfaction slipping over my face.

He smiled back, disarming me with what I saw in his gaze. His eyes lingered on my face and trailed down the rest of me with fascinated approval. It was a look of desire that caused me to pull back my sword and step away sharply. He wore it openly, standing up straight and staring right into me as he did.

"I yield, princess," he said, bowing low.

A cheer erupted from the crew so loud I was sure that they could hear it in the next port over. I glanced at Georgette, who had stood up on her barrel and was clapping for me enthusiastically. I looked back at Absalom, who wore a face of both worry and approval. I felt the weight of Elias's stare and knew better than to look back into his eyes.

When he had looked at me with open awe and want, a warmth had blossomed in my chest to meet it. It wasn't something I could allow to happen. For the sake of my country and the sake of his life, I would not allow it.

Seventeen

Georgette

I didn't say a thing to him all the way to the port. He had kept his distance, which suited me fine because I was going to give him the tongue lashing of his life if he even entered my line of sight. And while he was impossibly sanctimonious, he wasn't stupid.

I congratulated Mercy on her win, and the crew brought her a pitcher of spiced wine and sang a song for her. She had reddened during the whole thing. Jones presented her with another sword which was the twin of the one he had given her earlier as a winning gift. She looked pleased by them, and I was shocked. I had assumed the swords were from our store, not his private collection.

Most men offered to pay for her next round of drinks as she had just won them each twenty silvers. Also, something I winced about was thinking of opening our coffers and pulling out that much. Though it was a byproduct of the fun, and the loss would by no means cripple us. We could have wagered twenty gold pieces and still felt no sting.

I threw myself into preparing to port. While I usually allowed the crew to do most of the work, I felt the physical nature would do me good. I worked alongside them, snapping at them too quickly. However, they all took it well and did their best to stay out of my way.

When we finally got to Quizit, I was tying off, and my hand was burning from the rope when I first felt his presence behind me. I turned and glowered at him, heading back on the ship to grab my coat and hat. Absalom said nothing but kept close enough that I knew he was following me. I shrugged on my blue jacket, buttoning it up, and set my hat on my head. I ignored him still as I went to leave the ship.

"Wait," Elias called out to me, and I almost groaned.

I was in no mood to play guide and wanted to be left alone. If I said I wanted to be left alone, Elias would know that I was still in a foul mood. The only times I preferred solace were when I was in deep thought, tired, or in a terrible disposition. I didn't want to appear petty or, worse, have Elias try to help in that way he did. So, I forced a smile and looked up at him, nodding.

"Georgette..." Absalom started behind me in a soothing voice.

"Hurry up, Elias! I want to show Mercy that tavern we like so much here," I yelled out in response.

"Jones, be sure the crew hurries with the supply gather, we may have outrun the men after us for now, but we can't dally for long. Gather enough for a fortnight's journey, just in case." I said when my first mate passed.

"Yes, Captain," he nodded, toting Jamie behind him.

"That tavern is the only good part of Quizit," Elias said, coming up behind with Mercy following him.

She was wearing the hat we had gotten her in Liven. I realized it had replaced the circlet today, and I eyed her and my brother, wondering why the change had occurred.

"There is a fair gem trade here," I said, trying to keep a cheer to my voice that I wasn't feeling.

I dared not look back at Elias, who would know the false note.

"Yes, I suppose when thinking of riveting things to show a princess who has been hidden away her whole life, my mind would immediately go to gem trade," Elias quipped.

"I haven't been hidden away," Mercy argued with him, "Princesses are generally just protected and not allowed to wander about as they please."

"Hidden away for your protection," Elias amended, and Mercy let out a frustrated breath.

"George...," Absalom was next to me now, and I gave him a sideways look.

"I'm not ready to have this conversation." I waved him off as we walked down a street, passing several people hocking fish and fresh-caught ocean life.

The roads in Quizit mainly were dirt; it was a relatively poor city and not known for very much. It was a port for the roughest bit of trash that sailed the seas. You could get things cheap, as the people were starving, and could hire desperate people to do almost anything you needed.

"It wasn't my intention to anger you so terribly," he said, speeding up as I quickened my pace.

"Oh, you just meant to anger me slightly. I'm sorry my reaction to you making me look foolish in front of my entire crew doesn't suit your fancy, Absalom. Perhaps next time, you can tell me to what level I am to be upset so that I can meet your expectation," I hissed at him, and any attempt at hiding my sullenness died.

"George...," he called, the plea strangling his voice.

I ignored him again, my temper building after I had convinced myself I had worked it off. I walked faster, and he kept up still. I didn't see or hear Elias or Mercy but knew they had to be close behind. Absalom was quiet for several minutes while I led us deeper into the streets. There was a market like the one in Liven in the middle of the city, only much smaller. People here were apt to be more friendly, but the selection was not nearly as impressive.

I came out of an alley into the city center, where there was a giant sculpture of Jilor. They had painted her with ebony skin and braided hair, looking as fierce as any goddess would. The statue depicted her teeth bared and a harpoon in one hand as if to attack her foes. She was also completely naked in this sculpture though parts of her had crumbled and eroded over time. A spot near the bottom of her feet wholly worn away where locals would come and place their hands to pray to her.

I had noticed that depending on the city, their gods and goddesses were depicted differently. If the city was wealthy and affluent, their deities were depicted as kind and benevolent. If the town was small or struggling, they were illustrated as fierce and warrior-like. The blessed gorged on comfort, and the broken cried out for justice.

It was one of the things that I hated about the land so much. While prosperous cities thrived and often held their king's good favor and received contracts for their goods, impoverished cities and towns suffered. Their kings didn't so much as deign a look in their direction. The crown was supposed to protect them, and taxes were taken to support the armies and supposedly for the people in need. These people were forced to deal with rulers that they didn't choose. The rulers who took their seats handed to them by birth; each bloodthirsty successor was worse than the last.

I hated kings, and court, and land.

I wandered to a small shop whose sign heralded fine clothing. I had hoped its contents would deter my pursuer, but to my dismay, they did not. The doorway was too short for him, and he had to duck beneath it to get in. If I wasn't so irritated, the sight of him against the dazzling fabrics and glittering ornaments in the shop might have been humorous.

"How long will this go on?" he asked.

As if he had any right to be irritated with me. I was not the one who backed down from a fight. I was not the one who made a fool out of him. I was not the one who hinted at the weakness of the other due to their sex. I wondered how he would feel if I showed up and made him look a twit in front of the men under his command.

"In what way can I apologize that will soothe you?" He tried again.

"I don't need your soothing apologies," I bristled, "I need you to know me well enough not to offend me in such a way in the first place."

"If you want me to apologize for doing what I felt was right, I won't." I saw his guard start to raise, and his voice took on the edge of anger.

"Well, then it seems that neither of us will come to terms. For I cannot imagine you think so little of me to reduce me to a soft-footed maiden on my own ship. While you don't seem to think you did anything wrong."

"You're being ridiculous." He threw an apologetic glance at the shop owner who was ogling us.

"Being that I'm a woman who cannot defend herself, that should account for it. Women are known to be ridiculous and hysterical." I picked up a scarf woven from silk in bright orange and red swirling patterns.

Maybe I was a bit dramatic. However, the last week of him keeping his distance from me and pulling away whenever I tried to talk to him had frayed my nerves. Watching him share meals with Mercy and laughing with her in confidence had grown a jealous knot inside me. A feeling that I now realized was more extensive than I had thought it was. Then he had yielded our match without so much as even giving me the respect of facing me; my patience had broken. Now he was suffering the anger of all of that at once.

"I don't think you are hysterical," he said as I went back deeper into the shop.

Elias and Mercy showed up at the door. Elias peeked his head in and looked at us with a pained expression. However, he and Mercy stepped into the store and pretended to browse while Absalom and I continued to argue.

"I could not in good conscience raise my sword to you, George. Can you not understand that?" he asked as I ran my hands over some beautiful flowing shirts in soft tones of blue. They laced up the front and billowed out at the sleeve.

"No." I stopped browsing, focusing all my energy on him.

"I cannot go back and change my choice," he sighed. "And even if I could. I would not. We've disagreed on such decorum in the past, and it has not come to you not speaking to me. I'm sorry I belittled you in front of your crew. Though I would hope they know you better than to think it a reflection of you instead of myself."

He was right. My crew would not look down on me for it. At least most of them would not. I had proven a thousand times over that I was capable of my position over them. Absalom's one action had not undone years of influence.

"It isn't just that." My tone was softer, and he looked warier now than when I raised my voice.

"What is it then?

"It's the last week since I saw you at Odie before we started this blasted journey." My voice still small to keep emotion from it. "It's you keeping yourself from me and hiding away when I try to talk to you. It's you pulling back from me when I seek out your company. Then you take meals with Elias and Mercy as if I have done something to offend you, but you won't tell me what it is."

"This is about jealousy?" he exhaled.

I glanced at the door where Elias was now holding some ladies' pantaloons with pursed lips as if he had just picked something up in haste to look busy. Mercy didn't bother; instead, she stared between us and the shop owner in discomfort.

"If you'd like to reduce it to that, then fine," I shot at him, "If your fragile ego wants to dwindle it down to jealously so you can claim it to be false, then so be it. Though I know you, Absalom, and I know you are hiding from me. What I don't know is why."

"George...." If he said my name like that one more time, I would retch.

"When you decide to tell me what it is, we can continue this exchange." I grabbed two of the blue shirts and took them to the shop owner pulling payment from a pocket. "But if you think we are going to return to Odie and forget all about this while you go back to following me around like a mewling kitten, you are mistaken."

"Georgette." It was Elias, this time throwing a warning out after me.

"You needn't worry about that," Absalom said, raw and hurt, "When I return home, it has been arranged for me to be married to a woman of the higher court. It wouldn't be prudent for me to follow a pirate woman around like an animal while I am married to another."

Despite the sun outside and the dissipating anger in my belly, my blood ran cold. I leaned into the table where the shopkeeper had just taken my money. I was frozen to the spot, thinking I might have retched on the floor of the beautiful shop. It was as silent as a graveyard during a full moon.

"Mercy," Elias said softly, "I think I should show you another thing you may find interesting."

"Of course," she whispered.

I assumed they left and even the man behind the table made an excuse to go into the back storeroom for some parchment and twine. The silence was consuming and heightened every breath and word unspoken. Neither of us moved, and neither of us spoke a word into the void between us.

I finally let out a long breath as a despairing ache in my chest began to build, and I warred with tears that fought their way to freedom. A life I never had unraveled before me, and it tore something from inside that I didn't know was there, leaving a chasm.

"Georgette." Absalom stepped behind me until he was close enough that I could feel his warmth.

I turned slowly and looked up into his pleading blue eyes. He was asking for forgiveness. Not for the wager or the match he forfeited but what he had just told me and how it had come out. The desperation was apparent on his face that he regretted using it as a sword to my knees as he had. It had worked, and he had stolen my fire from me.

"You what?" It was all I could manage.

"I am to be married," he paused, raising his arms to touch my shoulders and then thinking better of it and releasing them back to his sides. "In three weeks, to a lady of the court. Her father has come upon hard times; otherwise, he wouldn't even think of allowing her to marry a foot soldier."

As if he were somehow her inferior. As if this woman was above him in any way. His father only promoted his King's blasted court standings by setting his son to be married to a woman of higher birth to improve his rank.

"What is her name?" I asked, still small, and he looked pained as some of my tears slipped down my face.

"Her name is Norissa," he answered softly.

"Is she kind and beautiful? Will she make you a good wife?" My tears flowed then as I looked down and away out of what felt like self-pity.

"She is not ugly, but I cannot speak of her character. I have only met her twice," he answered me dutifully like the good soldier he was.

It all made sense now. It all came together. Every moment he pulled away from me and every chance he got to evade my company. Every hollow look and regret-filled moment. His face at the table with his father at Odie when he knew he would be with us in close quarters. It was the thing I couldn't read on his face. The something he had tried to tell me several times during our journey. Why he was able to take meals with Mercy, she wasn't a threat to his future; I was.

"Please say something," he pleaded, "Anything, yell or scream or tell me what a dolt I am. Please. I shouldn't have told you like this; I'm an idiot, you know I'm an idiot. I couldn't seem to tell you whenever I set out to do it. I'm sorry, I'm so sorry. It's just when you and Elias leave on your grand adventures, I get lonely. I don't want to be miserable and alone for the rest of my life, pining after a woman who would never choose me."

"I..." I started searching for something to say as his words brought fresh tears to my eyes.

The thought of him being downcast when we left Odie broke something in me. Why hadn't he told us sooner? And how could I deny him any chance for that pain to go away?

"I am happy for you, Absalom. I only wish for your happiness, and if this is it, then I will be glad for your sake."

"I'm not sure why, but that is somehow much worse than you yelling at me," he admitted, and I saw a sadness in his eyes that matched my own.

I was never one to sit with my feelings. Like a wool coat that was rough and itchy, they made me uncomfortable. I couldn't express the depth of what I wanted to say as I looked up at my dearest friend and into the future that I knew we couldn't have. I had known before that moment, of course, but this was a change that validated what neither of us would ever speak. So, under the weight of the words I couldn't grasp, to describe feelings that were too uncomfortable, I smiled.

"I am going to get Mercy and show her that tavern. We shall buy you a round of drinks for you are newly engaged, and that is a celebratory occasion indeed. Elias won't let you hear the end of this; I hope you know."

While I held a smile, the worry on his face only deepened. I stepped away from him, hating myself for not being able to face him. I couldn't meet his raw admission about how our absence affected him. I couldn't confront the possibility that I may be responsible for any of his sadness.

Instead, I walked out of that shop like the coward that I was to drown my emotions in liquor.

Eighteen

Mercy

It seemed best not to press about her and Absalom's argument earlier. When Georgette had come to fetch me, Elias had said he would go back and make sure Absalom was still breathing. Georgette had not found that funny and stared coldly at him until he left. She had led me across the small city to a tavern with a dragon painted on the sign.

It seemed rather busy for the middle of the day. Georgette didn't hesitate walking into the establishment, and people cleared a path for her as I had realized they always did. It didn't stop me from seeing the way they looked at us. Though they may have given her a wide berth, they still looked at her as a woman in a room full of men, not all men with good intentions. However, no one approached us as she went up to a bar where a barkeeper was standing behind a counter.

He eyed us with little more than irritation until Georgette put several silver pieces on the counter, and she ordered something I didn't recognize the name of. He set four cloudy glasses in front of us and poured amber liquid in them. She took the first glass and emptied the contents without breathing. She shook the empty glass at the man who filled it back up. She slid two of the glasses in front of me.

"For your win." She nodded and smiled at me, but her smile didn't light up her face like it usually did.

So, I raised one of the glasses and attempted to drain it as she had. I sputtered and coughed about halfway through. The alcohol was like fire in my throat. It savored of wood and spice and coated my mouth, making my eyes water. I looked over at her as she drained her second glass, not noticing my struggle.

"Pirates," I said, shaking my head, finishing my first glass, and reaching for my second.

I had never been very drunk before. The spiced wine the night of dancing on the ship had warmed me, but I had not felt the effects alter me much. However, on my third glass of whatever the man behind the counter was pouring, my cheeks were inflamed. When I sipped the liquid, it no longer savored of fire, only pleasant spice. I had seen my brothers drink themselves into a stupor and always found it childish. With my head swimming and the room warming, I could understand the appeal of it. I finished my third glass, and Georgette slid me a fourth.

"Are you..." I fished for the words.

"Fine?" she asked me, drinking from another glass.

I wasn't sure how much she had drunk, but she seemed to be holding it better than I. She waved down the man who just set the bottle in front of her instead of answering and walked away. She looked pleased by that and poured more on top of what she had just been drinking.

"I will be," she decided.

I didn't think it was the truth. Georgette was good at half-truths, but she didn't seem exceptionally skilled at lying. I stared at her, and she looked vacantly out a window across the bar. I thought she might need a change of discussion. Something less invasive of her personal life. I decided to ask something that I had been too afraid to ask my mother before I left. With only younger sisters, I had assumed they wouldn't know either.

"May I ask you a question of a personal nature?" I asked, and she turned to me immediately interested.

I smiled. Georgette seemed to enjoy people's questions and problems genuinely. She wasn't reserved with her words and was as easy to talk to as Elias was. While Elias felt like a listening ear that would give you sound advice somewhat hesitantly, Georgette was like a mouth of a river. What came to her mind first was what she would say. It was a certain kind of honesty, I realized, and I had started to admire it.

"I never have…" I started finding myself more embarrassed than I thought I would be.

"You'll have to be more specific than that." She raised her eyebrows at me. "I feel there is a fair amount you've never done."

"Yes, thank you. Can you ever be quiet for one moment?" I barked at her, covering my mouth after the words had left it.

She sat back and took a sip of her drink, nodding, not looking the least bit offended at my outburst. I took a deep breath and gathered my courage. The alcohol helped a little, and my head felt lighter than usual.

"I've never… been with a man… in the married sense," I scraped out, and the amused look that came over her face was enough to make me regret asking.

"I would imagine that to be pretty common… as I'm told, among the higher court. Don't women lose a certain amount of value once their virtue is gone?" She didn't seem to be making fun of me, and I relaxed a little.

"Generally, yes."

"So, King Kosdel… your husband to be… will be your first then?" she asked, and I nodded.

She was silent for a bit, just looking over at me. She looked kind of sad about the prospect on my behalf. She pressed her lips together and took in a long breath.

"Have you ever... kissed a man?" she asked, and I shook my head again, her eyes going wide, but she didn't make any sarcastic remarks.

"Have you ever wanted to kiss someone or thought of anyone in a romantic sort of way?" Her voice was slow, as if she were talking to a child, and I gave her an incredulous look.

"Okay, well, it will be hard to explain because it is all so different depending on your partner. If you like the person or are attracted to them and they are kind to you, it's a much... different experience than if you are with someone who is using you only for childbearing or personal use."

"Please, I feel as if you are withholding the truth for the sake of my feelings. I asked you for your directness, and I wish you would be direct with me." I investigated the bottom of my empty glass.

So, she was. She explained things to me that ladies' maids tittered about behind closed doors of tea rooms. Something my mother had alluded to but never quite had the ability to tell me. It was both a horror and comfort, and when she seemed to be satisfied with the amount of information she had shared, she sat back and finished off her glass and poured another. I took a moment which she graciously gave me in silence.

My mother, and ladies' maid Alita, had always talked of the marriage bed as a duty for a wife. Like an inconvenience that one had to endure in marriage to bear children and please one's husband. However, Georgette talked about it like something reverent and enjoyable. It was a different interpretation than I had ever heard before. Though I supposed that was another difference in our lives. Perhaps because of her freedom, it was something for her that it would never be for me.

"Thank you for your honesty," I said finally.

"I wish more people thanked me for it." She held up her drink in toast.

She opened her mouth to speak again before narrowing her eyes at something behind me that I couldn't see. I went to turn, but she grabbed my arm tightly. She shook her head, telling me not to look as she sat up in her chair and sat forward at the counter. She hunched over slightly and nodded for me to do the same. So, I did, and she kept her eye on whatever had concerned her. Her gaze got darker until I felt the presence of several people behind us.

"What are two lovelies doing in such a wicked establishment?" a man's voice came from behind me.

"I think you best take your curiosity elsewhere, gentlemen," Georgette said with teeth clenched.

I did my best not to look behind me. When I looked over, she didn't look worried; she looked angry. A frown set deep into her face like she was used to this happening, and she was rather tired of it.

"Darlin', I'm just asking. There is no need to get nasty without getting to know us," he spoke.

"It would be one thing if I didn't," Georgette said, standing up from her chair and turning around.

I finally turned back to look and saw four men had us semi-surrounded, causing panic to leap into my throat. The one who had addressed us was tall and broad-shouldered. He stood a head taller than Georgette, but she looked up at him defiantly. He stared at her with a sickening delight as if she were already in his possession.

"The thing of it is, I saw you coming. I would know your entitled expression on any man anywhere. Like you are owed our company and anything else you decide to take." I was transfixed by how her words cut when another man set his hand on my shoulder.

Georgette didn't miss it and her gaze whipped to the man as I sat frozen with his hand on me. His fingers dug into my shoulder like a vise. I tried to shift to be rid of him, but he held me tightly. I watched Georgette's eyes turn from anger to danger. The feral pirate came forward in her features, and the female companion stepped back.

"Get your hand off of her if you don't want me to cut it off," she growled out.

The man's hand only tightened, and I begged her with my eyes not to cause a scene. My lifelong training kicked in automatically as I tried to make myself small and inconsequential. If she didn't fight them, perhaps, they would leave with minor damage done. But it was too much to hope for. It could have been her argument with Absalom bubbling under her surface, or maybe it was that she didn't like men taking liberties they shouldn't. She was buzzing with the want of a fight. I could feel her daring them to make a move so she would have an excuse to tear into one of them.

I sized up the four men knowing that even she couldn't take them all. They were bigger and heavier, and neither of us had our swords with us. My head was spinning with alcohol, and I cursed my stupidity. There was a beat of silence while the man clawed his dirty fingers further into my shirt and skin as he defied Georgette's warning.

That was all the pirate captain needed.

She moved away from the man in front of her and pulled a dagger from its' sheath, using the surprise to her advantage. She yanked the man whose hand was on me away, and he was so startled that it fell away. I thought she was going to cut his hand off for a moment, and I gaped in the seconds it took her to react.

She pulled his wrist forward and held it on the bar as she slammed the handle end of her dagger into the top of his hand. I heard the distinct crack of bones.

"You bitch!" the man howled out, and all eyes turned to us in the establishment.

"I told you not to touch her," she said as the man was cradling his wounded hand, and the other three were staring in disbelief.

Her stance was wide, her dagger brandished, and she curled her lip slightly. She stepped in front of me, forcing them back.

"Leave now with a few broken bones and your wounded pride," she spat.

"When we're through with you, we'll take turns having our way before we throw you to the city dogs." The large man who had addressed us first thundered, and to her credit, she smiled at him.

She glanced to the door and back at the men. I looked to the door and watched as Absalom and Elias walked in, talking to each other, before quickly realizing what was happening. Absalom's friendly face shifted into a soldier's as his eyes narrowed on the man in front of Georgette. They made their way toward us; our attackers were unaware.

"Very well," Georgette said to the man, "Though if you wish to reconsider, I will offer you one last opportunity to leave unscathed."

"Stupid girl," he said, coming at her as she slashed out at him cutting his hand as he pulled it back.

He charged her, using his weight to crush her against the bar, and she grunted in pain as his arms hit her ribs. He pinned her there smiling before his head was yanked back by his hair and a knife appeared at his throat.

"I don't take kindly to men putting their hands on my sister without her permission," Elias said calmly to the man though his blade bit into his skin.

Though he was a bit shorter than the man, he handled him with ease. Georgette had raised her chair and struck him against the knees. Elias pulled his blade back quickly as the man fell to the floor.

He turned and gave her an exasperated expression, and she shrugged as if she had no idea what he was upset about. I giggled a little at the exchange and then hiccupped. Elias looked up at me and turned back to his sister, pointing to me with the same look set on his face. Georgette winced a bit, turning back to me, and then gave Elias an apologetic look. They were doing the bit where they spoke without speaking.

"How did I know you were going to be in the middle of this?" Elias asked his sister.

"You always arrive at precisely the right time." She smiled at him, setting the chair back down casually.

I stood up, and the man who had grabbed my shoulder earlier came at me once more. Instinctually, I kicked him where I knew him to be most sensitive and grabbed the bottle of spirits Georgette had been sharing. I slammed it against his temple, and it shattered as he staggered backward. I looked at the broken bottleneck in my hands and up to Elias and Georgette, who were now staring. A proud smile spread over Georgette's face. I turned as I heard another grunt from the man, realizing Absalom had hit him in the face knocking him to the ground.

Chaos erupted between the four of us and the three remaining men. The man on the floor got up from his knees and tried to go after Elias. One went for Georgette, and one came for me, but Absalom stepped in front of him quickly. He blocked a few blows from the man, swinging in with some punches of his own.

I looked down to realize that when I had smashed the bottle, part of the glass must have cut my hand.

"Why can't you just stay out of trouble?" Elias asked while he was in a headlock from the largest man.

"I didn't start this fight." Georgette elbowed an assailant in the ribs as he doubled over in pain.

She picked up a metal pitcher off a nearby table and hit the man holding Elias in the head.

"You always say that, and I have a feeling that most of the time, it is untrue," he said, hitting the man in the gut once he got free and then once more in the face.

He wielded a chair and slammed it into him as the man fell, struggling to get back up. Georgette kicked him in the side and then again over his head with the pitcher, so he fell flat on the floor. In front of me, Absalom had managed to pull the man's arms behind him and spun him toward me.

"Excuse me, my lady," he grunted as I moved, and he slammed the man into the counter.

He took his head and smacked it hard against the surface. He let go of him, and the man slumped to the floor. All four men were on the floor: a couple of them moaning and a couple still out cold. The three of them looked around the room to see if anyone was thinking of joining. Though when the commotion was over, most of the other patrons returned to their drinks without another glance in our direction.

I marveled at the three of them as they started picking up the things that the fight had disturbed. Georgette even started picking up bits of the bottle I had broken. They set some remnants of items on the counter, and Absalom apologized to the man that had served us.

Elias filled an empty glass with silver pieces and nodded to the man. He picked up Georgette's glass with liquor still in it and drained it. Setting it back down on the bar carefully and walked out without another word. Absalom looked around to see if anything else needed to be done before he looked back to check on me. I was leaning against the counter, letting it support my weight. I thought of walking to him and realized it would be much harder than it should be.

I vaguely understood that all the drink had caught up with me, and the room was spinning, and I with it. I took a step toward Absalom and faltered. Georgette was at my side, suddenly holding me steady.

"I hit a man with a bottle," I said, and my voice sounded proud.

"And very well at that," Georgette said, slipping her arm around my waist.

It seemed I could not walk on my own. Absalom was at my side also but looked hesitant to sling his arm around my waist. I smiled at his propriety against the setting of the tavern and found it rather humorous at that moment.

"Did you have to get her to drink so much?" Absalom asked worriedly.

"I didn't think she had that much."

"I think I rather like that drink; can I get it in Urorah?" I asked, tripping in the doorway of the tavern as they led me out.

I squinted against the sudden onslaught of the sun. Through my half-closed eyes, I saw Elias standing in front of us, looking at me. He was terribly handsome, I thought. His hair pushed off his face, and his grey eyes looked worriedly after me. The split in his lip did nothing to detract from his perfectness. It was the first time I had ever allowed the thoughts to flow through me unchastised. My swirling brain wasn't working well enough to catch them as they danced around my head.

"Did she hit her head?" he asked Georgette.

"Give me some credit," she said, "She's just had a bit to drink."

"I hit someone on the head." I remembered and shared again, "And I do feel slightly unsteady. I don't think I can stand on my own. Isn't that funny?"

"You've broken her," Elias chuckled, and he motioned for Georgette to let me go, and he took her place.

It felt more natural with him, as Georgette was shorter and awkwardly holding me up. Elias fit to my side perfectly, throwing his arm around my waist, and I slid my arm around his shoulders, letting my weight settle into him. He didn't seem thrown off by it, and we all started walking away from the tavern.

"I've never had such fun in my life," I said out loud.

Georgette erupted with laughter, and Absalom grumbled a curse under his breath.

"Maybe you're more pirate than princess after all," Elias turned and whispered into my ear.

Something inside me begged me not to be so pleased by the words, but I drowned my self-scolding out by letting warmth radiate through me.

Nineteen

Georgette

It was well into the evening when our ship left the docks. Elias handled it as I was in no shape to do anything. I had cleaned myself up and had gotten into a night dress. I took stock of my wounds while I forced down a whole pot of thick tea spiced with a root that tasted of licorice. My knuckles felt bruised, but no broken fingers. My ribs were also bruised but I didn't think they were broken either. I eyed my reflection in a cloudy mirror and traced a cut I had received from a bottle along my hairline no more than a token long.

By all accounts, I had gotten out relatively intact other than my throbbing headache. I had enquired about Mercy's wellbeing several times, and Elias had assured me that the only injury she had received was a cut along the top of her hand. He said she was lying down after retching up all the alcohol she had consumed. He promised to keep an eye on her for me when I retired to my room.

I slipped under the blankets of my bed and unwound my two tight braids. I found myself strangely sad thinking of when we would have to say goodbye to our ship Princess. I thought she had proved herself to be one hell of a pirate, and there was a shortage of female courage in the world. I would likely never see her again, and I realized I had grown rather fond of her during her time on board. I hadn't been fond of many women in my lifetime, my mother and perhaps two or three others I could think of. She was the least despicable courtier I had ever encountered.

There was a knock on my door. I rose to answer it, assuming it to be Elias giving me an update on how Mercy was doing. The man standing before me was not my brother but Absalom.

"Have you come to lecture me on the dangers of fighting in taverns?" I asked, looking up at him through a crack in the door.

"No," he said simply.

"Perhaps to remind me that Mercy is a Princess and that I should have been more careful with her?" I enquired.

"Seems like from what I saw, you protected her quite well," he said, and I knew he was trying to soothe me to gain entry.

"Perhaps to tell me of what a fine lady your new betrothed is?" I asked, and he cringed.

"No, Georgette. I have neither come to lecture you or to boast of my future life. May I please come in?"

I nodded, stepping behind the door to open it wider.

"Would you like something to drink?" I asked when he closed the door. He turned and frowned.

"Oh, it's just tea Absalom; there's no need to look at me like that." I poured him a mug of the bitter tea and handed it to him, but he didn't drink it.

He looked somewhat disheveled. He usually was much more polished and put together. He wore a pair of boots, trousers, and a plain linen shirt he had left undone at the top. His hair was a wreck, as if he had been running his hands through it.

"If you haven't come to lecture, which you are remarkably good at, what have you come for?" I asked.

"I just came from looking over Mercy and thought I would look you over too."

"If I needed a medical assessment, I would call for Jamie."

"Will you please," he motioned for the table, "just indulge me."

"Very well."

I rolled my eyes and clambered up onto the table in the most unladylike fashion I could manage. Seeing how I was already exposed in only a nightgown, I couldn't get much less dignified. He seemed to notice and did his best to look unaffected. He was merely a commander looking over a fellow soldier for injury.

"You know this isn't the first fight I've been in, and it certainly won't be the last. You shan't be there for every one of my many brawls."

"Yes, please don't remind me."

He started with my head, inspecting the cut near my hairline and feeling the back of my neck, making me pull my hair back to examine. His fingers were cold and as soft as a sigh. His eyes roamed my arms down to my knuckles, where he frowned, bringing my hands up to inspect them. He poked and prodded the bruises. He bent every one of my fingers, watching my face for more than the occasional aching wince. When he finished, he used his fingers to press down my sternum and then squeezed my ribs. I let out a low moan of pain. His eyes shot to mine.

"They're just bruised, not broken," I assured.

He nodded, pulling my nightdress up to my knees and inspecting both my legs. There was something distant about the way he touched me. I didn't think we ever had been that close, and he had definitely never inspected me in a nightgown before.

While I should have been focusing on how his fingers grazed my skin, I only created a mental picture of how his future wife might look. I painted her hair muddy brown and stringy and straight. I gave her a crooked eye and a wart. I smiled at my mental picture, erasing it and replacing it with an average pretty face. The image was now of a girl with a demure posture in a white gown with an apron. Hair pulled back practically. She had a kind smile.

"Where have you gone?" He stood up and went back to inspecting my fingers.

"Not so far away." I looked up at my Commander, keeping the same smile on my face.

He brushed the pads of my fingers gently. The efficiency he replaced with a softness that cooled my blood.

"Stop touching me as if I am some priceless glass vase, Commander," I said, pulling my fingers away from him.

"How would you have me touch you, Captain?" he asked, and his arms fell to his sides, though he was still close to me.

Whatever was happening before had shifted, and we stared at each other. His briny blue eyes were looking into my storm, asking a question. Was it permission? Permission to lean forward or permission to pull away? I wasn't sure. My emotions were as muddled as they had been before the tavern escapade. I raised an eyebrow at him not sure what he is looking for.

He leaned closer to me. I held my breath as he pressed his forehead against mine, and my chest tightened. I closed my eyes as the feeling of something I never had, slipped through my grasp. The emptiness of a life I could have lived. He raised his hands and put them on either side of my face tilting my head up. Before his mouth came down to meet mine, I shot my hand up, and I placed my fingers over his lips.

It wasn't that I didn't want what he was asking for; I did. To know just once what it would be like, just once to have him hold me. My aching heart screamed to let him. What was the harm in one kiss after years of him being my friend? I didn't owe his father or his future bride anything. Wasn't I due this one thing?

He looked at me with my hand on his mouth and nodded as I lowered my fingers. He was not mine. Now not only was he not mine, but he also belonged to someone else. There were lines that even I would not cross. I was owed nothing.

He stepped back slightly. Not too far to cause a chasm, but far enough away to signal that he understood. We sat there for a long time. I thought I would cry again, but no tears came. He did nothing to soothe me. We just sat in the heavy silence together, acknowledging things that we hadn't spoken.

"It wasn't that I hadn't thought to ask you," he began finally, and I looked up.

"No?"

"Certainly, it's crossed my mind nearly every day since I was of marriable age and even before then. Perhaps as early as thirteen years old, I would try to work it together in my brain how I would trick you into marrying me." His hand rose and went back to rub the back of his neck.

"I'm flattered." I covered my smile with my hand.

"You're mocking me." He raised an eyebrow.

"No!" I defended. "No, not mocking. You know I love you." I said the second bit softer and without humor.

He stared then, looking as if he wished I hadn't said it.

"You must know... of course, you must know, Commander Absalom Church, how deeply I adore you." My fingers were picking nervously at the edge of the table.

"It's just that," he sounded desperate as if he could, by will alone, make me understand. "It's that when my father told me of the marriage with Norissa, I fought him on it. I told him I wouldn't, and he told me that I needed to let you go. That I needed to move on from the childish fancy I had of you."

I was silent, allowing him to say what he needed to explain. Though I already understood. We both had always understood.

"For days, I fumed at him, but I realized he was right about one thing. While what I feel for you is no childish fancy, I do need to let you go..."

"What if you asked and I said yes?" I interrupted his thought.

I was thinking of my daydreams. It was a selfish question, and I wished I could pull it back. Though he just offered me a sad smile full of knowing.

"I thought of that too. More often than I would be proud to admit. What if I asked you and you said yes? What if Georgette Anne Baine, Captain of The Siren, agreed to marry me? What if we were married and we had a house together and children?"

I got off the table and huddled myself in one of my chairs. It was like hearing someone recite back to me the secrets I hadn't told anyone. The longing in his voice paired with the desperate ignorance of reality. I pulled my knees up and wrapped my hands around myself. I rested my chin on them, letting him recant my private thoughts.

"What if I captured her and locked her away in a house with our children? Locked her away while I was gone for half the year, and she was forced to integrate with traditional society as a soldier's wife? What if I took away from her grand adventures and stole her freedom?" His voice was dark with blaming himself for our unhappiness that did not exist.

"I wouldn't think of it as captivity," I argued.

"Maybe not at first," he nodded, "but over time, when I settled back into my life, working for a King that you loathed. When you were in our house, alone, surrounded by people that judged you every day for what you are, you would learn to hate me. And I realized the only thing worse than being married to someone who wasn't you would be to be with you and see hatred grow in your eyes for me every day."

"I don't think I could ever hate you, Absalom."

I looked over to him, and his sad smile had fallen flat. Absalom had never been drawn to the dramatic. While I could never imagine myself hating him, I wondered if I could grow into it. If

I were to marry him and live a more straightforward, somewhat dull life, would I grow to hate him?

Yes. I answered myself. Perhaps not hatred but resentment, and every day would be worse than the last. Then I thought of what he said back at the shop, of how he wished to be happy, too.

"I cannot become your jailor, George; I couldn't bear it," he said, sitting across from me in one significant movement as if he could no longer be asked to stand.

"So, you agreed to be married to another," I finished for him while he nodded.

"Well, I hope she likes a bit of adventure; otherwise, you'll be two rather boring people living a much too sensible life together." I played with the hem of my nightdress.

"I'll let you know."

"Will we...," I asked hesitantly, hating how weak I sounded, "still see each other?"

"Oh, George, certainly. Of course, we will. What I said back in that shop... That was just to be hurtful. Of course, I will see you as much as I see you now. You and Elias are my family." He laid his hand across the table to me, the one with his scar, too painful to look at then.

I was relieved. I'm sure our relationship would change, but my heart might heal from that. I couldn't recover from losing his friendship. I wondered if I would like his wife or if I would hate her on principle.

"You have to know that no woman is above you because of her station in life. This woman might be a lady of higher birth, but that doesn't mean she deserves you," I huffed.

"That you believe that for me is why I love you," he said, leaning back.

There was something else in his eyes. I could see him waiting to mention something else. He was giving me the time I needed to say anything else that I needed.

"There's something else?" I accused, tilting my head up to him and sitting straight.

The look on his face all but confirmed it, and he looked guilty.

"I came to tell you about the correspondence we got from my father at Quizit."

"What does the great Master Gerald and his master have to say to us now?"

"We have been instructed to forgo all other port stops and head straight to Brits."

"He wanted at least two correspondence check-in between then," I said with an eyebrow raised. "What are they up to? What is the rush to get you both there?"

"I don't know. It doesn't sit right with me, but there isn't much we can do about it."

I was starting to feel how Elias had only days ago. Like we were the pieces in a bigger game. It was our fault, and we had set ourselves up for this. When one played a King's game, everyone but the King would lose. I wondered about the Island and if it were still in the realm of possibility. If we dropped them off in Brits and the Southern Ralice military were no longer a considerable concern, it may still be possible.

"Well, that's fine; the men will have supplies for the next week worth of travels. While we are about to lose the current, it should only take us a week to get there. Maybe less. We have traveled through that long. Though we don't prefer it, I suppose it will be of greatest benefit to get the king his bride. Will there be a company to meet you there?"

"I have been instructed to take her out of town to the edge of Hallow. A company of soldiers will meet us there."

"Why wait so long to meet you? Won't you be in danger without other men to protect you and Mercy?'

"I'm not sure why we aren't at least waiting until we come back around to the Northern border to safety. All I can hope is that they get our correspondence about Dalion's men in time and send more men, or hopefully, there is correspondence waiting for us in Brits."

"We will take you both to Castorica if you feel more comfortable," I answered. "I am quite sure Elias would agree."

"If I defy the King's orders and take the princess up to Castorica, he'll have my head." He frowned at me. "It isn't my place to question his orders, or my father's for that matter."

"'I'm glad you have such faith in him."

"He's a good King, George. I know you and Elias don't trust any royalty, but he's a good man. He'll protect Mercy."

"He'd better protect you both, or he'll have me to answer to." I ran my hands through my loose hair and yawned.

"I should let you go to sleep; you've had a long day." He stood up.

"Yes, finding out my childhood love is marrying another and starting a tavern fight," I mused.

He winced at my words as a hollow laugh came from me. Humor was one of my better defenses against emotional pain. He knew this and shook his head, making his way to the door. He sauntered like he still had more to say. I wasn't sure how much more I could take while still being able to make ill-timed jokes.

He stood with his hands on the door, hesitating for too long. I was still sitting with my arms wrapped around my knees. I knew he wouldn't leave. He couldn't rest until he felt like he had done his best to fix whatever was wrong. It would plague him all night.

I waited for him to speak, for whatever the last thing he needed to tell me to make it better.

"I would like you to know…," he paused, looking back at me, "that I don't think I will be capable of loving someone else as I love you."

"I hope for your sake and the sake of your betrothed, you find that is not true." I stretched my legs out in front of me, getting ready to stand up. He was still hesitating.

I pulled my insides together and thought of something to say that would reassure him that it was okay for him to walk out my door. I told myself it didn't even have to be true. If it was true enough, then I could live with a half-lie. If I had to pretend for the rest of my life that I was okay with him being married to someone else, then that is what I would do. For him, I could do that.

"Absalom," I started. He looked at me hopefully. "It's going to be alright. No matter what happens, you will always have Elias and me. This doesn't change that."

He took a step toward me quickly. Before I could react, he grabbed me and lifted me into a tight embrace. He held me fast as if I were no heavier than a small child with my feet dangling. I rested my head on his shoulder as best I could. He continued to hug me.

"You couldn't get rid of me if you tried, George."

"Is that a challenge?" I asked as he set me back down.

He walked out of my room without hesitating and without looking back.

Twenty

Mercy

It had been two days since Quizit. There had been word from my betrothed and his army captain, Absalom's father. We had agreed to the terms set by the letter, and I agreed to be sent off with Absalom to my future as a king's fourth wife. We would port in Brits, and the Captains Baine would send us with enough rations for two days ride. They had also decided to send Bram with us for extra protection, and he would ride on and meet them in Castorica just above the Northern Ralician border.

When we had met in the navigation room, we had all concurred that it was the best course of action. However, I couldn't help but feel the heavy weight of something over the room. I tried to tell myself that I imagined it. I looked at the faces of the three people I had been in the company the last week and a half. I couldn't help but think I wasn't the only one wishing for something else.

I was in my room, the sun had gone down, and the majority of the crew were asleep. I was trying to decide exactly what it was that I wished for. Certainly, I wished that I could spend more time with Absalom, Elias, and Georgette. I wanted more than that. The adventure and the sea called me by name. I was leaving, and it felt like I was abandoning something I was meant to do.

After my win against Elias, the crew had accepted me more like their own and spoke to me freely. I would miss Georgette's candor. Eventually, when Absalom left me at my new home in

Urorah, I would miss his kind and protective warmth. They felt like friends to me, and I was more upset about leaving them than I had been about leaving my own family.

Then my mind turned to Elias. It was more of an ache when I thought of leaving him. My mind played out the scene, waving as the two pirate captains watched from their ship, and we walked away. I couldn't quite get myself to imagine saying goodbye to him. Whenever I thought of it, my chest squeezed painfully, and a sort of breathlessness filled me.

I wished I could sketch so that I could trace his likeness to remember him. The charming pirate captain who had at first vexed me so. His wise eyes, having seen things in me, things I thought hidden away and secure. I felt silly having developed such warmth for him. The pirate that no doubt had left a trail of brokenhearted ladies in his wake. I was just another woman who had fallen victim to the inviting silences and provoking grins.

I thought of how his hand touched mine as we danced when there was a knock on my door.

"Yes?" I called out. There was no answer.

I was still in that day's clothes, having not thought to change into my nightdress yet. Too lost in fanciful wishes. I walked over to the door and cracked it open to find Elias smiling at me. I flushed at my thoughts that had just been centered on him, and I worried that somehow, he would see them on my face.

"Captain?" I questioned. "What is it?"

It was late into the evening, and I knew that he and Georgette were taking turns at the wheel to reach our destination faster.

"It may be the last clear night," he said as if that explained it all. "The clouds are coming, and I thought it might be the last opportunity to show you something."

"Oh?" My voice sounded too intrigued by half.

A smile slipped over his face, stretching lazily across it. He wasn't wearing a vest or a coat, and he had even left his cutlass behind. He looked more like a boy now and less like a pirate. A man dressed in brown trousers and a linen shirt coming to ask me about an adventure. I felt like I had mere days to savor the taste of what The Siren had to offer me, so I opened the door wide and followed him without another word.

I hadn't seen beauty that equaled the sunrises and sunsets on the ocean. The colors and light of them were almost lurid in their detail. I would likely dream about them when in Urorah, along with a great many things I had seen in my short time with pirates.

I looked up to the wheel and saw Georgette leaned against it, hat tipped back, looking distantly at nothing. She was lost in another world and didn't seem to notice us, or acted as if she hadn't.

Elias brought me to the ship's main mast, the tallest with three large sails attached to it. He stepped into a webbing of net that ran up to the top of the mast. It ended at a large bucket at the top that was large enough to hold two or three people, I had heard them refer to as the crow's nest.

"Can you climb?" he asked, jerking his chin up to signal the destination. "Do you have a fear of heights?"

"Not that I'm aware," I said, eyeing the top of the mast. "Though I've never been up quite that high with nothing but my own hands keeping me up."

"The ratline is situated so it will catch you if you fall," he assured.

He held his hand out to me, and I hesitated only a moment before I took it. He helped me up, and I started to climb up in front of him. I was slow, and I knew it, but my pulse thundered in my ears with excitement. I would never have been able to make the climb in skirts, and I sent a prayer up to the goddess Loripta for Georgette and her unorthodox fashion choices.

I had to stop a few times to catch my breath and close my eyes against the slight fluttering in my stomach. It reminded me of the trees I climbed at home as a child. I was experiencing the rush of reaching the very top branches with the crisp views that seemed incredible.

When I finally reached the crows' nest, Elias was patient and waited in the net below for me to get inside. I wasn't sure what the ladylike way to climb into it would be, but my attempt was less than graceful. I landed on my butt with a hard thump. A chuckle came from Elias, who I glared at as soon as his face came into view. He swung onto the platform with ease and offered me a hand up, which I took.

He let me adjust to the view and the height. He eyed me, I assumed, because he was worried about me fainting. I got my bearings looking down on the ship deck below but surprisingly did not feel lightheaded or sick. I looked over at him as he took a seat on the bottom of the platform and leaned against one of its curved walls. I sat next to him and followed his gaze heavenward.

The skies onboard the ship were magical. I had thought there couldn't be anything to top them. I let out a long breath as I stared at a fathomless sapphire painting. Bright stars covered the canvas in varying sizes and luminosities, dancing in and out of vision. They felt close enough to touch, and the ache in my chest opened once more.

"Do you like it?" he asked, sounding like a preening child.

"I'm not sure there are words, Elias," I exhaled, letting his name slip off my tongue like a comfortable endearment.

"This is the best spot on all the ship." His voice had gone slightly rougher than it had been a second ago.

"I have grown very fond of the front deck. I feel as if I can see everything before it happens."

"The forecastle deck," he acknowledged.

"And I'm very fond of my room," I admitted to him. "Though it's not my room... rather, I have grown very fond of your officer's quarters."

He looked like he would offer me something again, and his mouth opened slightly with it. He looked into my eyes, and I saw raw yearning before he closed his mouth and looked back up at the stars. I wanted him to ask me or offer me whatever he was about to. I desired to accept whatever parts of himself he was willing to give with gluttony.

I wondered if he had stopped as a kindness to me. Could he see that I craved it? When we were alone, he didn't feel like a pirate who had seduced many a woman on the high sea. I felt as if his heart was attainable if only I proved patient enough to wait out the guard he kept on it.

"Tell me a tale of the day and the night," I said, unwilling to cut our time short.

"What kind of tale are you looking to hear?" he asked.

"A tale of love despite born differences."

There would be no way that he could mistake my meaning. A flush of intimacy flitted across my features, but I found myself not caring. I heard my mother's harsh scoldings in the back of my mind and ignored them. I gave myself over to my adventure and my want of a pirate captain.

"Very well, Princess, I shall tell you the tale of the Lord of Night and the Lady of the Day." One of his warm, calloused hands slipped over the top of mine.

"Mind you, this story starts back when there was no transition between day and night." I heard his voice find itself as the story unwound in his mind. "When the day was over, you would simply blink, and it would be dark, and likewise when the night ended you were simply bombarded by bright sunlight...it was shocking and harsh."

I nodded, closing my eyes against his words.

"The Lord of the Night was a very handsome man; some would say the most handsome in all the realm," he continued.

"Oh, is that so?" I asked, laughing.

"You asked me for a tale... do not interrupt." He squeezed my hand, and fire radiated through me as I pursed my lips and nodded.

⸻ ❦ ⸻

While many admired the countenance of the Lord of the Night, the Lady of the Day was fairer still. While night held secrets and mystery, the day held warmth and honesty. Each was gifted with the duties of their realm, responsible for making sure both the days and the nights were in order.

Though neither of them had ever met, they had been raised to loathe each other. The night had been told that the day was prudish, stiff, and proud. The day had been told that the night was careless, heartless, and chaotic. So, they were enemies without having even spent a minute in the others' company.

One afternoon Lady Day was picking flowers in a field, and Lord Night happened upon her quite accidentally. Being the rake that he was, he figured it a farm maiden and walked up and asked if she'd like a good romp in the field...

⸻ ❦ ⸻

"The cad," I said, my laughter barely contained behind a smile.

"Indeed," Elias said gravely.

Lady Day had never been so offended in all her life and assumed all the tales that had been spun about the night were accurate. Lord Night, who had been about to apologize, was so put off by her lecturing that he walked off, sure that she was the most prudish woman he had ever met in all his life; it was an accident, after all.

So, they hated each other even more.

And though they hated each other, Lady Day kept going back to the same field, and Lord Night made sure that he passed along its borders almost every day on his travels. At first, they merely hurled insults at each other. Day after day, they found new ways to express their utmost disdain for one another.

Until, one day, when Lord Night went to pass the field thinking of the slander he would hurl, he found Lady Day sitting in the middle of the field crying. He thought of just walking by and leaving her to her misery. After all, shouldn't he rejoice in her suffering? But he wandered over to her, convincing himself it couldn't hurt to see what was wrong.

She sniffled for a bit, but upon some prodding, Lady Day revealed that she was to be stripped of her power and given over to a cruel man to pay her father's debts. It was her last day she would be free to run through the wildflowers in the sunshine.

Lord Night was troubled by this. While he had thought he loathed Lady Day, he felt a blossoming warmth and a desire to keep her from sadness when seeing her now. He asked if she would like haven among his realm until he could think of a more permanent solution. She agreed.

And so, Lord Night stole Lady Day away to the Star Kingdom. There was complete darkness over all the earth for several weeks, and the Day Kingdom began to crumble under its blackness.

Lady Day was distressed for both her kingdom and her people. Her heart ached to fulfill her duty to them. Though her heart also ached when she thought of leaving the Kingdom of the Night. For, it was evident that she had fallen in love with the stars and their mystery.

⸎

"Evident to whom?" I interrupted him, too lost in the tale to be embarrassed.

"To the night, of course." He had leaned in and whispered it, and his breath was warm against my cheek.

⸎

And while the Lord Night did not wish for her to leave, he neither wished for her to feel a broken heart over her Kingdom. He could not hold her captive if she wanted to return to her home. So, he offered to pay off her father's debts from his stores so she could remain Lady Day.

He made a vow never to steal her again so the world could benefit from the day and the night. For each had their duties to perform and could not plunge the world into darkness for their feelings alone.

They did find places to meet in the cracks of the end and beginning of each day. They would hold each other until they could no longer. Thus, dusk and dawn were born, and these are places where day and night profess their love for one another.

⸎

"That is a rather sad tale," I said when it was evident that he would add no more.

"Really? I find it rather hopeful."

His eyes were closed as I opened mine. His head was leaning against the wood. He hadn't pulled his hand from mine, and I was glad for it. I turned my palm up and laced my fingers with his around his rings which had been warmed by his skin.

"The day won't ever be able to revisit the night realm, even though she loved it." I started knowing full well that he knew I was no longer speaking of the story.

I hadn't realized it, but my eyes filled with tears. They spilled over onto my cheeks. More came as I thought of the prospect of my life in Urorah. Before, when I had left my home in Molina, I had been so sure that I could live a contented life at the side of King Cyril Kosdel. Being one of his many wives in a foreign country had almost been spun as a privilege. That was before being kidnapped by these pirates, before trousers and dancing, and before Elias. Now I was unsure of everything and despising the very future I had been resolved to weeks before. His other hand reached out and brushed tears off one side of my face.

"I can't stay. I can't ask that of you, your sister, or Absalom. It would be putting you directly in harm's way," I said though my resolve wasn't firm. "Also, continued peace with Northern Ralice depends on my marriage to King Kosdel. If I don't, a war hangs in the balance."

I was just going on as if he had asked me to stay, I realized, suddenly embarrassed. I sat up straight and pulled my hand away from his wiping my face. He let me go, but his face looked as pained as my heart felt.

"Thank you for sharing this with me," I said, gesturing up to the sky.

I scrambled up and went for the edge throwing a leg over. I was running away before he had the chance to unravel whatever willpower I had left, or worse, say nothing at all.

"Mercy..."

I scrambled down the ratline with him calling softly after me. About three-quarters of the way, my hand slipped, and I lost my footing. I tumbled into the net below. It burned my hands, and while it did catch my fall, it wasn't a pleasant safety. The rope was unforgiving, and it bit into my limbs. I untangled myself from it, stepping away in haste.

When I looked up, I saw Georgette sitting on the bottom step of the quarter-deck. She looked like she had been in the middle of sharpening her sword when I had taken my tumble. She had an eyebrow raised at me and looked back up at the crow's nest. If I thought she hadn't known Elias and I were up there, I was now aware that was wholly untrue. She sent an irritated scowl to the top of the mainmast before looking back at me.

"Are you okay?" she asked, running a stone over her blade.

No. I answered in my head but just nodded to her and smiled, turning my back and retreating to my room. I closed the door behind me and sat on the bed, taking off my boots and stockings. I threw them aggressively against the wall and watched as they slumped in the corner as dejected as I felt.

I did not sleep well that night.

Twenty-One

Georgette

It had been a day shy of a week since Quizit and the tavern brawl. We had sailed around Hesteige's finger and entirely out of Hestiege waters into Southern Ralice territory. Elias and I had both taken turns staying up to sail day and night to get there as quickly as possible. We had all agreed upon the plan to have Mercy and Absalom depart at Brits' port. We would rendezvous with Absalom in Odie to make sure everything had gone smoothly. We also agreed to send Bram with them for added protection. Though as the days passed, I watched Elias's demeanor change from casual acceptance to reluctance.

The night before we were to port, he announced to me that he was no longer in agreement about dropping Absalom and Mercy off at Brits. He hadn't asked me about it. He hadn't posed it as a question. He had come up and told me that we wouldn't be letting them off. He had confronted me on the quarter-deck with his guard up and his determination set. I knew arguing with him in front of the crew wouldn't have gone well, so I allowed him to leave unchallenged.

When I came to his quarters that night, he was as defensive and unreasonable as he had been when he changed plans earlier. I had tried to talk to him. To explain what kind of position that was putting Absalom in. I didn't dare accuse him of emotional influence, only tried to reason with him. He was utterly opposed to every idea I brought up.

He would not yield. He told me it was too dangerous to drop them off. That he now planned to sail up to Odie with them both. I had balked at him. He had stared at me, barring me from entering his room with the door only opened slightly as we argued quietly there.

He hadn't budged on the idea or even considered any point I had made. If he thought he could tell me what we would do without discussing it first, he was mistaken. This was our ship, not his ship. We made choices together. So, he had brought what I was doing on himself. That's what I tried to convince myself of.

I went to Mercy's room after he had slammed his door in my face. I told her that she and Absalom would be leaving early the following day before the sun rose. I explained to her it would be safer for them under cover of darkness, and if they went that early, they would reach the rendezvous point by midday. She had nodded, accepting the information. I noticed she had already packed her things in a sack I gave her. The silver and emerald circlet sitting on top had sent a pang of guilt through me.

She had complained of tiredness the previous two days and so had been sleeping on and off throughout. The voyage was taking its toll on her, and she was almost half asleep when we spoke. I smiled, leaving her to slip into a dream closing her door behind me.

I explained my plan to Absalom, who was hesitant to do it behind Elias's back but agreed that the King would see it as a punishable offense. I told him I would deal with Elias' wrath after they had gone. The plan would have worked had he not confronted us as we were executing it.

"Will Elias not rise to say goodbye?" Mercy enquired for the third time as Absalom looked at me with guilt eating away at his features.

She looked confused and hurt as her eyes shifted between Absalom and me. She had asked where Elias had been that morning, and I kept brushing her enquiries off casually. As if he had just not roused in time to see her off. I knew the cruelty of it as I saw the hurt in her eyes. I had schooled my thoughts back to uncaring. I would not put mine and my brother's life in jeopardy because they had formed some sort of attachment to each other. Not to mention the trouble Absalom would be in defying a direct order from his King.

Mercy looked exhausted with bags under her eyes. Her usually pale skin had gone greenish, and her cheeks were inflamed red. The quicker we got her on land, the better it would be for her. She was not used to enduring such long sea trips.

"He might have had his sister and his best friend not conspired behind his back." His voice came from behind me.

I looked up at Absalom, who paled under the light of the lanterns that we had hung on the deck. I rubbed the tiredness from my eyes. I had not slept the previous night, worried I would not rise in time before my brother. My attempts had been in vain. I turned to face him and the consequences of my actions.

"You are just making decisions on your own now, then? Using your influence over Absalom to get him to go along with it?" His voice filled with deadly anger.

"Elias, that's not what this is," Absalom said, "We have to go."

"Elias, I thought we agreed to this?" Mercy asked quietly, but I heard the hesitation in her voice.

He ignored them both as he fixed his rage on me.

"Listen," I said as if talking to a cornered animal, "You aren't thinking about this. If we don't drop them where Gerald instructed, we won't receive the money the king promised, and our crew won't get paid. Absalom will have consequences for defying Cyril. She isn't regular cargo we are hauling, Elias. This is the King's wife."

"It isn't safe," he hissed back at me.

"When I brought up these concerns days ago, you told me that it wasn't our problem," I said back to him, and he flinched away as if struck. "Not to mention, if we don't drop them off now, we may lose access to the island altogether; we may still have a chance to get to it."

"Damn the island," he said.

I sucked in a breath. The anger rose in me to match his. I heard the crew stirring below deck and knew it was only a matter of moments before some of them began trailing up. The sun was hinting at rising, and we were losing our window to get everything back to the way it was supposed to be.

"You cannot keep her here!" I all but yelled. "She doesn't belong here; she belongs to a king."

"She doesn't belong to anyone." He took a step forward as I gave him an exasperated look.

I turned my back on him as I heard more footsteps come up the stairs and onto the top deck. I looked down the pier for Bram, who we had sent out first to make sure the port was clear. There was no sign of him. I turned to look at Absalom when I heard the distinct sound of a sword being pulled from a sheath. Absalom's eyes went wide as I let out a breath.

I turned and saw Elias with his sword drawn. He hadn't raised it in an aggressive attack, but the message he was sending was clear. The few crew members that had come up deck stared at the scene in surprise, and the deck went as silent as the grave.

"Elias," I warned. "Don't do this."

"If you are going to openly defy my wishes and disregard them as lovesick musings without talking to me, I see no other choice."

"I tried to talk to you," I said. "I tried. You didn't want to listen to a thing I had to say. You forced this. You are accusing me of making decisions without you, but that is what you did yesterday when you just decided we would ignore the terms we agreed upon. Everyone else be damned except you and your affections."

Our voices were raised. It felt wrong, as it always did when we argued. Except for this time, he had drawn his sword against me.

"It won't be any easier," I said, voice lower, "to hand her off to him at a different port."

He didn't deny my thinly veiled accusations. Though he still looked at me as if I had betrayed him, and I supposed that I had. He stepped toward me, sword still out and raised.

"No," he said finally, "We wait."

"No," I said, drawing my weapon. "We don't."

He looked hesitant, but if it was a fight he wanted, it was a fight he would get.

"Elias, please," Mercy said from behind me, and his eyes flashed to her and then back to me.

"Let them," I heard Absalom say to her.

"We can't be sure they'll be safe," he said.

He stepped forward and attacked first as I sucked in a breath. I met his eyes, still unsure, but he had raised his sword to me, and I caught it with my own. It was the first time we had ever disagreed publicly with swords drawn and rage building between us.

"That's not our concern, you said so yourself," I sneered as he pressed into my blade, face coming closer to mine.

"Don't you care for their safety?" he asked, stepping back as I pushed him off.

We had drawn a crowd. While most everyone stayed back, they were watching and listening. We had strict rules about fighting in front of the crew. We had regulations more stringent about drawing our weapons on each other in anger. It caused dissent among the ship. It made us look weak. It was something our parents had made sure we understood. We did not fight in front of them.

But there we were with swords drawn.

"As I recall, you had a very private discussion with me while our voyage had barely started about letting affection get in the way of our ultimate goal." I attacked him with force and anger.

"It's not the same," he spoke.

"Of course not." I swung at him with every word, pushing him further and further away from the people watching.

We spared no bit of energy as we took out our frustrations on each other. The clang of metal rang out against the dead silence of the harbor, interrupted only by the distant squawking of birds. None of the crew spoke. When I could catch a glimpse of Mercy and Absalom, they were just as we had left them, staring after us with concern.

As we wore on and our anger dissipated with the effort of fighting, our blows lessened. We were up on the quarter-deck when I nearly missed a strike from his blade, and I tripped backward. He took advantage of the fall, pinning me to the wheel of the ship with his blade on my chest. I growled and slammed my head into his, and he stumbled back and off me. I dropped my sword, rushing him and slamming him into the doors of the navigation room.

"Is it worth this?" I whispered so no one else might hear. "Is it worth breaking every rule? Every promise that we have made to each other? You would defy everything we have been trained to do for her?"

He had no answer, only looked at me empty and pleading.

"You would put Absalom and me in harm's way for it?" I shook his shoulders. "For what? Another week with her?"

He showed nothing, just despair.

"I've always put this ship first. I've always put you first, without hesitation. I have always given up anything I wanted to do what they taught us." I had started whispering, but the end of my sentence came out harsher and more loudly than I meant it to with emotion on its heels.

"I've never asked that of you," he said, "Don't blame me for your unwillingness to do what you want. That's your own martyr story, and I have nothing to do with it."

"You think I feel like a martyr for doing what I am supposed to do? For keeping my promises to you and our parents?" I fell back from him, more than a little wounded by his accusation.

"You think I can't see it?" he said, looking right at me.

This conversation was disintegrating into something that I feared. The mere thought of it always stopped my daydreaming in its tracks. My fitful fancies of land life cowered in front of facing my brother. My fear and an unsure resolve regarding our life together.

"Why would you try and hide it from me?" he asked, staring down at his hands. "Don't you know I only care for your joy in life? You needn't go out of your way to keep your word to me if it makes you miserable."

I didn't want to talk about that with him. I wanted to be rid of Mercy and Absalom from our ship. I wanted to be on our way to a treasure so legendary that it would make everything better. So, it would go on just like it had. I would find happiness there amongst a lost pirate's hoardings, and it would be a savior for my wayward heart.

Elias's words sparked a softness in me, and my anger with him melted. *Don't you know I care only for your joy in life?* I cared for his joy beyond that of my own or any normalcy that I craved to feel. I cared for his happiness far beyond any treasure or safety. My love for my brother was more substantial than any pull I had ever felt.

It was a profound thing, as sure as the river Cras leading to an ocean, connected by upbringing, memory, and lineage. Our eyes fastened us, and the matching beauty marks we shared under our left eyes. We were two sides of the same coin. Nothing in this world could drive me to seek my happiness in the face of his sorrow.

"Why?" I asked him without having to explain.

"I think I might be in love with her." Quiet as if it were the first time he had said it aloud.

"Oh no," I said, rubbing my hands over my face. "Not with a princess, Elias, surely?"

It evoked a promise between us. It was the pact of love. Something Elias had invented as he was the one more likely to believe in its existence. Love was a great romantic and passionate thing that swept you away with its charm and heat in his mind. He believed in one true match for everyone. That if you ever found them, it was a minor miracle. The vow was to defend each other's soulmates with as much dedication as we did each other. When I made the vow, I hadn't believed in soulmates, even if Elias had. I hadn't thought I would be called upon to fulfill it.

"I'm sorry that it offends you," he said, the hint of a smile coming to his mouth.

"Don't," I said, pointing a finger at him. "I'm still angry with you."

"What if we send her off with Absalom and harm comes to her, George? I will never forgive myself," he said, and for what I saw in him, I believed it.

I had seen a connection between them. I had seen it and brushed it off as Elias's charm or her soft footedness. I thought perhaps it was just attraction or passing fancy. Maybe Elias was trying to prove to himself that he could win her affection. Though, when he looked at me unguarded, I saw what it was that he felt. It was no passing affection. How could I have been so stupid?

"What of Mercy?" I chewed at my lip in worry. "Does she wish to stay with us?"

"I don't know," he said, "I think she feels the pull of the duty to her brother, but... I think she would stay if she could."

"Neither of us knows the weight of being royalty," I said to him. "What if you ask her to stay, and she still decides to go?"

"Then I will let her, of course," he said firmly, but now that I saw what was in his heart, I was afraid it might break some part of him.

"She may," I said. "She's been taught to serve her country. To the point of imprisoning herself in an unwanted marriage for the rest of her life. You have to know that it may be nearly impossible to sever that desire."

"I would never assume to keep her here if she wishes to leave. I only wish to offer her the choice with your blessing."

"Next time, just ask for my blessing instead of being such a pain in my ass first."

"There won't be a next time."

He was determined, and as I looked at him again, I saw that he believed it. He was either sure or very nearly close that Mercy was the love that he sought. After our father filled his head with stories of love that could move cities, he was sure that he had found it.

"So be it," I nodded to him as we both gathered ourselves and our swords and went to go back to the main deck.

"What are we going to tell Absalom?" I asked.

"I don't know."

There was a commotion, a shuffle, and a few shouts. We both looked at each other one last time before rushing down to see what had happened. When we came into view, we saw Absalom supporting Mercy, who had passed out. He was setting her gently on the deck. She was limp and white as a new sail.

"What happened?" Elias asked, rushing to her side and felt her forehead with the back of his hand.

"She was starting to complain of the heat and a weakness. I suggested we wait in her room to rest, but she insisted on staying here until you both sorted things out. She just collapsed," Absalom said, still holding her up a little, looking down at her, concerned.

"Captains!" It was Bram who came up the loading plank.

He was out of breath, and the new sun highlighted the bright pink of his already ruddy cheeks. He looked distraught and kept looking behind him as if someone were approaching. Seeing as how there was only one enemy after us, I paled, knowing what he was going to report.

"Southern Ralice military has almost the whole port surrounded. They have guards at every exit into the city."

"We have to leave," I said, and Jones appeared before me as if he knew I would need him.

"Jones, pull up anchor and tell crew we leave as quickly as we can," I ordered. "Elias, take Mercy to her room, and I'll find Jamie to look her over."

He had already taken her in his arms and headed in the direction of her room. He stepped away with her leaving Absalom kneeling where he had set her down. The commander looked at me amidst the commotion. His eyes wandered to Elias and back to me with a question in them. I sent no response. It was not my truth to tell.

"Let's go, you lazy siren fodder!" I shouted to my crew. "Ship out as quick as you can. There's a round of drinks at the next port in it for all of you if you hurry!"

I walked to Absalom and held my hand out to help him up. He got up on his own as my stature made my offer of help rather silly.

"My father is going to have me hanged," he sighed, but that was his only resistance as he gathered his and Mercy's things and wandered toward her room.

I hustled below deck to find our young doctor so he could start earning his keep.

$$\mathcal{Twenty\text{-}Two}$$

Mercy

I was in and out of fitful sleep for the next two days. Jamie came and checked on me every couple of hours, constantly waking me up and making me drink some clean water. I went through hours where I felt fine and almost normal, and then I would get unbelievably cold and feel as if I was about to faint again.

Georgette brought me books and warming alcohol. Absalom brought me tea and good company. Elias brought me fantastic, contrived stories and worried glances. The lot of them never left me alone for a moment. They took shifts sitting at my side. Absalom talked of his home and what he thought I would like, not minding if I was strong enough to respond. His solid voice helped me sleep. Georgette mostly read from books of pirate nature, teaching me about ship terminology, sailing techniques, and the like. Elias was the only one who sat on my bed, at the end, where he wouldn't disturb me. He looked up at the ceiling and told me magical tales laughing at himself during the humorous bits.

Though I was feeling rather poorly, my spirit soared from their warmth toward me.

"And that's the tale of Penelope the sea witch and Vlad the Admiral," Elias finished another tale with a smile in my direction.

It was late the second day, and I was feeling relatively well. I was sitting up in my bed wearing a black silk nightdress that Georgette had given me. It was softer against my skin than any of my nightgowns at home. She said it had never really suited her when she laid it before me. I pulled my hair back away from my face and had used some cold water to wash the sweat from my skin.

"Pity it didn't end better for them," I said.

"You and your happy endings. Life rarely ends happily."

He didn't have to remind me of that.

"That's what I like about a story," I said, sitting up straighter. "For a moment, you can pretend it does."

"We'll reach the port by morning; we are working our way against a strong current, but as soon as we dock, we will take you and find a healer. Jamie knows of a couple in Skirttown that his father knew before," he assured me, though all three of them had told me this.

"What then?" I asked for the first time, enquiring about his fight with Georgette without asking the question directly.

"Then...," he said, slowly outstretching his hand and drawing light circles on my knuckles with his pointer finger. "Whatever you choose."

"Whatever I choose?" I marveled.

"Yes, if you wish for Absalom to take you home, then we shall provide you with men and provisions to make the journey safely. We will drop you at Castorica where we can be sure Dalion's men won't attack you."

"What's my other option?" I asked, and he looked up slowly, the pain of a timid hope on his face.

"If you don't want to go to Northern Ralice...," he said slowly, "You'll have me and my sister's protection, and we shall come up with a ruse to ensure your safety. I am sure Absalom would agree to it as well if it's what you want."

"What would that require?" I put my hand on his, trapping it between both of mine.

"I have not a single inkling," he said, looking directly at me, "I hadn't allowed myself to formulate even a semblance of a plan."

He stopped, taking a breath, and let it out quickly. His legs were crossed in his brown trousers, and his feet were bare. His shirt was untucked, and his hair was more disheveled than I had ever seen it.

"Do you know a tale about a princess that dreamed of being a pirate?" I looked down and whispered the words like they were between a prayer and a secret.

"I'd like to," he said, "Does it end with this princess-turned pirate swallowed by the guilt of leaving her people and country to suffer?"

"I don't know," I said honestly, "It may."

"That is one sorrowful ending I could not endure."

When I looked back up, he was smiling with something that seemed was just for me. I wanted him. My heart ached for it as it ached for the sea. His smile calling me just like the stars did when I gazed upon them.

"Would you mind if I asked for a small favor?" The words bubbled out of my mouth almost on their own.

"Any favor you like," he said generously, "If this small favor is within my power to give."

"Would you...." I stopped suddenly hot as I started to pick at the edge of the blanket on the bed.

"Are you feeling alright?" he asked, moving from his seated position to place his hand on my cheek. "Your face is very flushed, perhaps you should lay back, and I'll fetch Jamie."

"No," I said, quickly reaching up and grabbing the front of his shirt. "I mean, I feel fine."

"Oh," he said as my meaning dawned on him.

His eyes flitted to my mouth for half a second before he shook his head and looked back into my eyes. If I hadn't been flushed before, I was sure that now my fair skin was aflame with distress.

"I just," the words were clumsy and strange, "I have never kissed… a man, And I thought that perhaps it would be nice to, at least once, kiss someone I wished to."

I let go of his shirt and covered my face with my hands. I let out a groan of frustration at myself for being so idiotic. His hands wrapped around my wrists and tugged my hands down gently. He looked so softly at me with a kind, closed smile. Kindness, I would have never known a pirate could offer.

"Certainly, though…" Each of his knees were on either side of my legs. He had moved, so he was no more than a handbreadth from me. "To you, it's a kiss stolen from a pirate, and to me, it's the dawn."

The tightness in my chest squeezed again, almost causing me to gasp. I couldn't offer what he was offering. I couldn't promise myself to him or this life. I couldn't sail the enchanting seas by his side, wholly free and myself. I couldn't, while I knew my people might suffer. I felt a pull of duty as strong as the pull of the ocean and to him.

"No matter," he said, no doubt seeing the hesitation in my face, "I can live with a single moment of dawn."

I squeezed my eyes tight, and my breath stilled as I held it. Though after seconds of nothing happening, I opened them. He was pursing a smile, and humor lay in his eyes.

"You look like I'm about to attack you."

"I've no experiences with such things." Flushing deeper, I cast my eyes down.

"Well, first, you needn't close your eyes so tight, as if prepping for assault." His hand came up to my face raising my chin, so I was looking into his eyes once more. "Second, are you sure? You owe me nothing, Princess."

"Quite sure," I assured him, but my voice was higher and breathier than usual.

He leaned in closer as the pad of his thumb brushed over my bottom lip. Hotness pooled in my stomach, radiating everywhere he touched me or was close. I was aware of every inch of my exposed skin. His nose brushed my cheek, and my eyes fluttered shut on their own against the touch. He placed a kiss on either of my eyelids, as soft as a summer breeze. Though my eyes were closed, I could feel the warmth of his mouth just above mine. I let out a small exhale of breath, and his lips were on my own.

I hadn't realized that I would enjoy it. Or perhaps I thought I would but could not know the way my body would react to his. His mouth was soft and gentle on mine, and I met him with a ferocity that I was surprised by. Though I was inexperienced, my body proceeded naturally. My hands came up to tangle in his unkempt hair trapping him to me. My mouth was needier than his, too, pushing back with fervor.

He pulled away, resting his forehead against mine.

"Oceans deep." His breathing was ragged.

I didn't let him say anything else as I took one hand from the back of his head and grabbed his shirt, pulling him to me. I kissed him against his grin. A swift knock came at the door, but before we could react, quick footsteps came in.

"We have port history tonight, Mercy..." Georgette's voice stopped mid-sentence as she surveyed the scene before her.

Elias and I had somehow gotten tangled in one another. Both our faces turned to her, but evidence of what had been happening was entirely on display.

"Well, this will be branded into my memory until death," she spoke.

"You could have knocked and then waited a moment," Elias said.

"You can unbind yourself from our sick princess and be on your merry way before I murder you," she growled, having emphasized the word sick.

Elias shook his head but began extracting his limbs from mine as Georgette tapped her foot with impatience. I was half flushed with passion and half with embarrassment, so I said nothing.

Disheveled, Elias stood up next to my bed. Not feeling pressured, it seemed, by his sister, he leaned in and placed one more lingering kiss to my mouth. I accepted with a smile.

"Goodnight," he whispered.

"Goodnight."

"Elias!" Georgette yelled.

He whirled on her, put a hand out, and pinched one of her cheeks. "Ocean knows I've walked in on worse, little sister."

He left as she batted his hand away.

"Is he older?" I asked when Georgette had closed the door, hoping to change the subject. "In the way that twins are, did he come out before you?"

"No," she huffed, pulling out the desk chair and sitting down. "Well, he could have; we don't know. He claims the title anyway."

"Didn't your mother ever tell you?" I asked curiously.

"We weren't born of my mother," she said easily. "We are children of a prostitute on Puddle Island. Our parents adopted us when we were only three."

I was thoroughly surprised, not at the information but that Georgette had given it so willingly. Getting information from her had been like ripping a cat from a tree branch. But I could sense something had changed. A comfort sat between us now, and I could not name the reason for it.

"Ports," Georgette began, and I laid back in my bed, suddenly very tired.

⸎

When I woke, it was morning, and Georgette was in my room rummaging for clothes for me. She laid some out as I got my bearings. She motioned for a glass of water on the dresser. I stood up on unsteady legs and drank as much of it as I could. I felt dreadful. I was freezing despite the warmth I knew was around me, and my legs felt unable to carry my weight.

"We are ported at the far end of the port at Skirttown," she informed me, "Get dressed. We are going to take you to a healer Jamie has directed to us to see if we can get something for you to make it to Castorica."

"Oh," I said, winded at the idea of leaving.

"Only if you want to leave," she said, nodding. "No one will force you to stay or go; your life is yours. You'll have time to decide. It will take at least four days to get there. Absalom and Elias are going to post mail to Gerald and King Kosdel to let them know we deemed your safety in jeopardy here in Southern Ralice."

"If I don't go, you will both be hunted. You would endure that for me?" I asked.

"For my brother, there is little I would not endure." A determination set in her eyes.

It had been Elias then that had caused this warmth between us. Georgette would protect me because of whatever feelings Elias had for me. Admiration and jealousy surged through me. Their love was a weighty thing.

When we both emerged, Absalom and Elias were nowhere to be found. Georgette explained they had already gone into the town, part to send the letter and see if there was any correspondence waiting for them and part to make sure it was safe.

"So far, we haven't seen any military presence, but we must be careful as we are in that blasted king's country now," she said as we walked off the ship. "We should bring Jamie, but I am trying to afford you as much anonymity as possible."

Before we started into town, she paid a port boy to come to get us at the healer's when Absalom and Elias came back to the ship. It was slow going, and Georgette stopped patiently with me every several hundred feet so I could take a break. I felt less and less well, and I could see in her eyes that she was worried. We were taking a particularly long break when Absalom found us.

"Where's Elias?" Georgette asked.

He pointed ahead. "He's gone on to the healers, no correspondence from my father. We must have finished before you. I thought you would beat us there."

"It's my fault," I said, standing up." I can't seem to go far without taking a break."

"Nonsense, a princess cannot be blamed. You take whatever time you need."

We had just started going again when the boy came up to us. I didn't know what he planned to say with Elias at the healers and Absalom here with us. His eyes were wide as anything, and his breath was quick and ragged.

"Miss Captain." He bent over, putting his hands on his knees.

"What is it?" Georgette asked.

"Your ship," he said, panting, "Someone has boarded your ship."

"What do you mean, someone?" Her tone was too high, too panicked.

"A lot of someones," he said, "King Dalion's men."

"Thank you, you go home, and don't you go back to that pier."

He nodded and ran off past us in the opposite direction of the port. Georgette was breathing slow. It looked as if the weight of the world crashed in on her, and I saw the unflinching sarcastic exterior crack slightly.

"Your call, George," Absalom said

"We can't take Mercy back there," she said, "They'll take her."

"Okay," he said, and I could tell he heard her panic as much as I did.

"But I have to go back; I can't leave the crew," she said, "to whatever fate we forced upon them."

"You aren't going alone," Absalom said to her.

"You have to stay with Mercy," she argued.

"I'll be fine," I said, doing my best to stand straight. "He must go with you. I'm not in danger here, and I can find my way to the healers."

"Are you certain?" Absalom asked me.

I saw in his face that while he was duty-bound to protect me, he would not leave Georgette's side. He would never send her off into danger by herself, and I would never ask it of him.

"Commander, you go, and I shall retrieve Elias and warn him."

"Yes," Georgette breathed, "Elias, he'll know what to do."

"I remember the directions; you two go." I waved them off, still holding myself tall despite my waning strength.

I was so cold.

"Straight to Elias," Georgette said, putting her hands on my shoulders and tugging me in close to her. "Be careful."

"Go," I said, my eyes pricked with emotion.

So, they did. I looked in front of me and the long walk to the healers that was still ahead. I was lightheaded and weak, but I could do this for them. I could do it for me. I was strong enough, I told myself.

Though my resolve didn't matter a few hundred feet later when I came to the market center as Jamie had instructed us. I sucked in a breath, stealing myself back into the shadows of a building. The open areas were teeming with men in blue military uniforms. They were flashing pieces of paper at passersby. There wouldn't be any way I would get through them. I weighed my options. Perhaps they were just looking for Georgette and Elias and wouldn't recognize me.

No. I knew I couldn't wade through them; it was me they were after, and they would know what I looked like. So, I made my way back the way I had come, hoping Elias had seen and kept himself safe. I was practically limping along, drawing long, ragged breaths. I used walls and stalls to prop me up as I made my way back to the port. I wandered in a fever haze back to The Siren, looking for its tentacled woman as a marker.

I was stopped suddenly by two military men. I saw the ship just behind them. I had made it so close, but I was starting to fade. I felt the darkness closing just as it had on the deck two days ago. I was too weak to fight them, and they seemed to sense it. One of them grabbed me around the middle hoisting me over his shoulder and carrying me a few steps toward the ship.

"Unhand me!" I used the last of my strength to shout. "I am the Princess Mercy of Adamas, and I demand you unhand me this instant!"

A few moments passed while I flitted in and out of consciousness. The man holding me had laid me on the dock, and I shivered there as cold as I could ever remember being. I was too weak even to lift my head to see what was happening to me. I hoped I would die before being taken by them. I prayed for it.

"What have you done!?" I heard a familiar voice say, "I'll see you hanged for this."

It sounded like Atticus, my brother's personal guard. It couldn't be, and I blamed it on the fever.

"I think she's sick..." I heard someone else say before I gave into the dark.

Twenty-Three

Georgette

I crept aboard my ship, trying to control my breathing. Absalom followed closely behind me. His presence was like a comforting weight that I wasn't alone. I didn't know what I was walking into, but I hoped Mercy reached Elias in time. He always knew what to do, and without him, I felt unequipped.

There was almost no sound coming from the main deck. No sound of crewmembers shuffling about. Just the sound of a bell somewhere in the distance and other harbor sounds that my beating heart thundered over. They had not removed the boarding plank, and when we came in view of the deck, my heart dropped.

My crew was all sitting on one side, surrounded by five men dressed in nondescript attire. Their weapons had been taken, and I saw the pile of swords, daggers, and pistols off to the side, like discarded trash. A few bodies were scattered around in broken, lifeless positions with pools, drag marks, and bloody flowering evidence of a struggle. I breathed through the wave of loss and nausea, trying not to identify them. I saw Jones and Bram were among those still alive. I made eye contact with Jones, who nodded once, signaling that the whole ship had been taken.

I stepped aboard confidently, never letting my chin drop from its defiant position. I turned and was faced with the two men from Liven. The handsome one with a scar on his mouth and his serious counterpart. Both were looking much too smug for my taste. About fifteen men in total meant they took my crew over by surprise and not overwhelming numbers. Most of them dressed in the Southern Ralice Military wear, and the others dressed as civilians. I glanced at Absalom and watched him try to make sense of it.

"A ship takeover, and I wasn't even invited," I said, schooling my face to indifference.

"I was upset not to find you aboard, Captain," the man I had fought in Liven said. "Though we assumed you would return shortly. Where might our stolen princess and your treacherous brother be?"

I went to open my mouth to say something snarky, but I heard shouting and hollering behind me on the pier. One voice was unmistakably Mercy's. I closed my eyes and took a deep breath. They had caught up to her. I hoped it was before she reached Elias, so at least he was safe. I felt terrible for the thought as soon as it intruded my brain.

"Unhand me!" I heard as the princess shouted. "I am the Princess Mercy of Adamas, and I demand you unhand me this instant!"

The man who addressed me turned to one of the men dressed in casual ship wear.

"You best go handle that." The man gave him a nasty look but nodded, rushed down to the pier, and started yelling as Mercy's cries stopped.

I tried not to let the panic fill me. Everything was getting worse by the second. I moved further on deck as I heard two sets of footsteps coming up, and men in the same military blue as the other two men stepped aboard. They addressed the man who spoke to me with respect and stiff straight posture.

"The princess has been secured," one said to him.

"We shall send correspondence to The King that she has been located," the man said, and the two men nodded and went back the way they came.

It was as we had suspected. Mercy would be transported to King Dalion's court, and oceans only knew what he would do with her. That led to the thought of what his plans were for my brother and me as we were expendable pirates. While I could no longer protect myself, Absalom, or Mercy, there was one person I could still shield.

"You may have found my stolen princess," I said, playing along to his verbiage of Mercy being stolen. "My brother will be harder to recover."

"Oh?" the man asked, raising an eyebrow at me and looking to Absalom, whose face I knew would not betray me.

"Where was it that we dropped the former captain's lifeless body, Jones?" I called over to my first mate with a voice as cold as the black depths of the uncharted sea.

"Deep in the Kortel Ocean just after our port at Brits, if I recall." Jones didn't have to respond because Absalom picked up the lie as smoothly as I had started it.

"I'm impressed," the man responded.

"I got tired of splitting coin and fee," I said, bored. "Family he may have been, but he was also a bloodsucking leech and a stupid one at that."

"You murdered your brother for money?" he asked, "The ruthless tales woven of you don't do you justice, Captain Baine."

Both his eyebrows raised, and the man with him gave me a disgusted look. I glanced over at the crew again, heart sinking as I realized I didn't see Jamie amongst them. I ached, not daring to glance at the fallen bodies. If I saw his face among the lifeless, I didn't know that I would be able to keep up this facade.

Absalom stepped away from me and warily began looking at the dead crewmen. I wondered if he sensed my anguish. Though he did not have to pretend to be indifferent, and I saw the pain of loss cross his face when he happened upon each. While he had only known them for two weeks, he had become friends with several of the crew. No doubt some of them lay dead on The Siren's deck. He made his way around, and the silent tension was palpable. He eyed the men surrounding the crew, hand on his sword in a warning.

"You are being arrested for the kidnap of Princess Mercy Landlight of Adamas. You shall serve the penalty for piracy in Southern Ralice. You shall forfeit your life for this heinous crime," a man not in uniform said to me with more authority than he looked to possess.

The penalty in Southern Ralice for piracy was death.

"That's rich, seeing as it looks as if you intend to kidnap her yourself," I spat at him, and he drew his sword, looking somewhat offended for a kidnapper.

I drew mine in response and took a fighting stance. The man I fought with on the pier stepped closer to me. He hadn't removed his sword, and his hands were up in surrender. He looked to be pleading with me.

"I thought you were going to kill me next time we met." I leveled my sword flat at him, but he didn't make a move to remove his.

"If you come with us, they won't kill anyone else," he said low.

Though the others could hear him, he didn't say it for their benefit but for mine. I wondered if he saw the fear deep in my eyes. Could he see my panic just beyond my cold words?

"It's your life for theirs. My King only wanted you and your brother; these men need not suffer." His words nudged the part of my composure that was too fragile as I lowered my sword.

"George, don't," Absalom warned, "The King of Southern Ralice is not to be trusted."

"You have King Dalion's word that no one else shall be harmed if you come peacefully," he said to me again, promising me and me alone. "He has instructed me to take you and Elias Baine to the capitol. If you were to surrender, any bloodshed could end."

"That means nothing to my men lying lifeless on my deck, Sir," I said evenly, but my uncaring front had started to crumble.

"Men that resisted," he assured me as if that was a warrant for their deaths. "No one else need die. If Elias is truly dead, I will take you to our capital of Hallow, and these men will be left alive."

I turned to look at my crew and Absalom standing a hundred feet away. I felt the trade worth their lives.

"Very well," I said, sheathing my sword. "If I have your word, soldier."

"You do, Captain."

The man next to him closed the gap between us and grabbed me firmly. He turned me around, clasped my hands together behind my back, and began to bind them.

"George!" Absalom shouted, and I watched the men who were not in uniform become defensive.

"Absalom," I said, trying to calm him, but I could see the wild panic in his eyes.

"You have it wrong," he said to the man who held me.

"Absalom, don't," I warned.

I didn't know why but I knew no good would come of him trying to explain. We may know part of what was going on, but politics were too messy to get involved in. I wanted to beg him to keep quiet and keep his life. To wait for Elias and keep the crew safe. To go after Mercy if there was still time for her. To get King Kosdel to help.

"These pirates were hired by my King to retrieve the princess," he said, and I closed my eyes against his words.

He was betraying his King for us, for me.

"Who is your king?" the man who convinced me to surrender asked.

"King Cyril Kosdel of Northern Ralice, I am a commander of one of his companies, and I was tasked with escorting this ship."

"You're King Kosdel's soldier?" a man behind him asked, and I looked up to see the man who had his sword drawn behind Absalom.

"I am and..." he went on.

"Absalom!" I screamed as the man thrust his sword into Absalom.

I watched the blade protrude out the front of him. His face quickly dissolved from surprise into realization. He reached up and gingerly touched the sword coming out of his chest before falling to his knees.

"From our King to yours," the man growled and pulled his sword from Absalom's body.

"No!" a scream clawed up my throat and out into an unintelligible cry as I watched my friend crumple to the ground.

I pulled away from the man that held me. I knocked him back, but he reached out and grabbed one of my braids, and pulled hard. I yanked against it feeling the sting on my scalp. Without a thought, I grabbed the toothed dagger at my belt and swiped up with the jagged edge. I wasn't sure if I had cut my hair or his hand, but I found myself free. I ran to Absalom and slid the last several feet on my knees.

"Let her go to him," said the liar who promised me no harm would come to any of my crew. "I gave this woman my word that no crew member of hers would be harmed. If you raise your sword again, sir, you shall forfeit your life."

"He wasn't her crew; he was King Kosdel's man," the man said but stepped away.

"You've been warned," the liar spoke.

I looked over at Absalom, who was gasping for air. However, he smiled a bit at me as I came into view. I smiled back, looking at the blooming bloodstain on his clothes. He had already lost so much blood so quickly. My heart said he could sustain it. My head knew he couldn't. The tears streamed down my face, and I didn't do anything to stop them as I reached out to touch his face.

"I knew you'd be the death of me." He reached up with a painful smile but coughed, and blood came with it. "Don't cry, George, no, it's okay."

"Don't," I said, my voice breaking.

"Don't let them break you. Don't you let them; you promise me? George, you fight them every minute of the way."

"Absalom, please don't," I whispered as that was all I could manage, and he lifted his hand with a groan and put it on my face.

"Promise me."

"Yes," I whispered, my throat almost too tight to speak. "Yes, I promise."

"There's my fearless pirate captain." He smiled again, closing his eyes, and let out a hard breath.

His hand fell from my face, and a harsh final breath left him. His features were the same as before, but he didn't seem the same to me. His eyes were closed, but something about him was missing.

"Where have you gone?" I whispered to the empty shell of my friend.

I expected to be filled with rage, but there was only a hollow emptiness that consumed me. Grief immobilized me to where I could do nothing but hold his face and let my tears fall on him. I was taken back to that night on the dark beach in Odie only weeks after Absalom's mother had died.

⸎

Elias and I had dragged Absalom out of the ocean, screaming for his mother. Though she had been dead two weeks, he came to the edge of this beach every night and called for her. Every night we were there to drag him back to shore as he dove in, begging the sea to give her back.

We were all three soaking and sitting silently in the sand. Angry tears streaked down Absalom's face, and neither my brother nor I did anything. We looked away to give him the honor of grieving in peace. Our parents, who had known we needed to be with him, had found several things that 'had' to be done in Odie. Though they had warned us this was the last night we would be docked there. I had cried to Elias the night before that I was worried Absalom would drown out in the ocean without us there.

He had assured me, as he always did, that he would take care of it. So that night, we went to the beach where we had found him every night prior and stayed a ways away to let him grieve. Absalom was usually a strong child. He was always standing up for us, and whenever other children would taunt or tease us, he would always put them in their place. He never started a fight, but he finished plenty. However, when his mother had died, we had seen the brokenness inside him. The bond that he and his mother shared had snapped, and there was an emptiness to him after.

We had both gotten up and ran into the ocean after him calling for his mother that night had ended with him wading in too far. The waves were reaching much above his head. We dragged him back and sat with him. I waited for Elias to say something. Whatever it was that he had come up with, I had complete faith that it was the right thing to say.

"Listen, Mate," Elias started after a while.

Absalom looked up at us, eyes red and fists bawled up with rage and grief.

"Our parents say this is our last night that we are to be at port," Elias explained, "Now, I don't want to have to comfort my sister every night. Assuring her that you haven't gone and drowned yourself in the ocean until we get back."

Absalom sniffed, wiping his face on his wet shirt sleeve. He seemed to square off his shoulders and sat up a little straighter. I could tell he didn't want to disappoint us and was doing his best to look brave.

"We don't want to leave Absalom, but we have to," I said, "I just want to know that you're safe, please."

"We do have to leave, but we'll be back in a couple of weeks like we always are," Elias added.

"I won't come here anymore," Absalom promised us, "You won't have to worry."

"Good man," Elias said.

It was something our father always said. I knew he was trying to sound more grown-up than he was. I knew he was sad and worried about Absalom just as I was. Absalom's father left him and his mother alone frequently, and I didn't think he would stop going just because Mary had died. More than likely, Absalom would be alone often.

"Well, I think it's time we took the pirate oath of friendship," Elias said out loud, and both Absalom and I looked up at him.

"I haven't heard of it," Absalom said.

"Oh yes," I said when Elias raised an eyebrow at me, "The sacred pirate oath of friendship."

I could go along with the lie, but it was nothing but gutter water. There was no such pirate oath. Pirates did not make oaths of friendship to each other. It was absurd, but I trusted Elias.

"If you think we can include him, of course, George, he isn't a pirate after all." Elias eyed Absalom warily.

"He's our best friend," I said as if defending him.

"Maybe..." Elias pretended to think about it.

"I'll keep it very secret," Absalom promised, looking as eager to know what the oath as I was.

"Hold out your hands," Elias demanded of us.

I set mine out first and didn't flinch away when he pulled his knife out. He set the tip of it into the soft part of my palm. I winced as he cut but didn't pull my hand away. The waves rolled in, getting further and further away as the tide rolled out, and we each took turns cutting an X into our hands. I did Elias's hand and then moved to do Absalom. He held his hand out for me without hesitation. I was proud of him as I set the tip of Elias's knife into his skin.

When we were done, Elias instructed us to rinse them in the saltwater. He told Absalom to pick off any scabs as they formed, and Absalom nodded solemnly. We threw our arms around Absalom's shoulders and started walking him toward his home.

"Friends unto death," Elias had repeated.

And so, the sacred pirate oath of friendship was complete.

❦

I don't know how long they let me sit there crying over his body as my mind ran through memories that I would never be able to recount with him. Eventually, they pulled me away from him with tears still wet on my face.

"Are you the first mate?" I heard a man ask.

"I am," Jones's voice answered.

"This is your ship now," the liar said.

"Aye, glad to be rid of that bitch of a captain," Jones said.

I looked up slowly to make eye contact with him. None would be able to note the false note in his tone. Once we locked eyes, he nodded once slow, eyes full of promise. He would take care of the crew. He would find Elias and make sure the ones that lost their lives were taken care of. Absalom would be honored as he deserved.

"This is the crew you would sacrifice your life for?" the liar asked.

I let them take me away with no more fight than a broken doll.

Twenty-Four

Georgette

They took my dagger and sword, and we walked down the harbor. I prayed to whichever gods were listening that we didn't see Elias. He wouldn't be able to stand by if he saw me like this. I hoped he wouldn't come upon the ship until I was long gone, and there was nothing he could do but accept my death. I prayed it so hard I didn't notice where I was being taken.

One man helped me onto a horse behind the man I had thought beautiful, but now he was just *the* liar. We rode for what seemed like hours. When we finally stopped, we had reached a caravan of horses and carts. I looked around, disinterested, unable to muster so much as a sarcastic jab. I realized that none of the men wearing plain clothing accompanied us; only the men dressed in the blue formal military attire. The camp abounded with dozens of other men dressed the same. They all stared as I passed.

I was loaded into the back of an uncovered cart. The edges had been stacked with hay bales, and the bottom padded with hay as well. I sat on a bale and looked out over the encampment. We were on the edge of a forest, dark and thick. Its trees loomed over us, and its empty darkness seemed the unfriendly kind. I couldn't remember the last time I had been that far inland.

The man I rode with got up in the cart with me. He settled into the opposite corner of mine to keep an eye on me. He stretched his legs in front of him and leaned against the cart as if he planned to remain.

"Why not just kill me here?" I asked.

"That's not what the king commanded," he said simply.

The blind following of orders reminded me painfully of Absalom.

"What's your name?" I asked.

He looked up at me with his dark eyes and dark lashes. He had a gaze of what was either disgust or concern, but I didn't care enough to ask.

"Cassius," he spoke.

"Cassius, you lied to me," I managed to choke out.

"Yes, unintentionally, but yes, I did."

"I don't think I have it in me to forgive you for that. No matter how handsome you are." I closed my eyes against the forest air and the dimming sky.

"I would understand if you couldn't."

"I shall be dead soon anyway, so what does it matter to you if a soon-to-be-dead pirate hates you."

"I prefer to be a man of my word."

"Then that shall be my curse on you, in death. Cassius the liar, and that wicked king that you serve; I curse you with knowing you were not a man of your word." I chuckled without any humor.

Even to me, it sounded broken.

"Brees!" Cassius called, and the one who had been next to him on the deck walked over quickly.

"How long before we leave?" Cassius asked him.

He was irritated, I decided, his mouth pursed in an angry line and his scar gone pure white against the pink of his mouth. I thought he must have had authority over the man with how he had spoken to him on the deck of The Siren. That and how all the men looked at him now. He must be a commander of some sort.

"Not long, my..." Brees stumbled a bit. "Captain."

"Very good." He nodded, and Brees left, throwing a wary glance in my direction.

Minutes later, the caravan began to move. All the carts and horses were going together in a tidy line into the forest. It was a haunting place with birds that screeched and a constant groaning I might have been afraid of the day before. Whenever I looked at Cassius, he was staring at me darkly. His eyes never seemed to leave.

Eventually, I got up from where I was sitting, and Cassius sat up straight, eyeing me suspiciously. He or Brees had never bound my hands again. Maybe they saw my defeat and figured I wouldn't fight back; they would have been right. I shook my head and sat down, laying against the hay bale, and closed my eyes. I was more tired than I could ever remember being, and the ache in my chest threatened to swallow me whole. Some fresh tears came and slipped down my face. Cassius did me the courtesy of keeping silent.

"What are your royalty-ordered murders like?" I asked against my closed eyes.

My throat felt dry and sore. It was a struggle to keep my question even.

"How do you mean?" he asked.

"Hanging? Tortured for a few days and put on display? Torn apart by horses? What's your King's preferred method."

"It's hardly ever quick, I'm afraid."

I just nodded. Usually, I would have had some quick answer but couldn't think of anything at that moment, so the bobbing of my head was my only reply. Fear crept into my soul at the thought of the death I was to face. It wasn't the actual dying of it but of a King notorious for his cruelty, a King who liked to torture his captives first. Torture before death struck fear in me that took over my grief for a few moments.

"Does everyone gather around to watch?"

"People love a good show," he said without humor.

"Yes, that they do." I paused. "What will happen to Princess Mercy? What does King Dalion want with her?"

"Why should you care? Are you so concerned for the well-being of all your captives?"

"Mild curiosity," I said casually, knowing I couldn't mention her illness without sounding more concerned.

"I cannot speak for the King or his plans for the princess." His tone was final, as if he would field no more questions about the subject.

I wasn't sure whether it was because he didn't know or because he was a loyal dog to his master.

"I suppose I won't be curious when I'm dead," I said finally.

I tried to sleep then. But sleep did not come to me. It danced just beyond my eyelids, tormenting me with its promise of forgetting the day's events for a mere moment. I don't know how long I lay there with my eyes closed, but Cassius did not try to make conversation with me.

When my back started getting stiff, I opened my eyes. We were in the thick of the forest, and the light was dim around us. I sat up again and ran my fingers down my braids. One was still intact while I had shredded the other with my serrated dagger. I felt the ends gingerly. Where I once had waist-length hair, pieces of it had been severed to above my shoulder. I could feel the unevenness of it and sighed. I took all my hair and plaited it back in a single braid as best I could.

I took Cassius in, and though he watched me watch him, I was too tired and grief-stricken to care. He was still lovely, even with a bit of facial hair starting to appear on his face. I hated to admit it. I noticed small eight-pointed star tattoos on either set of his knuckles. Each finger held one except his middle knuckles, which each baring a small symbol of three inter lapping circles; two filled in and one just an outline. Eventually, he seemed to get uncomfortable under my scrutiny and instead looked up at the trees with a dark look as if he were cursing them wordlessly.

"What is this forest called?" I asked, hating myself and my avoidance of silence.

"Bronog Forest," he answered. "The Capitol city of Hallow is just on the other side. We will be there in two days. The forest terrain will slow us down a bit, but it's still faster to go through than around."

He said it as if I were just an acquaintance, and we were having a casual conversation about the cursed forest. As if he weren't taking me to die. As if I weren't asking how long I had left to live. I reminded myself that Elias was safe. Most of the crew was safe. My life in exchange for theirs was worth it to me. I would die knowing they were alive, and that was enough.

We sat in silence until night fell. Cassius grabbed me a blanket from another cart and a rolled horse blanket to sleep on. He nestled himself in the corner and watched as I tried to get into a comfortable position. His eyes were on me all the while, even as I slipped into a fitful sleep.

⁘

My dreams were full of me reliving Absalom's death over and over. Only now, he lay on a white marble floor, and his blood seeped out of him. When he coughed, his blood splattered on a pure white gown I was wearing in my dream. He called out for me as if I weren't there, and when I screamed to tell him I was, no noise came from me.

"Captain!" I was startled awake by someone shaking my leg.

It took me a second to remember where I was and come to the full realization that my nightmare was not just a nightmare.

"What is it?" I asked, pulling a blanket up around me, feeling the chill of the forest.

"You were screaming," Cassius said and slumped back into his corner.

"Is it morning?" I sat up, letting out a breath, and wiped fresh tears from my face.

"It's almost impossible to tell in the forest, but I would say it is, or it's about to be."

It was the last thing he said to me all day besides asking if I needed to relieve myself in the forest when the caravan stopped for a break. They brought me food and water, and they never once attempted to bind my hands again.

I was still exhausted, and I flitted in and out of sleep leaned up against a bale of hay with Cassius watching me most of the time. He seemed to have gotten bored though, because he left the cart a few times. He always returned. He seemed entirely at ease, not talking, and the silence itched at me though he seemed oblivious. What I assumed to be that evening, I looked over at him and caught his eye. He raised an eyebrow at me, anticipating something.

"What's your King like?" I asked, "Other than terrible, malicious, heartless, wicked, and mad as a box of frogs."

With every insult to his ruler, he blinked and pulled his head back a little. If I had any good humor left in me, I might have laughed.

"I'm surprised pirates keep apprised with politics and rumors about kings."

"We don't," I said, "it was a byproduct of having a princess aboard... and Absalom..." I choked, forming his name.

I couldn't put words to why I was telling him anything. Why was I even talking to him at all? Maybe I was reaching out on the off chance that he was the last human I would ever speak with. Perhaps it was the gaping wound and horrific scene of Absalom dead on the deck of my ship. I was reaching out for any sort of comfort.

"Are all the things people say about you true?" He evaded my question with a question.

"Tell me, Cassius the Liar, what have you heard about me?" I sat back and folded my arms.

"I'm not overly fond of that title," he said, but for some bizarre reason, a smile slipped over his face.

"You aren't supposed to be."

"I've heard you and your brother are greedy and merciless and spare neither woman nor child when you take a ship."

"Hm." I nodded thoughtfully, though the idea of children aboard a pirate ship was preposterous, save Elias and me.

"I've heard you have lived unnaturally long lives; that you've both discovered the fountain of youth."

"Yes, I feel I've aged rather well; I must be what?" I looked up into the trees thoughtfully. "Seventy?"

"That your ship can outrun any ship in any fleet," he continued, "Though we've proven that a falsehood."

I scowled, and his grin skittered across his face once more. He was mocking me. I shook my head, done with my own game, and closed my eyes.

"King Dalion is a new king, young and untested," he offered after a few minutes. "Though I suppose he will grow into the kind of king his father was before him."

"That is a shame." I yawned.

"Why is that?" he asked, and it sounded as if he were intrigued to hear my answer.

"The way I hear it, no one liked him, not his people, and certainly not the other royals of Marecult."

"One doesn't need to be liked to be king."

"Perhaps not, but tell me this, did your king's father die alone? In the dark with no one by his side? And I would wager not a single soul was sad to see him pass over."

There was only silence. A silence that continued until we reached Hallow.

It came upon us like the shock of cold water when you weren't expecting to be submerged. When we came out of the forest, there was a small town with muddy roads and people who looked as if they hadn't eaten in months. When we passed, most of them had hopelessness that burned in their eyes. They tried their best to get out of the caravan's way, and aside from a few brave souls and most children, they did not look up at us.

"How far is this place outside the city?" I asked, staring down at a small girl. She had gaunt cheeks and mud covering the hem of her dress up to her knees.

"Not two miles." Cassius's face was cast down, away from the people, with a pained expression visible.

"I hope I shall have the opportunity to look your bastard king in the eyes before I die and tell him just what a worthless coward he is." I passed several more children, my heart wrenching at the sight of them.

I knew some cities and towns suffered, Quizit for example, but I had never seen it like this. These people were dying. Minutes away sat their king on a throne made of finery while they died in the mud like animals. The blooming hatred I had for King Dalion grew into a hot red flower.

Cassius said nothing, only shot a look of pity at me as if I didn't understand something. Like there was some greater truth behind their suffering that I was too uneducated to understand.

I shook my head at him and reached in my pockets for three gold coins I knew were there. They would be nothing to a dead pirate but everything to a starving family. I climbed up a bale of hay and leaned out. We were almost to the end of the town, and I made eye contact with a woman looking at me brazenly in the eye, defiance written in the fabric of who she was. I held my hand out to her, and she raised her chin at me in rejection. I looked to her left and saw who I assumed was her son. I nodded to him, and he ran forward as she bristled, mouth agape.

"May Baya bless you, sweet lady," he said, and Cassius snorted.

"You too, boy." I dropped the coins in his palm outstretched as he did his best to keep up with the moving cart. "You tell your mother I admire her spirit."

I winked at him, and he stopped running. I settled back into my seat as the town, the boy, and my last three pieces of gold disappeared.

"They'll squander it and be back to their growling bellies before the week is out," Cassius snapped.

"Kindness is not squandered on those that are desperate for it, soldier," I chastised him, and he went back to his brooding silence.

The city of Hallow was surrounded by a stone wall nearly triple my height. The pink stones were laid with mortar of the same color and topped with a shining brass border. The metal was fashioned into spikes, both beautiful and off-putting, and the early sun shone off them, welcoming me into its glowing gate.

If the town before was desolate and underfed, this place was cultivated and fat. Our cart rolled along a stone street, and the two cart-horses shoes clacked loudly against it. Cassius slipped down lower in the cart, putting the collar of his uniform up. I stared at him, trying to figure out if it was embarrassment, and if not, what then would cause him to retreat from this city's people.

Though we traveled into the city and with every foot, the weight of my future pulled on me. Instead of looking at the fantastic city before me, I started imagining the litany of tortures that might lie ahead. I winced against my imagination, sparing no gruesome detail.

We came upon another stone wall made of the same pink stone that protected the city. This one was taller, and the brass spikes atop the wall seemed larger as well. We stopped at a gate, and because we were close to the end of the caravan, I didn't see the armed guards until we were passing through the gate itself. There must have been at least fifty of them milling about and twenty standing at attention by the mouth of the entrance.

A large blue flag was hoisted above the gate with a depiction of a snake. Its mouth hung open with a forked tongue flicking out. Three matching stars embroidered to its right, and the Southern Ralician war motto written below: *Venom and Will*. I had always thought it was apt for a kingdom that fought its way out from under another, only to become cruel and worse than its mother kingdom.

Hallow Manor was a misleading term. To me, manor suggested a large house or perhaps a couple of large houses owned by a lord or lady. Hallow Manor was a castle, the likes of which I had never seen. Granted, I had only seen pictures and never an actual castle, but I would imagine even if I had seen one, it would still be stunning. Grey stone with menacing spires and towers rose before me, and all I could do was stare in awe.

"Hallow Manor, Captain Georgette," Cassius said.

"It's... irritatingly impressive," I said, taking in the grassy grounds as we got closer.

Hedges, waterfalls, and entrances to gardens passed us as I looked at them in amazement. It was massive and one of the loveliest things I had gazed upon. We stopped after coming around the back of the castle to a rear entrance, and I looked over the stone building with its high windows, wondering where the dungeon or keep would be.

"Shall I be given a formal tour?" I asked Cassius, who had climbed out of the cart.

"Would you like a tour?" His mouth flicked up in a handsome smile.

"If my cell isn't paved with silver tile, I shall be thoroughly disappointed," I said.

"I'll see what I can do to accommodate that, Captain," he said before walking off.

I looked around and wondered if I could run for my life. I would no doubt die. I wasn't hoping to escape with such a heavy guard presence, but perhaps an arrow or sword to the back would be an easier way to die than the torture that they'd planned.

Don't let them break you, you promise me, George...

Absalom's words shot through me like a hot poker through the gut. I would not, for his sake, go out like a coward. If torture was in my future, I would endure it with defiance in my eye and a curse on my lips. So, I sat there waiting for them to take me away.

Finally, the man named Brees came back to retrieve me. He looked up at me with the same disgust-filled expression he had on my ship. Though now, he looked much more agitated than he had before. He motioned for me to get out of the cart, and I obliged him.

"Follow me," he grumbled, walking swiftly away.

I was surprised he wasn't going to take me by force or tie my hands at this point. There were no more guards that accompanied us, only him. I looked around for Cassius to see if his face held any more answers, but I didn't see him in the glance I cast. I followed Brees into a set of double wooden doors with large metal ring pulls.

They opened into what I assumed was a cellar stocked with so much food my gaze lingered on sacks piled with vegetables and fruits and what looked to be baking supplies. Canned things were lining the colder shelves, and some stripped dead animals hung up waiting to be butchered and roasted.

"Please," Brees barked out, "I have better things to do than wait for you to inspect the food stores."

After that, I kept up with him, wondering what kind of castle didn't have its own entrance to its dungeons. We passed a large kitchen with a dozen people flitting about. They didn't even notice us as we passed and a robust man with a large mustache barked out orders. He was covered in flour, and the people about him tried to keep out of his way. Whatever they were cooking smelled excellent, and my stomach grumbled loudly despite having eaten a breakfast provided to me.

Brees took me past the kitchen through a dining room of sorts. I didn't have time to admire the general splendor of the room because Brees was moving quickly. He was stomping through the place like an angry hen, but I stopped dead when we reached the main hall.

It was lit with so many lanterns and candles; so, while hardly any natural light came through, it sparkled with fire. It was tiled with the same pink rock as the wall, veined in black and polished. Two staircases were winding up, carved of shiny black granite. In the middle of the room was a pool and fountain; at the bottom of the pool was a giant tiled serpent that matched the flag. I walked up to it despite Brees's impatient huffing. I watched the candlelight sparkle off the water and caught the reflection of the ceiling.

"Ocean deep," I said, careening my head up to the vaulted ceilings that glimmered in gold paint. Murals of naked revels splayed across the expanse, and tiny cherub babies were painted flying about with silky white wings.

"Yes, Yes, I assume you'll have time to ogle the expansive rooms and their many attractions, but that time is not now," he said.

"I'll have time to see the castle?" I asked, but he didn't answer me as he drilled up the stairs.

"Sir?" I called after him taking the stairs two at a time to catch up.

He said nothing as he led me through a maze of hallways. Everything I saw was as impressive as the main hall. Ostentatious drapes, tables, and paintings dripped from every surface. I addressed Brees several times, and he ignored my questioning tone as he led me further into the castle.

Finally, he came to a large set of ornate doors painted white and gold and stopped before them. He glowered at them a moment before turning his contempt on me. He pushed them open and gestured for me to enter. I stepped past him, half expecting him to pull a dagger and stab me in the back.

It was not a single room but a room attached to several. The main room looked like it was intended for women that took tea in velvet chaises and intricately woven rugs. I could see down a hallway to a room that held a bed piled with soft blankets and decorative pillows. It was all immaculately kept though I could tell it was not a lived-in set of rooms.

"I..." I choked out, swept up by the finery. "Is this a prisoner's cell?"

"Believe me when I tell you, lady, that the confusion in your voice mirrors my feelings exactly. Please wait here until I send someone. If you try to escape, I will be sure you die with the thought still fresh in your mind."

"You are rather unpleasant."

"If you liked me, I would be concerned." He stepped out and shut the doors, leaving me in a lavish room.

Decidedly not dead.

Twenty-Five

Georgette

I had fallen asleep on a chair before anyone came back for me. Someone nudged me gently, and I opened my eyes wide, recoiling from them in fear. The room was dark, save for a candle lantern the woman held.

For it was a woman that stood before me. Her head shaved, almost bald with beautiful sable skin. She smiled without teeth, and her eyes held a kindness that caused me to relax slightly.

"Lady Georgette, I am Devika, your principal grand lady."

"I'm not a lady," I said instinctually though perhaps I could have said something a bit more cordial.

"Yes, I know." Her voice was soft but firm.

"Why are you here?"

I had searched the room earlier when Brees had dropped me there. He had locked the door; that is the first thing I had checked. There was another door down the hall in the bedroom that was locked as well. However, I had grown tired and sat in a chair to sleep, not daring to lay in the fine bed.

"To get you a bath and clean clothes. I also brought some food," she said, slender fingers gesturing to a tray behind her set with silver serving plates.

"Are you...a servant?" I enquired, seeming to have lost all the politeness my mother had ever taught me.

"Certainly not." She almost shrieked, and I smiled a little, watching her regain her composure. "My father is a Lord. An

Ambassador of Hestiege. He lives here; King Dalion is our King. I was promised the title of Principal Lady to the first wife of the King. I am neither a servant nor am I a maid. I am a Lady of high court."

"So, you're the queen's principal lady?" I asked, rubbing sleep from my eyes.

"I think it best you get in the bath and eat something, Lady Baine; it seems they have told you nothing."

I couldn't think of any reason to object, and I was sore and hungry. So, I watched as several people filtered in with vats of warm water to fill a bath as I ate a scone as unladylike as possible in my chair.

Once my bath was ready and full of suds, I undressed at Devika's command and got in the warm water, groaning as my muscles strained. I had slept in the chair very awkwardly as well, and my neck was stiff.

"So, where to begin?" Devika said, starting in on me before I had any time to relax in the water.

She was as lovely as I imagined any courtier. Pearls dangled from her ears, and the creamy white of her dress contrasted with her skin marvelously. She was the subject that goddesses were shaped after.

"Perhaps I could start with a question," I offered, noticing her hesitation.

"Of course, My lady."

"Why am I not dead? Or locked up in a cell somewhere? Why am I in these elaborate rooms?"

"That was three questions." She smiled.

"Feel free to answer whichever is easiest." I submerged myself entirely underwater, feeling the unevenness of my hair once more. When I came up for air, she extended a bar of soap to me that smelled of clove.

"You..." she hesitated again. "You are to be married to the King of Southern Ralice."

I stopped washing my arms and looked up at her. My mind went completely blank as what she said wrote itself on the space.

"Pardon me?" I asked, voice coming out breathy and slow.

"You are to be married to the King of Southern Ralice," she said, "My King."

"What kind of lunatic King marries a pirate?" I asked her. "Is this some form of strange torture?"

The only man I had ever considered marrying was lying cold and dead somewhere. It was an offense to me and his memory to suggest I would be married to someone else.

"While our king may not always have a... traditional approach to a ruling, I do not put myself in a position of questioning his commands."

"Well, he isn't my king, and I'll marry him when the depths of the ocean turns to ice."

"Would death be better?" she asked, not unkindly.

I opened my mouth to tell her that yes, death would be preferable to being married to a mad cruel man who I had never even met. To be trapped in court life would be worse than death. Then I thought of my brother, who I had assumed I would never see again. If I lived, there was a chance I would. There was even a chance I could escape. If I were dead, both of those things would be inevitably impossible.

Then Absalom's words came to me. *Don't let them break you.*

The king wouldn't break me, but I would fight to break him. If he thought he would trap me in a loveless marriage and dictate my life, he had not known many pirates.

Over the next several days, I learned so many things. I had headaches every night I fell into bed. I learned all Southern Ralician traditions. I met other ladies who were assigned to me. I learned better than to call them maids or servants, for it seemed their place beside me was a noble one. I saw Brees a handful of times, and he seemed to like me just as well as he had the first day. Though now he seemed resentful, and I didn't fault him for it. I learned what foods they served at balls and which dances started them off. I even had a tour of the castle, the likes of such a place I had never seen.

They also cleaned and groomed me as I had never once been in my life. They had removed my hoops from my ears, though they had so much trouble with the one in my nose they ended up just leaving it. They also cut my hair to the length of the shortest pieces I had severed on my ship. It was now above my shoulders, and the slight wave it had when it was long turned into an unruly curl. Though I thought my locks might be afraid of Devika because whenever she tamed them, they listened.

Devika had become a sort of companion in the last couple of days. I liked how direct she was. I had dismissed my other ladies from being in my chambers at every waking moment, but I had leaned on Devika like a crutch.

She showed me a hallway lined with portraits of previous rulers when I came upon one of a blond woman with fair skin dressed in a deep red gown.

"She's lovely," I said, stopping to admire her.

Her eyes harsh and cunning. They were dark brown but seemed to look at me like she thought me beneath her, and I had to remind myself that it was a painting.

"That was Queen Desdemona," Devika said, her tone darkened.

"Not a kind woman?" I turned to her.

"Queen Desdemona poisoned her husband The King a year after their marriage," she said, "She wore that very red gown to her wedding. It is now considered bad form for a woman in Southern Ralice to wear red to her wedding."

"What happened to her?" I asked.

"She was drained of blood a little at a time and forced to drink it for days before the king's brother cut her head off in the front courtyard."

"Naturally," I laughed, and Devika looked at me as if I were nothing short of insane.

"You seem rather well educated, my lady but know nothing of our history." She said it, but I heard the question.

"Our parents raised us and educated us as well as any courtier, though they left most court history out. So, when it comes to kings and queens and history, I am at a loss. Do you know of a soldier or a guard here named Cassius?" I didn't meet her eyes, having finally mustered the courage to ask.

Devika went rigid as a cat who I had just provoked. Her spine straightened, and her eyes shifted to mine.

"I don't believe so, Lady."

I nodded, letting her lie stand, though I didn't understand it. I would find him. Another person in this castle that I thought I could become friends with. I could use all the friends in the foreign place I could get.

"What is on my wedding list today?" I asked her, hoping the question would put her at ease.

"We go to the tailors today, and you pick what you would like to wear to your wedding ceremony."

"Perfect," I said, looking up at the portrait of Queen Desdemona once more before following her down the hall.

Twenty-Six

Mercy

They had given me some sort of drug. I only knew because it felt like the medicine my mother gave me when I was young. I could tell what was happening but didn't have the will even to lift my head. What I did glean was fuzzy and too warm. Someone had been trying to calm me down, their words assuring.

The drug did wonders for my fear, hardly leaving any room in my head for anything at all. I knew only fever and drowsiness and the occasional worried voice pushing their assurances on me. I could have been taken advantage of or killed, and I would have had no recollection of it.

I started becoming more conscious when I was moved. I felt strong arms carry me and the biting cold after being so warm. The drug still made me drowsy, but they placed me in what I thought was a carriage if I could judge by the rocking of it. Whoever had me forced more syrupy herbal liquid down my throat, and I tried to cough it up only to slip back into sleep.

When I finally woke, I was so startled by my surroundings that I bolted upright and screamed.

The walls were decorated in pink wallpaper with deep orange and blue floral designs. I was in a four-poster bed with sheer peach draping, and a window was open, the breeze causing the curtains to flutter slightly. I saw myself in a large ornate gold mirror that hung on the opposite wall. I looked horrid.

But I was in my room. Or my old room.

I tried to make sense of it, tried to piece it back together, and for half a second, I thought I had made it all up. I might have gotten sick and had a few terrible nights of fever dreams that had turned to lovely dreams that had turned sour once again. Though one look to my left suggested that that wasn't the case.

Two sets of eyes, the same clear blue as mine, stared back at me.

"Prudence, Temperance," I breathed out, jumping out of bed, and I hugged them both tightly.

"Mercy!" they said in unison.

Aside from their physical features, which were almost identical, they couldn't have been more different. Prudence was wild and warm. Even now, with her hair unbound in a dress with grass stains, she looked like a fresh field of flowers as the sun cascaded upon it. Temperance was colder and more calculating. She had her hair pulled back harshly from her face and wore muted shades of brown, grey, or black. She was like a rigid schoolteacher at only seventeen years old.

I had never been happier to see either of them. Their shock was evident by their stiffness as I held them. However, I became very weak and had to sit back on my bed quickly.

"How..." I faltered, unsure of where to even begin.

"We'll go get Holt," Temperance said.

"He said to come as soon as you woke," Prudence said with a kinder nod and reached out to touch my arm tenderly.

I nodded. My oldest brother and King of Adamas would know. I hoped he would understand what had happened. I hoped he would know where Elias and Georgette were. Had their ship survived? Did King Kosdel send men to protect them? I would ask about King Dalion and tell him how he had been the one to kidnap me. I wondered if I would still have to marry King Kosdel.

I pushed the thought from my mind, swiftly unwilling to think on it so soon.

I smoothed my hair back the best that I could and waited for my brother to come.

"My sweet sister." His booming voice came to me before I saw him.

My brother was the very picture of a king. He had darker auburn hair than I and a full well-kept beard. He also had kind brown eyes like my father had and the stature of royalty. He was only twenty-six, but he held the crown well.

"Holt," I breathed out as he entered the room, instantly relieved.

He sat in one of the chairs that the twins had at my bedside. He reached out and grabbed my hand tenderly. It was a softer touch than he had ever spared me, and I was surprised at the contact.

It wasn't that my brother was a cruel man, just preoccupied with the throne and being a diligent son.

"I cannot imagine the pain and torment you have been through the last couple of weeks," he said, sitting back, letting my hand fall from his.

"Well..." I said, unsure how to respond.

"And I cannot tell you enough how happy I am to see that you have been returned to us alive, and now that we have nursed you back to health, you are the picture of beauty. Our healer said you had traveling sickness. He's done his best and said you should make a full recovery." He smiled.

I raised an eyebrow at him. This was his voice he reserved for political speeches or court deals. It was the way he talked to courtiers, not to me.

"Yes, brother, thank you... I was wondering..."

"I will reign Yezreth's fire upon that King and his country, and they will rue the very day they thought they could steal something from me. That he thought he could trick me, the venomous viper."

It seemed I would be the catalyst of a war between our country and Southern Ralice. No doubt my brother had already gotten King Kosdel to agree to join him.

"What of King Kosdel? Has he been informed that I am alive and safe?"

Holt furrowed his brows at me and tilted his head a little. He had a look of pity on his face as if he were sorry for my stupidity. Two weeks ago, I would have just let it go, but now a tiny spark of irritation bloomed in my chest.

"Kosdel?" he asked.

"Yes…" I said slowly. "King Kosdel? Won't he be glad to know that his betrothed is not dead?"

"Did you not just hear me swear my wrath upon the man? Why would you think you are still engaged to be married to him?"

The world slowed a bit as the information I had compiled crumbled like a poorly built castle of sticks.

"What?" I asked.

"Oh, sister, your fragile mind had been rattled by all this. I shall fetch Alita to draw you a bath. I should have given you more time." He got up to leave, and panic surged through me.

"Holt!" I shouted his name, and he stopped and sat back down.

"Why…" I couldn't piece together why the King I was going to marry would have kidnapped me.

"That bastard liar staged a kidnapping and tried to make it seem as if the King of Southern Ralice had done it. However, I know King Dalion from childhood. When I had guards sent to his palace to accuse him, he denied having anything to do with it and even assisted us in locating you. Though when Kosdel came to me, I acted as if I believed every lie he spun. Dalion has a spy in his court and said he had two pirates in his employ that he didn't care for anyone to know about. The knave would stoop so low as to consort with pirates." He spat the words out as if they tasted of poison.

"That's why Dalion's men were pursuing us," I breathed out, "Not to take me for himself but because he was helping you."

"Yes," he said it as if I should have known it.

"Why, why would King Kosdel do it?"

"I can only guess his goal was to get me to aid him in a war against Southern Ralice. When his pirates brought you back to him, and he claimed to be the hero. Either that or he planned to kill you all along and blame that on King Dalion as well. After he staged your abduction and forced you to live in torment and torture for weeks, I'll have his head for it; his blood will run on his paving stones."

I didn't hear what he was saying. I only saw the faces of my new friends. I knew in my heart that they had known none of it. They wouldn't have been able to lie so entirely. Absalom had believed his King to be a good man.

"The pirates," I whispered, "The pirates and King Kosdel's man aboard their ship, where are they? What happened to them?"

I could hear the shakiness of my voice. My brother looked at me, and his face softened. He was mistaking my panic for fear; he reached for me once more.

"You needn't fear, dear Mercy; Dalion took the pirate captains back to the Capital of Hallow to be executed. No doubt word will come any day of their deaths. As for the man of King Kosdel's aboard the ship, Hestor reported that he ran the bastard through himself. His head was delivered to King Kosdel as a declaration of war."

Bile rose to my throat, imagining Absalom's head rolling on a throne room floor. I felt violently ill, and my hands were shaking. My eyes welled with tears.

"They're dead?" I said, my words choked out of me.

"Certainly, by now. The notorious Captains Baine shall terrorize Marecult no more," he said, reassuring.

He got up and leaned in, kissing my forehead.

"How boring all this must be for you. I'll have Alita come run you a bath, and then you can move on to more feminine and delicate things."

He left. I lay down on my bed and stared at the side of the room, my heart breaking in two. My endless tears slipped down my face. When Alita came, I pretended to be asleep, and when she left me alone, I cried more. It felt like I cried for two days, and when I wasn't weeping or wishing to vomit, I was dreaming of the ocean, and tavern brawls, and the soft touch of a pirate captain I would never see again.

❦

I asked not to be bothered day after day, but on the fifth day, I woke up to my little brother and sister staring back at me over the side of my bed.

"Were you tortured and raped by pirates?" my brother asked, and Charity smacked him on the back of the head hard.

"Prudence said to be nice," she scolded him, "It's not polite to ask if someone has been tortured and raped."

"Sorry," Harold said, rubbing the back of his head.

I looked to the door, where Prudence and Temperance stared in obvious curiosity.

"I was kidnapped," I said to Harold and Charity, "But they did not torture me."

"Did they feed you moldy bread?" Charity asked, eyes wide.

"No," I chuckled, my throat dry as a desert.

I thought back to the conversation I had with Elias about how I didn't like my sisters. About how I envied his relationship with his sibling. As I looked at my sisters and youngest brother, my heart softened a bit. Perhaps the blame for our lack of closeness should settle on my shoulders. I was, after all, the oldest sister. While I knew I could not make up for the lost time, I could start forging relationships.

"Would you like to hear the tale of how I was recovered by the fearsome Pirate Captains Baine?" I asked, inviting them to come to sit on my bed with me.

"Oh yes, please!" Herold said, jumping up almost immediately.

Charity was slower and more delicate, and I recognized the restraint in her eyes of wanting to act like a proper princess. She sat next to him though eventually, the excitement shone in her eyes.

"It includes dancing and duels, a tavern fight, and even a kiss," I said, wonder in my voice.

"Yuck," Herold said, sticking his tongue out at me, and I smiled.

"You went to a tavern?" Temperance asked from the door, and I beckoned both my sisters to me.

"You were kissed by a pirate!?" Prudence asked fancifully. "Oh, how romantic. Was he handsome?"

"Oh yes, very handsome indeed. Shut the door, and I'll tell you all about it," I said, situating myself back against the pillows.

They gathered around, the twins sitting in chairs to my left and Herold and Charity up on my bed. They all looked at me expectantly.

"Holt sent me off to be married to King Kosdel on one of the fastest ships in our fleet…"

And so, I began my tale, hoping to capture some of the magic Elias possessed.

Twenty-Seven

Mercy

I had been fully recovered for several weeks. That morning my ladies' maids had come in and bathed me like life hadn't changed. Like I had never left. While I went through the motions, my heart ached, still thinking of the friends I had made and how I would never see them again.

The kiss Elias and I shared lingered on my lips and burned into my memory. If I thought about it too long, I began to wallow. So, I allowed them to dress me as they had always done. I was laced into a dress a little too tight and primped until they deemed me satisfactory for my brother's presence. They had placed a heavy silver and emerald crown on my head and turned me to view my reflection.

I saw a girl drowned in a metallic green dress with abundant skirts. A crown too heavy and too adorned sitting atop her head. While it was a reflection I had seen several times, the girl looking back at me was a stranger.

I met Holt outside my door. He looked regal, dressed in a green buttoned coat to match mine with a decorative sword at his side. He took my arm as we made our way down the hall.

"You look well," he chirped, awaking in me anger I hadn't realized was hidden away.

I said nothing, and we continued.

"I have gathered Lords and Ladies of all Adamas to show them how strong we are. To show them that King Kosdel cannot take advantage of us. To show them that we will fight this war and win." He said it with conviction.

"I am to be the proof of our resilience? Your war token?" My voice held an edge, but he didn't seem to notice.

"You will be our trophy of strength." He beamed at me as if he thought I had done something admirable. "Songs will be written of how you survived kidnapping at the hands of detestable pirates and endured for weeks despite their endless torture. How Cyril set his dogs on you, and you resisted."

"There will not be if I contradict such stories." I bit out the words, and as we stopped in front of the doors to the throne room, he finally turned to me.

"I've heard reports that you have been spinning stories of those pirates' innocence, Mercy, and I tell you now, I shall not have it." His voice had gone cold and sharp.

It was something I was used to. One minute he was praising me, and the next, he was bullying me into his opinion. I could tell him they weren't stories. Tell him how I had felt more at home those two weeks on a pirate ship than I ever had in this castle, but it wouldn't matter. He wasn't listening. He just wanted blind obedience. He wanted my silence. To use me as a representation of a war he planned to start.

The doors opened.

"Say you understand," he ordered, "That you'll stop the childish petulance and put your country first like the princess you are."

I looked at him, waiting for me to respond. He was waiting for me to pledge my allegiance to him and Adamas and deny the connections I had made. The message was clear, and if I didn't, consequences would follow. But I thought of Georgette's defiant eyes and confident demeanor as she did what she pleased.

"No," I said quietly, the word feeling awkward on my tongue.

"What did you say?" he asked, his brow furrowing.

"I said no." This time it was loud enough for some of the people inside to hear.

I reached up and took the heavy crown off my head and dropped it on the ground. The silence made the impact deafening as my brother stared after it in horror.

"You will not use me as your show horse, Holt. My answer is no." I turned and walked away, leaving him and the crowd of nobles behind.

Twenty-Eight

Georgette

"I am here to get you dressed, my lady." Devika came in as silent as a mouse.

I hadn't been sleeping. I was just lying in the large bed with too many blankets and pillows, drowning in goose feathers. I looked out the window into the magnificent garden thinking that Elias and Mercy would probably enjoy it.

"Devika, please call me George or Georgette. I've asked nearly half a dozen times now." I smiled as she shook her head.

"I couldn't, my lady. I insist on calling you Lady, and after today I shall call you, My Queen."

"That sounds rather terrible. What will happen today?" I turned back toward the window, and though she had told me already, I needed it repeated.

"We shall get you bathed, and I will do your hair and get you into the dress you ordered from the tailor. You will be presented before the priest, who will do a ceremonious blessing. Then you will walk into the throne room before all the noble families who have been invited and kneel before our faithful king. They will recite the wedding covenant, and the King will present you with a token. Since you will be the queen, the token is usually a piece of jewelry he has had crafted for you. Then you shall kneel before the throne and be crowned Queen of Southern Ralice and take the royal name. Normally your father and mother would walk you down to the King, but I suppose you shall just walk yourself." The last part was said quieter as if she were worried that I would take offense.

I thought of my father and mother walking me down the shiny black marble floor, tracking seawater all along with it, and smiled. Their swords would be hung from their belts in an act of defiance. I hoped I could make them proud.

"All the better," I said, getting out of bed and heading toward the large bathroom attached to my quarters.

The tub was so large that I had counted eight servants with vats of water to fill it up. However, Devika had them all lined up outside, ready to go. I sank into the bath, submerging my whole head, willing the warm water to wash away the tears I cried that night. Tears for Absalom mostly. His last words to me stuck in my soul and cried out to me whenever my eyes closed.

Don't you let them break you, promise me?

Every time his command came to my mind, I repeatedly promised that I wouldn't. I promised the memory of his face until the tears stopped flowing. Until a bit of him disappeared. I came up for air closing my eyes against the smell of white flowers.

"Miss Georgette!" A cry sounded from the bedroom, and I catapulted myself out of the bath in a panic, slipping along the marble floor.

"What is it, Devika?" I rounded the corner and saw the woman hunched over a box that now sat on my bed.

"Is this a mistake?"

"What mistake is worth that kind of panic?" I hastily wrapped a sheet around standing next to her and began to laugh with delight.

"There is no mistake." I finally got out around my laughter. "This is what I ordered."

She said nothing, only stared in horror. I felt a little sorry because it would be evident that I had only used the tale she told me to fuel my defiance. However, I would never betray Devika or let on that she had given me the idea. This was my fight with the King, no one else needed to suffer.

"Are you trying to anger him?" she whispered finally.

"Yes," I said.

"But why my Lady?"

"A promise I made to a friend." I walked back to the bath.

Devika followed me after a while, wearing a concerned expression. She washed my hair and poured some oil in the bath that smelled of the sweet white flowers that perfumed many of the things in the bathroom, making me wonder if it was a native flower.

I wondered if Cassius would be present at the wedding. When I replayed the scene of Absalom getting stabbed, I realized he had told the men to let me go to him. It wasn't a colossal kindness, but it had been something. Surely, we would meet again. Though he was the agent of a man I already loathed, my heart ached for friendship in this place where I felt so alone already.

I finally got out and dried off upon Devika's insistence. I put on some undergarments she had laid out for me. I sat in a chair as she brushed my hair out. Devika ended up pinning a bit of it back to make me look somewhat put together.

"What jewelry shall you wear with your erm... wedding attire, my Lady?"

"Do you know where my gold hoops are?" I asked, turning so I could gauge her expression. "For my ears? They took them from me when they cut my hair and took my clothing."

She paled.

"If you desire your earrings...," Devika said, putting the brush down.

She walked to the large room filled with clothing and jewels, and shoes. They had filled it up the past two weeks I had been there. Just when I thought there couldn't possibly be one more dress or gaudy necklace housed in the room, more showed up.

I walked over to the box of clothing I had called for from the tailor. I pulled out beautifully tailored pants with gold buttons on either side of the waist. Next, a completely sheer top with long sleeves gathered at the wrists and a brocade corset with the same beautifully detailed button closures. Lastly, a beautiful velvet military coat with golden buttons. All the clothing was in fabric the color of freshly spilled blood.

Devika came up behind me and dropped eight small golden hoops into my hand. She was staring at the clothing laid out on the bed. The expression of dread she had from earlier was gone, now replaced with reluctant acceptance.

"Well, if he kills you for it, it's been my pleasure," she said, and I laughed.

I allowed her to help me dress and lace up the back of the corset. It gave me more structure than I was used to, and the clothes fit like a second skin, save the sheer sleeves, which swayed about beautifully. I walked to the door and slipped on my boots that I had come in. They had been cleaned and shone so that I could see my reflection in them. I slipped the red velvet jacket over my shoulders and finished my wedding attire with my own earrings. Defiance in nine golden rings.

"How do I look?" I asked Devika.

"I'm afraid if I tell you how beautiful you are, you will take it as encouragement for this ludicrous behavior," she said, walking to the door and ushering me through.

We saw only guards as we walked the halls. Devika looked away from their gazes that followed me in disbelief. I stared at them right back, daring them to say something. They all bowed when I passed and were silent. We stopped outside what seemed like their place of worship.

"Don't speak to the priest unless spoken to, and don't look into his eyes," Devika warned.

"Does he have a third eye?" I wondered, "Horns?"

"He's a holy man of the goddesses and cannot be looked upon by mere mortals," she whispered, slightly angry.

"Hard life to live." I gathered my courage and walked through the door as Devika followed and closed it behind us.

"You come into the temple dressed for your wedding day in the color of disgrace?" A low voice boomed across the dimly lit room.

There were red candles lit all around that cast an eerie glow to the walls. A tall wall stood before me with a mural of goddesses upon it. Incense burned at the base, and several painted stones were stacked up as well.

I looked up to find the voice who called out to me but found my eyes were still adjusting. It made me uncomfortable, and something about the room caused anxiety to rear up in me. My heart hammered in my chest, and I tried my best not to look bothered.

"Pirate filth, put your head down!" the voice shouted again, and I did as he commanded though I scolded myself for it.

Who was this man to yell at me this way? Though in my experience, people valued their priests almost as much as their royalty.

"I will bless you but know that I disapprove of this blasphemous match. A thief of the sea should never be married into our pure bloodline of royalty." His voice was much closer now, and I avoided looking up to keep how nervous I was from him.

"Noted," I ground out, "This morning, I asked myself, whatever will I do if their lunatic priest disapproves of me? Perhaps I'll cry myself to sleep."

"Lady," Devika warned, but my blood was already boiling.

"I have no desire to be your queen, so by all means, defy your king on religious principle if you dare."

"You are as wicked as I tried to warn him you would be," the man whispered in my ear.

"Coward," I countered.

After a silence, Devika led me to an extended bench, where she directed me to kneel with my head down. The priest spoke in what sounded like gibberish. Nonsensical words forming songs came from his mouth. He could have been cursing me for all I knew, and I just knelt there and let him. He chanted for so long that my knees and back ached from kneeling in one position on the floor. I started reciting constellations in my head, tracing them under the bench with my fingers.

It was not over quickly after that, and my knees screamed. I could not say how many hours I kneeled there. I wondered about many things. About what King Dalion would be like. Devika had assured me that he was handsome as if that were the most important thing. How old would he be? I didn't know much about him other than his reputation for cruelty reached beyond that of an ordinary ruler. I wished then that I had kept more apprised on the royalty of Marecult.

Whatever he looked like, however old he was, my hatred for him grew the more I was locked in his massive castle. He had taken Absalom from me. He had stolen me from my family. Then he dared to dictate my fortune by marrying me as if I were his subject, as if I were his property. He didn't even have the character to tell these things to me himself. He was a coward hiding behind the religion of his people to avoid seeing me.

When we were done, the priest took a bit of charcoal and wiped it across either of my knuckles, leaving black marks on them. He hit me rather hard on the head three times, and I fought the urge to look up and sneer at him. I heard him recede into the shadows once more and prayed I would be allowed to stand up soon.

"By the power that the goddesses have placed in me, young pirate woman, you have been cleaned of your sins against them, and you can go and be joined with our beloved king."

"Excellent," I said, standing up without waiting to be dismissed. I walked quickly out of the room to the hallway beyond.

I waited for Devika there, catching my breath. I hoped I would not run into the vile man very often. When she emerged, she gave me a small apologizing smile.

"Is it normally that long, or did he just not like me?" I asked as we made our way back down the corridor.

"I've never been to one before, so I don't know," she said politely, but I had a feeling that she did know.

We reached the doors of the throne room and stopped before it. I was again much more nervous than I intended to be. I took a deep breath hearing the voices of many people inside. I closed my eyes and tried to focus on who I was. I would not be broken.

"I'll go in before you to announce your arrival. There will be a clear path with noble families on either side. Walk up to the throne and wait for the King to place the crown upon your head. You'll sit on the throne and be announced as the Queen."

"This is all very exciting."

Devika, who had now picked up on the sarcasm that I often used, just gave me an exasperated look. She adjusted my clothes and slipped a stray piece of hair behind my ear. When she was done looking me over, she nodded and slipped into the double doors, leaving me alone in the hallway, unsure of when I should follow.

Though a few seconds later, the crowd inside went silent. The doors were opened before me slowly by two men dressed in formal wear. They both bowed, and I supposed that was my cue.

So, I squared my shoulders, put my chin up, and took one last stabilizing breath.

I started the walk to the throne. It had seemed a much shorter walk the day before when Devika had shown me where I would be taken. I determined not to look at the nobles gathered to gawk. They had come to ogle the pirate queen that their king had chosen. I heard whispers and gasps sweep through the room, and I fought a smile. My offensive attire had hit its mark.

I stopped dead, finally focusing on the man seated on the throne, his wicked grin undeniable.

He was harsh as if any softness had been wiped away, and in its place, coldness was left behind. His dark brown curls were pushed back by a twisted crown made of dark metal and rubies. His freckles stood out more against his high sharp cheekbones. He wore all black, save for the silver buttons on his coat. The white of his teeth violent and mocking against his attire.

I started walking again and finally reached him, and he took me in with one eyebrow raised. His smirk held none of the anger I had hoped to incite. Instead, he looked rather pleased with himself that he had caused me to falter.

"King Cassius Dalion, is it?" I asked in front of him, rage barely contained.

The wrath building in me must have been evident because the smirk he had before turned into a full smile of arrogance. I seethed, hating every part of me for hesitating and hating him for taking something else from me. I had wanted to thank him for letting me sit by Absalom's side while he died. It was his fault Absalom had passed, and I had wanted to thank him.

I never figured anyone in my life the villain of my story. If anything, I assumed I was the villain of my own story. Now, this king, looking back at me as if he had won some sort of prize, was my villain. I had found my nemesis. I looked into the dark brown eyes I had thought held kindness and now saw only cruelty.

Standing before him, I watched as his slender fingers began to tap on the arms of his marble throne. His nails had been painted a void black, and his knuckle tattoos looked more threatening than they had before. He opened his mouth to speak, and I could tell by the glittering of his dark eyes that whatever he said would not be pleasant.

"There's my fearless pirate captain."

Twenty-Nine

Cassius

I had never seen hatred look so rapturous.

I smiled when she faltered. She was so sure of herself in her red wedding clothes. Of course, I had known what she was going to be wearing. The tailor came to Brees the second she had gotten the order from her. She had been too afraid to create the clothing without asking first. The tailor had been sweating, just relaying the order when Brees had brought her before me.

What shall I make for her? the tailor had asked. *Make her what she's asked for.* I had said and glad of it too, for she looked every bit my pirate queen.

She walked toward me after the recognition and betrayal set in. After she realized who I was and what it meant. Hatred dripped from her and was on display for all to see. I couldn't help the smile that slipped onto my face. I had won this battle.

Though there was something else in her eyes that I almost flinched away from. It was a loss, a friendship that had barely begun when I spent two days with her after I had taken her from her ship. When I was just a soldier and she was just a pirate captain. I had stolen that from her after taking so much already.

And she hated me for it.

I supposed it was better that she hated me. It would be easier to forget the way a small kindness shone in her grey eyes or the sarcasm that dripped from her lips that made me want to silence her mouth with my own. Better that she hated me to her very core. It made it easier to do what I had been raised to do.

"King Cassius Dalion, is it?" she asked, ice on her tongue; not an ounce of warmth lingered there for me.

"There's my fearless pirate captain." I smiled wide, using her friend's last words to her as the dagger to whatever had been forged between us.

It worked. The rage that I saw in her eyes was for me and me alone.

So, the ceremony proceeded. All the while kneeling before me, Georgette's eyes never left mine. When it was time for me to present her with her gift, a priest's boy came up clutching a wooden box lined with velvet. Inside was a pendant I had made for her. On a golden chain. It was the woman on the head of her ship. The ship I had taken from her. The lady siren with tentacles flailing dangerously. I had it cast in gold, and the siren's eyes were blood-red rubies.

Her hatred seethed as I slipped it over her head. She looked down at it quickly, then returned her gaze to me. A smile slipped over her features as vicious as any of my own.

She kept that smile there as she rose and was crowned with the ruby-encrusted crown of the previous queens of Southern Ralice. It didn't waiver when she sat next to me and the priest recited the queen's coronation text. She leaned in close, and I turned my head, intrigued to hear what she had to say to me.

"Is it a war within your own house you want Cassius The Liar?" she asked.

"My king is fine," I whispered back.

"I have no king, nor will I ever call you my king," she promised, and I believed it.

"I was bred for war," I informed her, "Do your worst, my Queen."

She pulled back at the title as if I had slapped her.

When the ceremony was over, we waited for the courtiers to file past us with their congratulations. It was a grueling process. The thrones had not been built for comfort.

Georgette said nothing, just stared coldly out at the room. Her hands gripped the arms of the granite throne so tightly her knuckles were white. Finally, when the line had diminished, and I stood up to leave, she addressed me again.

"If you come to my bed to consummate this marriage of ours, I'll slit your throat."

It wasn't crafty or poetic, but at least she told me where I stood.

"My Queen, I shall not enter your chambers for any such thing, nor will that ever be required of you. I shall not touch you in such a way unless a time comes where you beg me for it."

"I'd rather die," she spat.

"If you wish to die, that can also be arranged," I said in a bored tone. "I have far prettier maids than you willing to warm my bed who don't bring sharp weaponry with them."

"What is it then, I wonder, that you need of me."

"I haven't decided yet," I said, nodding to Brees off to the side as he took a few steps toward me, and I turned to leave.

"You will come to regret this. I'll rip your crown from you."

I looked back at her, half a grin still on my face. However, her features made me hold my breath for a moment. The words were not just a threat but a promise from someone who had nothing left to lose. Left unleashed, I knew she would fulfill the promise.

"War it is then," I said, turning and leaving her behind in the throne room.

Brees had the good sense not to say anything for several moments when the doors shut behind us.

"We will have to respond to King Holt's request soon," I said.

"Why didn't you just kill her, Cassius?" he asked, not addressing my statement, "We are on the edge of a war decades in the making, and you choose this time to make a political statement by marrying a pirate woman? It would have been best if you had beheaded her and been done with it."

"I have my own plans for her, Brees. Perhaps I should put you on the board of advisors since you seem so eager to offer me political advice."

"Our whole lives, I never thought you crazed, Cassius. I always thought it was a charade you played to uphold your father's reputation. Now I'm starting to wonder. You aren't your father. Why are you doing this?"

"Our people expect a mad king. Our enemies lay in wait to see if I will take up the title, and I hate to disappoint."

Thirty

Elias

I had pursued them into the forest called Bronog, but delirious with grief, rage, and exhaustion, I had escaped its dark clutches merely a day after they had. In a blind panic, I made my way to higher court of Hallow, looking like a half-mad sailor. I begged people to tell me if there had been an execution. *No,* was the answer I received. There had been no execution, but a decree had gone out that there would be a wedding.

My sister was alive.

So, I waited two weeks until George was married to the King of Southern Ralice. I paid a kitchen maid off who came into town for supplies to tell me how the new queen was fairing. She had been moved into the queen's quarters, and the King didn't even keep her bed company, so the rumors went. She was safe and well treated, and I was no use to her bedraggled and emotion swept as I was. One could not execute a rescue singlehandedly with no resources.

It had been four weeks since the attack on our ship.

Now standing on the main deck, I had just finished counting out a year's worth of wages to each of my crew. A double wage counted to Jones, who stood beside me.

"If you don't hear from me in four weeks' time, Jones, you find them. You know how," I said, darkness clouding my words.

"Yes, Captain."

Jamie, the young surgeon, was standing to my quartermaster's left, shuffling his feet in nervousness. The crew had hidden him in a cargo hold below deck when the ship had been overtaken.

"And if it comes to that, you be sure to give Absalom's ashes a proper pirate burial. On the fifth moon."

"Yes, Captain," he said dutifully. "Where will you go?"

"I'm going to kill that bastard King and bring my sister and our princess back."

Fortune of Emerald and Salt Playlist

Towards the Sun — Rihanna

Hey Brother — Avicii

The Last Shanty — Derina Harvey Band

Teir Abhaile Riu — Celtic Women

Hoist the Colors — Colm R. McGuiness

The Devil is a Gentleman — Merci Raines

Rewrite the Stars — Zac Efron, Zendaya

It's OK — Nightbirde

Booty Swing — Parav Stelar

Dharawi Nights — Secretpath

Dark Nights — Dorothy

Soldier — Fleurie, Tommee Profit

For the Lover that I Lost — Sam Smith

Already Gone — Sleeping At Last

Morning Sun — Melody Gardot

Authors Note

This is a dream. Seventh grade me wouldn't believe it if I told her one day, she would publish something she had written.

This story started as a work of grief. The original inspiration coming from losing my younger brother in 2016. I wanted to showcase a healthy and supportive sibling relationship because so often I see the opposite in fiction. This story is about the power of having a sibling who loves you fiercely.

This journey and these characters have changed me forever. I never thought I would finish a novel until this story swept me away in its current. Georgette, Elias, Mercy, and Absalom captured my heart and stole my free moments with their personalities and charm. Their story rattled around in my mind and exploded from me as soon as I put my fingers down to tell it. I can't wait to share the rest of their adventure with you.

If I could also encourage anyone who wishes to tell a story. If you think you can't or that no one will care about the story you have to tell, you're wrong. I told myself that I couldn't for years, that this wasn't a feasible dream. Working part-time with two kiddos and hectic life, I convinced myself I couldn't do this. However, with heavy encouragement from loved ones and a promise I made to myself, I have put out a piece of magic unique to me. You have magic in you, too, and we are all just waiting for it.

Thank you for reading my story. Thank you for following this adventure. You belong in the softest part of my heart where this story lives.

Acknowledgments

So many people to thank and so little page space.

I want to thank The Lord first; by grace and grace alone, I finished this novel. My editor, you are a miracle. Celeste, for being my alpha reader with all your words of affirmation and praise that I drank up like a dessert. To all my beta readers, thank you for your feedback and encouragement. Persephone Jayne, my critique partner, thank you for your priceless time and for making my story stronger.

My cover designer Primmepgx, you are a gem who made the wrapping of my book match the story inside; thank you for that. My editor Natalie Boyland with Shrimp books you made this book stronger and so much more polished, thank you.

Barrett, the love of my life, for taking the kids and letting me work on this craziness with unconditional support, till the end of the line. My sister Willow who was up for talking about plot points over the phone while I made absolutely no sense: I love you most. Brittany, my best friend, for texting about all things pirate and character development and such; I love you. Amanda Dykes, you softly blew on the embers of this story to coax it into a flame, and I will always be grateful to you. To my Uncle Domenic for the excellent literature conversations over my life, you are my Ka-tet.

To anyone who ever encouraged me during this project. I coveted those encouragements, and you met my need. You have no idea the way your words carried me through.

Thank you, thank you, thank you.

About the Author

Author Monroe Wildrose has been stuck between the pages of books since the fifth grade when her father bought her a copy of Eragon by Christopher Paolini. When she's not reading or writing, she can almost always be found with a cup of coffee in her hand as she enjoys time with those she adores. She makes her home at the base of the Sierra Nevada Mountains where she and the loves of her life, her husband and two rowdy toddlers, are fortunate enough to have Lake Tahoe at their fingertips.

Check out her other books!
Fairvein Novellas:
Clementine's Parlor of the Extraordinary and Curious
Tailor Troubles
Booker Brothers Duet:
Too Sweet: A Highschool Vampire Romance

www.ingramcontent.com/pod-product-compliance
Lightning Source LLC
Chambersburg PA
CBHW021103110726
47900CB00007B/2008